'Thank you,' she murmured.
'I think I will be able to sleep
now. I will be up and ready to
leave first thing.'

For a moment he thought she might rise up
on her toes and kiss his cheek, like a sister or
a friend, but it was his mouth where her gaze
lingered. Heat rushed through him. His blood
headed south.

The distance between them was so very slight
he could feel the graze of her breath against
his throat, see into the warmth in the depths
of her melting soft brown eyes. Could such
a kind, gentle creature, such a respectable
woman, really want a man like him?

## Author Note

I have wanted to write Caro and Blade's story for ages, and finally had the chance in *More Than a Lover*. Discovering from Blade that he was at Peterloo, a massacre of civilians at St Peter's Field near Manchester that was vilified in the press of the time, gave me lots of interesting historical background. Having a character tell you where he was and how it affected him is always the icing on the cake for an author. I hope you enjoy the journey as much as I did.

Also, I hope you enjoy this opportunity to catch up with the twins and their brides from *The Gamekeeper's Lady* and *More Than a Mistress*, because they are some of my favourite people. If you would like to know more about me or my books you will find me at my website: annlethbridge.com. I love to hear from readers.

# MORE THAN
# A LOVER

Ann Lethbridge

Published in Great Britain 2016
by Mills & Boon, an imprint of HarperCollins*Publishers*
1 London Bridge Street, London, SE1 9GF

© 2016 Michèle Ann Young

ISBN: 978-0-263-91696-6

Printed and bound in Spain
by CPI, Barcelona

In her youth, award-winning author **Ann Lethbridge** re-imagined the Regency romances she read—and now she loves writing her own. Now living in Canada, Ann visits Britain every year, where family members understand—or so they say—her need to poke around every antiquity within a hundred miles. Learn more about Ann or contact her at annlethbridge.com. She loves hearing from readers.

## Books by Ann Lethbridge

### Mills & Boon Historical Romance
### and Mills & Boon Historical *Undone!* eBooks

#### *Rakes in Disgrace*

*The Gamekeeper's Lady*
*More Than a Mistress*
*Deliciously Debauched by the Rake* (Undone!)
*More Than a Lover*

#### *The Gilvrys of Dunross*

*The Laird's Forbidden Lady*
*Her Highland Protector*
*Falling for the Highland Rogue*
*Return of the Prodigal Gilvry*
*One Night with the Highlander* (Undone!)

#### Linked by Character

*Haunted by the Earl's Touch*
*Captured Countess*
*The Duke's Daring Debutante*

*The Rake's Inherited Courtesan*
*Lady Rosabella's Ruse*
*The Rake's Intimate Encounter* (Undone!)

#### *Undone!* eBooks

*One Night as a Courtesan*
*Unmasking Lady Innocent*
*A Rake for Christmas*
*In Bed with the Highlander*

Visit the Author Profile page
at millsandboon.co.uk for more titles.

I would like to dedicate this book to all the wonderful
editors at Harlequin Mills & Boon who have
helped me write more than twenty-five stories to date,
and in this particular case to Nicola Caws,
who let me write the story my way
and then helped me to make it better. Thank you.

# *Chapter One*

*March 30th, 1820*

Bladen Read, erstwhile captain of the Twenty-Fifth Hussars, stretched his legs beneath the scarred trestle table in the corner of the commons of the Sleeping Tiger. Nearby, a miserable fire struggled against the wind whistling down the chimney while the smell of smoke battled with the stink of old beer and unwashed men oozing from the ancient panelling. He might have stayed somewhere better these past five days, but it would have been a waste of limited coin he preferred to spend on decent stabling for his horses and a room for his groom. After all, it wasn't their fault he'd been forced to tender his resignation from his regiment.

That was his fault, fair and square, for not

blindly following orders. And not for the first time. It was why he'd never advanced beyond captain and never would now.

Hopefully, his letter to his good friend Charlie, the Marquess of Tonbridge, would result in an offer of employment or he'd be going cap in hand to his father. The thought made his stomach curdle.

He nodded at the elderly tapman to bring him another ale to wash down the half-cooked eggs, burned bacon and day-old bread that served for breakfast in this establishment. Not that his rations while fighting for king and country on the Iberian Peninsula had been any better, but they also hadn't been that much worse.

He opened *The Times* and placed it beside his plate. The tapman wandered over with a fresh tankard. He slapped it down on the table, the foam running down the sides and pooling in a ring around its base. His lip curled as he pointed a grimy finger at the headline—the words were stark: 'Hunt. Guilty of Sedition'.

'Sedition?' the old man growled. 'It was a massacre. There was women there. Families. It's the damned soldiers what ought to be up on a charge.'

'You are right.' Blade knew, because he'd

been at St Peter's Field. Hunt had been invited to Manchester to speak to a populace suffering from the loss of work or low wages and high prices for bread. He advocated change. What the powers that be had not expected were the vast numbers who would come to hear the man speak.

People had come from miles away, the women in their Sunday best, many of them wearing white, holding their children by the hand and carrying the banners they'd stitched. They'd come to hear Hunt, a radical who was famous for his opinions and wearing a white top hat. Scared to the point of panic, the government had sent the army to break up the gathering because they had learned of the careful organisation behind the event. Curse their eyes. The crowd had been peaceful, not starting a revolution as the government claimed. Hunt had barely begun addressing the crowd from a wagon bed when the militia had charged.

The potman snorted derisively. 'You were there, then, were ye, Captain? Got a few licks in?'

Not this soldier. He had tried to turn the militia aside. As a result, he'd been deemed unfit to serve his king. His years of service had counted for nothing. Not that in hindsight he would have done anything different. Waking and asleep, he heard the screams of women and children and the shouts of men, as the soldiers, his soldiers, charged into the crowd, laying about them with sabres as if they were on the battlefield at Waterloo. Eighteen citizens dead and over seven hundred injured, some by the sword, others trampled by horses. Just thinking about it made him feel ill.

No wonder the press had labelled it Peterloo. Britain's greatest shame and a tarnish on the victory over the French at Waterloo a mere four years before.

The potman spat into the fire. 'The people won't stand for it. You wait and see. They might have put Hunt in prison, but it won't be the end of it.'

Blade's blood ran cold. 'I'd keep that sort of talk to yourself, man, if you know what's good for you.'

The government had spies and agents provocateurs roaming the countryside looking for a way to justify their actions of last August and the laws they had changed to reduce the risk of revolution. The Six Acts, they were called. The radicals called it an infringement of their rights.

He swallowed his rage. At the government. At the army. At his stubborn dull-witted colonel. And most of all at himself for remaining in the service beyond the end of the war. He had wanted to fight an enemy, not British citizens.

The man gave him a narrow-eyed stare as if remembering to whom he was talking. 'Will there be anything else, Captain?'

'Mr and, no, thank you. Nothing else.'

'That'll be fourpence.'

The waiter plucked the coins Blade tossed him out of the air and sauntered back to the bar. Blade finished the ale and pushed the food aside. He had no stomach for it this morning.

Time to check on his horses. With studied movements born of hours of practice, he carefully folded the newspaper and tucked it under his left arm. It never failed to irritate how the simplest things required the utmost concentration. He donned his hat and walked out into the sharp wind of a typically grey Yorkshire spring morning.

He strolled through the winding lanes, heading for the livery.

As he turned onto the main street, the walk of a woman ahead of him caught his eye. A brisk, businesslike walk that did nothing to disguise the lush sensuality of her figure, even though it was wrapped in a warm woollen cloak. In his salad days, before Waterloo, he might have offered to carry her basket. Women, young and old, loved the dash of an officer in uniform.

Well, he was no longer entitled to wear a uniform. He'd retired. Hah!

The woman stopped at a milliner's window, revealing her profile.

Caro Falkner. Pleasure rippled through him. Desire was certainly a part of it, a hot lick deep in his gut, but there was also a lightness, a simple gladness at the sight of her. Not that the gladness would be reciprocated. She had made it quite clear she wanted no remembrances of the past. Of youthful folly, before the carnage of war had taken his hand and killed her soldier husband.

He'd met her in a small village not far from Worthing, where his regiment had been stationed, but had been far too tongue-tied at her beauty to utter a word. How he had hoped, with the desperation of the very young, to ask her to stand up with him when he and his fellow officers had been invited to the village assembly. Naturally, she'd only had eyes for the older and far more charming Carothers. She'd been a delight to watch, though, as she danced and flirted her way through his more experienced companions.

These days the woman was far too prim and proper for her own good. And that made her a challenge to a man who had enjoyed the intimate company of several willing widows over the years. A challenge he had no intention of taking up because, for some reason, his very presence in a room made her uncomfortable. At Charlie and Merry's wedding, good friends of them both, she'd been far from friendly. Tales of his rakish ways passed on by Tonbridge, no doubt. And as the daughter of a vicar, she would likely be shocked by his antecedents. Horrified. Not even a smart new uniform would make up for such a background with a respectable woman.

He forced himself to pretend not to see her, as she had made it so obvious she would prefer. Never had he even hinted to Charlie of their past meeting. He could still see her, though, in his mind's eye, the sparkle in her eyes as she spun with her partners through the steps of every country dance that night. He'd been fascinated.

Not that he was about to force these memories upon a woman who shied away at the sight of him.

Besides, these days he preferred the kind of woman who enjoyed a bit of danger along with her dalliance. Widows or members of the demi-monde who were not looking for any sort of permanent relationship and were honest about it. Oh, his adoptive mother had forced him into a semblance of civility, given him polish and manners, and a degree of charm to go with it, but the ladies of the *ton* had no trouble sensing the ruffian who lurked within. Naturally, decent ladies avoided him like the plague. As did Mrs Falkner.

He stepped clear of her at the same moment she turned away from the window. Their gazes clashed. Her eyes widened in recognition. The flicker of anxiety in her eyes sent a chill down his spine, though she quickly schooled her expression into one of reserved politeness. Was it merely the response of a sensible respectable woman when faced with a man who could ruin her reputation if she wasn't careful? Or something else? Her reaction wasn't a shock; he was used to respectable women distancing themselves. It was his hurt that *she* would do so that momentarily stole his breath.

He buried the pointless feeling of rejection and flashed her his most seductive smile. The devilment of anger taking possession of reason. He was, after all, a good friend of her employer. He lifted his hat and bowed. 'Mrs Falkner, what an unexpected pleasure.' The purr of seduction in his voice caused her to stiffen.

'Captain Read?' There was something about her soft and low voice that affected him in a very visceral way.

Blast it, he really should have pretended he had not seen her. He did not need desire for a woman he could not have to make his day any worse. 'Just plain Mr these days, ma'am. I hope you are well?'

Pink stained her cheekbones with a becoming blush. He remembered that about her, the way she coloured. But that was all that remained of her from before. Her ready smile and happy laughter were nowhere to be seen. Respectable widows did not smile at rogues. 'I am well,' she said, lifting her chin. 'Thank you.' She hesitated a fraction. 'And you?'

Her politeness surprised him. He didn't imagine she cared how he was for one single moment.

'I, too, am well.' He glanced around, looking for a maid or a footman. Seeing no one nearby, he frowned. 'Are you unescorted?'

She stiffened. 'I am quite capable of doing a little shopping without aid.'

From the icy blast of dislike coming his way, he knew she didn't want to have anything to do with him, but he wasn't enquiring for her sake; he was doing what his friend Charlie would expect of him. And, indeed, Charlie's new wife, Merry. With the unrest among the population at the news in the papers this morning, even a guttersnipe like him knew better than to allow a decent female to walk the streets alone. He certainly would not allow his half-sisters to do so, though they, too, would likely baulk at his escort.

He grasped the handle of the heavy-looking basket over her arm. 'Allow me, please.' Not really a request, though at least he had enough manners to phrase it as one. Perhaps the countess, his stepmother, had done a better job than either of them had thought.

A moment of resistance held them frozen, but her expression said that while she did not want his escort, neither did she want to make a scene in public. She let go and stepped back. 'It is very kind of you, Captain…I mean Mr Read, but I have quite finished my errands.'

'Then I will accompany you back to your

lodgings. I assume you are staying in York overnight?'

Her eyes narrowed with suspicion. Then the sensible woman sighed, knowing there was no use arguing with a determined man. 'At the King George. I return to Skepton tomorrow.'

He transferred the basket to the crook of his right arm and, gritting his teeth, slightly winged his left elbow. Enough for her to be able to ignore it without embarrassment for either of them. She would not be the first to refuse his injured arm.

His heart gave an odd lurch when, without a moment's hesitation, she tucked her hand into the crook of his elbow. The feel of her hand seared his skin through several layers of cloth, including her gloves. He could not remember the last time he'd felt this shaken. Foolish sentiment, no doubt. After all, a woman who went about gathering prostitutes off the streets of Skepton, as Charlie had related to him, was hardly likely to baulk at a missing hand.

Even so, it was with a sense of doom that he realised that even for such a small gesture from this woman, he would walk barefoot across hot coals.

*Idiot.*

* * *

Caro could not believe her bad luck. Or rather she could. If anything could go wrong where she was concerned, it would. She had hoped never to see Captain Read—no, Mr Read apparently, her employer's friend—ever again, after the Tonbridges' wedding was over and done. Indeed, she had hoped she would not. For Tommy's sake. Of all the people she had met in her life, he was one of the few who might guess at her secret. At her shame.

She still did not know whether he recalled their meeting years ago. The uncertainty made her heart flutter wildly, as did the way he regarded her as if she was some sort of tasty treat.

'Who accompanies you on this shopping trip of yours?' he asked, his voice teasing, but also concerned, when he had no right to be concerned for her welfare.

If she kept her answers brief and to the point, hopefully he would take the hint and be on his way. 'No one. Merry is in London with Tonbridge, who was called to attend his father's sickbed.' Caro tried to ignore the sense of abandonment that had plagued her since her friend's marriage. The same feeling she had experienced when her father had turned her out of his house. Yet it was not the same thing at all. She and Merry remained friends and correspondents. She had heard nothing from her family since the day she had left.

While she did not look at Mr Read, she sensed his gaze on her face. Sharp. Assessing. 'You travelled to York alone?' he asked.

The note of disapproval in his voice added to her discomfort. Her father's voice had held exactly that note when one had a smut on one's nose or had misplaced one's gloves and kept him waiting. Instinctively her chin came up, the way it had so often in her girlhood, generally leading to further admonishment. What was it about this man that affected her so, when she had worked so hard on perfecting a calm demeanour? 'I drove here in the Tonbridge carriage with his lordship's coachman.'

He made a scoffing sound in the back of his throat that he then tried to disguise as a cough. 'Have you not *read* the newspapers, Mrs Falkner? The north is up in arms about this latest idiotic verdict—' He grimaced.

Mouth agape, she stared up at his face, once more overwhelmed by the height and breadth of him. In her mind she kept seeing him as the gangly young ensign from nine years before with large ears and a hook of a nose, hanging at the fringes of his fellow officers. The skinny fellow on the cusp of manhood was gone, replaced by a hard-faced, hard-eyed man who had grown into his aristocratic features. He'd become handsome in the way of a battle-hardened warrior, a face of clean lines and sharp angles. 'I read the newspapers,' she said with hauteur. It was difficult to look down one's nose at a man who was as tall as he, but if he got the message that she wanted nothing to do with him, it was worth the attempt. 'None of that has anything to do with my trip to York for household supplies.'

His expression darkened. 'A woman driving across Yorkshire's moors in a lozenged carriage with no more than an elderly coachman to guard her is hardly safe. Don't think your gender will protect you. No one was safe at St Peter's Field. Men, women and children died, and those wielding the swords were related to half the nobility in Britain.'

She recoiled at the underlying bitterness in his voice. 'You speak as if you have first-hand knowledge.'

His mouth tightened. 'I was there.'

'Is that why you resigned your commission?'

His jaw flickered. He turned his face away, looking off into the distance. 'In part.'

Clearly he did not welcome further interrogation. Nor did she have any reason to engage him in conversation. Quite the opposite. 'I am sure there can be no danger to me. Tonbridge made his disgust of last August's events quite clear.'

They crossed the square in front of York Minster, its spires pushing into the clouds like medieval lances.

He stopped, forcing her to stop, too, and look at his grave expression. 'Nevertheless I will escort you on your return journey as Tonbridge would expect.'

His autocratic manner sent anger spurting through her veins, despite that he was right. Tonbridge *was* exceedingly protective of his wife and, by association, her erstwhile companion. And it was not just the recent troubles that made him so. The establishment of the Haven for Women and Mothers with Children in Need had been highly unpopular with the wealthier of Skepton's residents. Until Tonbridge had taken up their cause, both her life and Merry's had been at risk.

'It is most kind of you, Mr Read. However, rather than put you to such trouble, I will hire outriders for the journey back.'

His face hardened as if he had received

some sort of insult. 'If that is your preference, then please ensure you do.'

She had not intended an insult, but surely he had better things, more important things, to do than serve as her escort? She bit back the urge to apologise. If he was insulted, he would likely leave her in peace. The longer she spent in his company, the more likely he was to remember he *had* met her before. She'd seen the puzzlement in his eyes as he tried to figure out why she looked familiar on the occasion of their first meeting. She had no wish to remind him or to reminisce about old times. Or old acquaintances. She repressed a shudder. And she certainly did not want him anywhere near her son.

He started walking again. He had long legs and towered over her by a good eight inches, but he adjusted his stride to the length of her steps. It was the mark of a well-bred gentleman. Or a man intent on making a good impression.

'How is Thomas?' he asked, to her surprise and trepidation. 'Is he with you?'

It was difficult not to be pleased at his recollection of her boy, when in truth she should have been terrified. Why would a man who was barely an acquaintance care about the whereabouts of her son? Was it merely commonplace conversation or a threat of exposure or simply a way of worming his way into her good graces? Whatever his motive, she did not dare show her worry, so she kept her voice calm. Her answer factual. 'He is well, thank you.'

Tommy had been impressed by Captain Read in his uniform when they had met. The boy had talked of how his father would have been just such a soldier. Subsequently, she had done her best to keep Captain Read at a distance in case he recalled the past she had tried to keep hidden.

'You should think of him if you will not think of yourself. He would suffer greatly if anything happened to you,' he said.

Her blood chilled. 'Are you trying to frighten me?' It would not be the first time a man had tried using intimidation to get what he wanted. 'It is not well done of you. I can manage to find my own way back to my hotel from here.' She could see the dashed place.

There was frost in his voice when he replied, 'What is it about my company you object to, Mrs Falkner? Have I done something you find offensive?'

Her words had hurt him. It was a vulnerability she would not have expected from a man who carried himself with such confidence, but he had asked and she was all for speaking the truth. 'I am a respectable woman, Mr Read.' A respect that had been hard-won in a town like Skepton, where the community closed ranks against outsiders. 'It will not serve my reputation to be seen junketing around with a single gentleman, no matter how worthy he may be. Or how well connected.' She had no wish to be the subject of gossip or idle speculation, for Thomas's sake, as much as for her own.

The hard muscles beneath her hand tensed, though his face gave nothing of his thoughts away. He was like a coiled spring. A weapon ready to fire. Perhaps if she insulted him enough, he would walk off in a huff. Let her escape from his unsettling presence. The flutters of attraction she felt each time he looked at her with those amazingly piercing hazel eyes were scrambling her thoughts. Was it because Merry and Charlie had deliberately warned her about his reputation as a ladies' man prior to their wedding? Could it be her tendency to wickedness leading her astray? After all these years? Certainly not. She would never become one of his conquests. Or let him expose her secrets. She dropped her hand from his arm.

He did not take the hint. With grim determination, he walked her all the way to the hotel entrance and handed off her basket to the footman waiting at the door with an easy grace that belied his missing left hand. After five years, he must be used to it, she supposed, but still, something inside her ached at the sight of the sleeve pinned at the wrist.

Not that his injury made him any less of a man. Indeed, he had the sort of lethal masculinity that warned the unwary to be careful unless they disturb a sleeping beast. And warned a woman to guard her heart.

'What time did you intend to set out for Skepton tomorrow?' he asked in a surprisingly mild tone given the heat of anger in his gaze. Or perhaps it wasn't anger at all, but something far more risky. Chills ran across her skin. Pleasant little prickles.

She ignored her body's reaction. 'I asked Mr Garge to have the coach at the door at eight. The haberdasher has promised to deliver the rest of my supplies later this afternoon. I will be home by mid-afternoon.'

He doffed his hat and bowed. 'Then I wish the rest of your day is pleasant and bid you good day.' He marched off, his bearing very much that of a soldier.

Dashing and handsome, in or out of uniform. Her skin warmed. Her body tingled in unmentionable places she thought she had firmly under control. The man was without doubt one of the most attractive she'd ever met. The kind of man…

Blast. How could she entertain such thoughts when she knew the danger of the smallest indiscretion? She had spent years creating an aura of respectability. Fought hard to maintain it, too. She wasn't about to throw her life away for the sake of a handsome man. Especially not one of the ilk of Mr Read, who, while not legitimate, had an earl for a father. For Tommy's sake, she could not afford to be noticed by anyone with connections to the beau monde. Not if she wanted to keep her son by her side.

If Mr Read should ever put two and two together she might well lose her son.

Charlie's timing was abysmal. The next morning, sitting in the snug at the Sleeping Tiger, Blade stared at the letter that had, according to his groom, Ned, arrived in the first post. It was exactly what he had hoped for and the worst possible news. If he had known about this yesterday, before he'd met Mrs Falkner, it might not now feel so damnably uncomfortable. Mrs Falkner was not going to be pleased.

Understatement of the year.

She might, he mused, even think he was lying to get his own way in the matter of her requiring an escort.

Too bad. Charlie had offered him a position, albeit temporary, and he intended to do all he could to prove his friend's trust justified. He needed this job. If he was successful, he might even be able to hold up his head and meet his father's gimlet gaze after the Peterloo debacle.

Serving in the army had offered him the chance to leave his unfortunate beginnings behind and he'd mucked it up. No doubt the earl would already have received word of his failure. This offer he'd received from Charlie was a chance to start again without the need to ask his father for assistance. Something he hated. He certainly wasn't going to let Mrs Falkner's dislike keep him from honest employment.

He glanced at the dingy face of the case clock in the corner. 'Damn.' It was gone nine, well after the time she said she'd depart. Still, ladies were often late. Or at least his sisters often were. As were his previous inamoratas. Lost hair ribbons and misplaced gloves generally delayed a lady's departure by more than an hour or two.

Unfortunately, Mrs Falkner did not strike him as a lady subject to missing articles. She was far too efficient or Charlie would not have left her in charge of the charitable establishment Merry and Mrs Falkner had founded. A home for fallen women and their children they called the Haven.

He downed a cup of scalding hot coffee and called for his shot. He'd have to hurry if he was going to catch Mrs Falkner before she left her hotel. The innkeeper ambled over with his bill. 'Thought we was to have t'pleasure of your company a few more days, Mr Read.'

'Change of plans.' Blade skimmed a glance down the bill and found it accurate.

'You'll be careful on the road,' the landlord said. 'I hear there are rabble-rousers going around the countryside stirring up sentiments as ought not to be stirred.'

'Do you know any specifics?' he asked casually as he got to his feet.

'Not me, sir. I hear things. Mutters and so forth. No specifics.'

Hardly helpful. 'Have your man come up for my valise in ten minutes.' Ten minutes he could hardly afford, but it would take him that long to pack without help from Ned. 'Have a note taken round to Shaw's Livery for me, would you please?'

Ned would have his horse ready by the time he arrived.

# Chapter Two

Blade hunched deeper into his greatcoat. Naturally, it would rain *all* day. And naturally he'd missed Mrs Falkner at the King George.

Fortunately, his batman-cum-groom had taken the change in plan in stride. An excellent fellow, Ned. He'd been with Blade since the day he set foot in Lisbon and had proved a loyal and worthy comrade-in-arms. Blade was determined to keep the man employed, since work for soldiers returning from war was scarce, there being so many of them. Hopefully, Charlie would agree with the extra expense. If not, he would have to pay him from his own salary.

'House steward' was what Charlie had called the position he'd offered. Not something Blade would have thought of doing in his wildest dreams. He'd never thought of any career but the army from the time he could handle a wooden sword. And with the army reduced to a fraction of its former size, there wasn't a hope in hell of selling his commission quickly. If at all. He could just see the earl looking down his nose in his autocratic way and pretending he understood perfectly, while not understanding at all. Likely wishing him in Jericho, too. It wouldn't be the first time.

Not that Blade cared.

The odds had been against him from the start. Even his mother hadn't wanted him. He'd been in the way from the day of his birth and likely before. *Nothing but a bloody nuisance.* His mother's words still had the power to carve a slice out of his heart.

He'd tried his best not to be in the way at his father's house when he'd gone there at the age of ten. Tried to do nothing that would make him or his lady wife regret offering him a place in their home. He hadn't stood a chance. What man wanted his mistake thrust under his nose on a daily basis?

Thank God and Charlie, he didn't have to return to his father like the beggar he'd always been.

He hunched deeper into the folds of his scarf, but it didn't prevent a trickle of rainwater finding its way down the back of his neck. And that didn't take his mind off the water splashing up from his horse's hooves and soaking his breeches. Pretty soon his backside would be soaking wet, too.

While the dry and warm Mrs Falkner, when he caught up to her, would not be the slightest bit pleased with him or his news.

The woman certainly offered a challenge to a man known for his charm when it came to lonely widows. A reputation he'd worked hard to acquire. Pleasurably hard. Those words in conjunction with thoughts of Caro Falkner had him shifting uncomfortably in the saddle. Was it her obvious disapproval that had him thinking of seduction each time he saw her or the beauty she tried so hard to hide behind her severe demeanour and dress? Or was it the mystery behind her facade of unbending respectability? The picture she painted of the vicar's perfect daughter, when he remembered her so very differently. Was she hiding something that might prove dangerous to his friend and his friend's wife?

An intriguing question.

He rounded a bend to a scene of utter disaster. A carriage tilted crazily on the verge. A shattered wheel some distance off. A team—

Tonbridge's team, for goodness' sake—trembling and shifting in the harness, ready to bolt. His heart rose in his throat.

He galloped the intervening hundred yards and leaped down. His gut clenched at the sight of the coachman sprawled face up in the ditch. Blade had seen enough death to recognise a broken neck. Why had he not caught them up sooner? Had the woman's distaste for him made him deliberately hang back? *Idiot.*

'Mrs Falkner?' His shout was met by a resounding silence. Heart in his mouth, he approached the carriage door swinging free on its hinges and peered inside. The sight of her pale face, her closed eyes and the way she lay on the floor in a heap brought bile to his throat. He leaped aboard. She groaned softly and her eyelids fluttered.

Alive, then. Relief flooded through him.

He rubbed her cold hands. 'Mrs Falkner?' he repeated. 'Come on, let's get you out of here.' It would be cold in the wind and rain, but he could feel the carriage shifting as the horses moved restlessly. At any moment the animals might take it into their foolish heads to run.

'Mrs Falkner,' he said again, more demanding this time. Louder.

She opened her eyes and put a hand to her

head. For a moment she stared at him blankly, then frowned. 'Mr Read? Where is Josiah? Mr Garge?'

He thought about lying, but she was going to see how matters lay the moment he got her out of the carriage. 'Dead, I am afraid. Broken neck. Here, let me help you up. Put your arm over my shoulder and hang on.' With only one hand, he had to get her to help herself. Fortunately, her eyes cleared and, with his aid, she pushed to her feet. He helped her to the ground, where she swayed slightly, then found her feet and her balance.

Out in the grey light of the morning, his blood chilled as he saw the red lump on her forehead, already turning blue, and the blood streaked across her chin. 'You are hurt.'

She stared at him blankly, then glanced down at her hand where more blood welled. 'A scratch, I think.'

He guided her to a boulder and sat her facing away from the coachman. 'I must see to the horses and then we will see what we can do about that injury.' He'd seen men die from less on the battlefields of Europe.

A quick check of the horses confirmed his impression that while nervous, they were unharmed. He found a length of rope beneath the coachman's box and used it to hobble the leaders. There was no way for him to repair the coach. They needed help.

He went to his own horse and pulled down his saddle pack before going back to Mrs Falkner. Her colour was already better. A good sign. He put a finger beneath her chin to lift up her face so he could see to tend her forehead. Her eyes widened in shock. 'You have a bump,' he said by way of explanation for his forward behaviour. 'Do you have a headache?'

She shook her head. 'It only hurts if I touch it.'

Another good sign. He pulled out a bottle of witch hazel and dabbed at the bruise and then at the cut on her hand.

'Did you say Garge is…?'

No sense beating around the bush. 'Dead. Yes.'

'How can that be?'

'He must have struck his head on a boulder when he came off the box.'

'But…he opened the door. Looked in on me. I heard him. I felt so dizzy, I told him I had to rest a minute. He left before I could open my eyes. But he was there. After the accident.'

Not possible. She likely imagined it. 'I am so

sorry, Mrs Falkner, but Mr Garge's neck was broken by the fall. It would have been instant.'

She stared at him, then turned her face away, clearly confused. And why would she not be after such a bang to the noggin. 'Is there nothing we can do for him?'

'No.' He kept his voice matter-of-fact. He did not want her going into a fit of hysterics after she'd been so stoic. She would not like him to see her in such a state any more than he would like to watch her fall apart.

She started to rise, swayed and put a hand to her head. Her face blanched.

He gently pushed her down. 'Sit.' He pressed her head to her knees with his forearm at the back of her neck, a beautiful vulnerable nape that begged a man's touch. He forced himself to look away and gaze off into the distance until her breathing evened out.

She took a deep shuddering breath. 'I am better now. Thank you.'

He released her immediately. He did not want her thinking he had anything untoward on his mind, because it would be easy to fall into such a trap with a woman as lovely as this one. 'He wouldn't have felt a thing,' he said. It was what they always told themselves in the aftermath of battle, though, given his own experience, he doubted it was ever true. 'There was nothing anyone could have done.'

She buried her face in her hands. 'What on earth am I to tell his wife?'

He grimaced. It was something he had always hated, but at least he'd only been required to write a letter. He'd never had to face anyone's widow with the bad news, though he'd met plenty of them since returning to England. Made a point of it. And they were grateful, most of them, when they should have taken him to task for not caring for their men better than he had.

'What happened?' he asked.

'I don't know. The coach bounced so hard it must have hit a rut in the road and then I was thrown against the door. I don't remember much after that.'

With a coachman as competent as Tonbridge's driving a team as steady as this one, it was hard to imagine Garge running foul of a rut. 'Did you see anything unusual?'

She frowned. 'What sort of thing?'

Clearly his conversation with the innkeeper had his senses on high alert. 'I wondered if something might have distracted Garge. Made him make a mistake?'

She frowned. 'I heard a crack. The whip. I

assumed he was trying to make up some time after the slow going in the valley.'

Ice ran through his veins. A shot? He bit back a curse, not wanting to scare her. He needed to look at the carriage. And the coachman. He rose and stared around him. 'Well, there is no moving the carriage with that broken wheel. We must find you some shelter.' He'd also have to notify the local authority about the death. 'Our best course is to hope someone travels along this road, sooner rather than later.' Once he knew she was safe, he'd come back before the local coroner arrived and see if his suspicions were borne out by evidence.

She touched a hand to her temple. 'Yes. Of course. That is best.' She looked hopefully up and down the road.

He couldn't believe her calmness. Most women in her place would be fainting all over the place and calling for their hartshorn. Not his sisters, though, he realised, suddenly missing them like the blazes, when he'd done his best to ignore them for years. She was like the women who had followed the drum with their husbands. One of the kind made of sterner stuff. The kind a man could admire as well as lust after. Curse his wayward thoughts.

'Sit here and don't move while I see to the horses.'

She stiffened and he realised he'd phrased it as an order. 'If you don't mind?'

Her posture relaxed. She nodded, trickles of rain coursing down her face.

'I don't suppose you have an umbrella in the coach?'

She shook her head, her eyes sad.

Blast, he needed to get her out of the rain before she caught some sort of ague. As soon as he was sure the horses would not make a dash for it, he would sit her back in the carriage.

And then he heard the sound of wheels on the road and the clop of hooves. For a change it seemed luck was on his side.

Rescue was at hand.


Sitting by the hearth in a tiny parlour of the small inn at a crossroads some two miles from the accident, Caro could not seem to get warm no matter how close she sat to the blazing logs. They had been lucky the carter had agreed to bring her to the closest inn while Mr Read stayed with the horses. The Crossed Keys, situated high on the moorland, was the only hostelry for miles. The carter had then gone off with the innkeeper to fetch the local constable.

In her mind's eye, she kept seeing poor Mr Garge, lying on his back on the rock-strewn ground. Kept thinking of his wife. She had no doubt that Tonbridge would offer the woman some sort of aid, but that wasn't the point. They were a devoted couple and now the woman would be alone. Caro knew the pain of losing everyone you loved. Even blessed as she was with Thomas, it had taken years before the agony of that loss had eased to a dull ache she rarely noticed.

The innkeeper's wife, Mrs Lane, bustled in with a tray. 'Here you go, ma'am. This will warm you from the inside out. I've taken the liberty of adding a tot of brandy. Put some heart into you, you look that pale.'

'Thank you, Mrs Lane, but I do not drink strong spirits.'

'It's medicinal,' the woman said and folded her arms across her ample bosom. 'Ye'll drink it like a good lass. One swallow. I'd do no less for one of me own.'

A will of iron shone in the other woman's eyes, but there was kindness there, too. How kind would she be if she knew the truth of Caro's past? But that was neither here nor there in this situation. She picked up the goblet and sniffed. The pungent fumes hit the back of her throat and made her eyes water. 'I don't think—'

'The trick is to drink it down quick, lass. The longer you dally, the worse it will get.'

Like the rest of the unpleasant things in life. Heaving a sigh, Caro closed her eyes, tipped the glass and swallowed. Her throat seized at the burn. She choked and coughed and gasped while Mrs Lane banged her on the back—until she caught her breath and was able to ward her off.

'I'm fine,' she managed.

'Aye, well, you will be. Now drink your tea and we'll await for the menfolk to return. Meanwhile I've a supper to cook.' She marched out.

Her husband, who was also the local undertaker, had sent his potboy for the local coroner. The Lanes were indeed practical folk.

Caro poured her tea and sipped to take the taste of the brandy away. She had to admit she did feel better. And warmer. A whole lot warmer. A welcome numbness stole over her. She leaned back against the plump cushion.

A sound jerked her fully awake. She opened her eyes to find Mr Read staring down at her with an odd look on his face.

She sat up, her cheeks flushing hot. 'Oh,' she gasped. 'I must have fallen asleep. I beg your pardon.' She glanced at the clock. Goodness. She had slept for more than an hour. The landlady had taken her tray away and she hadn't heard a thing. 'Is everything all right?'

Such a stupid question from the look on his face. She squeezed her eyes shut, trying to break free of the fog of sleep.

He grimaced. 'I hate to do this, but the coroner is requesting a word. About the accident.'

The last word had an odd emphasis, but when she looked at his face, there was nothing to see but a kindly concern. 'Yes. Of course. If it is required.'

'I'll fetch him.' He made a small gesture with his hand and let it fall. 'You might want to take a peek in the mirror. Your cap...' His words trailed off, but there was heat in his eyes she did not understand. He turned away smartly. 'I'll fetch him up.'

The moment he closed the door, she leaped to her feet and stared at her reflection in the mirror above the mantel. Heavens, her cap was askew and tendrils of hair were hanging in strings around her face. Mr Read must think her a slattern to be drinking and sleeping in such a state. Cheeks pink with embarrassment, her stomach dipping in shame, she quickly tidied herself barely moments before she heard the tread of heavy steps on the stairs followed by a sharp knock.

'Come.'

Mr Read ushered in a heavyset gentleman who appeared to be in his sixties with wind-roughened cheeks and a beak of a nose above a grizzled beard.

'Mrs Falkner, may I introduce Sir Reginald Walcombe. Sir Reginald, this is the lady of whom I spoke.'

Sir Reginald bowed, with a creaking of corset. 'Ma'am.'

'Please, gentlemen, be seated,' she said.

Sir Reginald sat, pulled out an enormous white linen handkerchief and mopped his brow. 'Stairs, ma'am,' he wheezed apologetically.

Behind him, amusement twinkled in Mr Read's eyes for such a brief moment she almost might have imagined it. Almost. But it was such a warming and comforting thing, she knew she had not. Indeed, she had a tiny bit of trouble repressing a smile. 'May I call for the tea tray, Sir Reginald?'

'No, thank'ee kindly. I had a shot of Lane's best down below.'

For some reason, Mr Read remained standing. His expression was blank, but he seemed to be watching her intently.

'Now, ma'am, I know thee's had a shock, but tell me, if you will, in your own words, what happened.'

She relayed the same information to him as she had told to Mr Read, whose gaze became more intense.

When she got to the part about Garge looking in on her, Sir Reginald frowned. 'You saw him, ma'am?'

'No. It took me a moment or two to come to my senses, but the door was open, as Mr Read will confirm.'

'It was,' Mr Read said.

Sir Reginald's bushy brows drew down in a way that would frighten small children and miscreants. 'He spoke then? Said something to 'ee?'

'No. The door opened. Nothing else.'

'Ah, probably the latch gave way. Coach is badly damaged.' He shook his head. 'Bad business all around.' With a laboured grunt, Sir Reginald pushed to his feet with hands braced on the chair arms. 'A terrible accident, then. And not the first time on that bend. I'll bid you good day, ma'am.'

'I will see you out, sir,' Mr Read said. 'I will return in a moment, Mrs Falkner.'

Something in the way he looked at her gave her pause. Was there something he wasn't saying?

Heart beating fast, she awaited his return.

A good fifteen minutes passed and still no sign of him. She got up and looked out of the window. There was no sign of any conveyance, but the windows of the rooms below cast their light out into the courtyard.

Finally, a light knock sounded at the door. She hadn't heard anyone mounting the stairs. 'Who is it?'

'Read,' came the low rumble of his voice.

'Come in.'

He entered with a frown on his face.

'Is something wrong?'

'I took the liberty of asking for dinner to be served in here and booking you room for the night. I had your valise and purchases taken upstairs.'

Her stomach pitched. 'I cannot be away all night. Tommy will worry.' He was a clever little boy. It had not taken him long to realise that most children had two parents as well as extended families. He knew his father had died and had become terrified she would die, too, leaving him completely alone.

Mr Read's expression darkened as if her anxiety was his fault, but he gave her no chance to explain. 'We have no choice,' he bit out tersely. 'It is too late to set out tonight. Sir Reginald has promised to send over his carriage for our use in the morning, but he needed it to return home. Lane's cart is required for funeral purposes.' His voice was harshly matter-of-fact.

They were stranded. She took a deep breath. 'I see. Well then, there really is no alternative.'

'Mrs Lane will show you up to your chamber to freshen up. Dinner is to be served in here in an hour.' He hesitated and went on in a voice devoid of all expression. 'If you don't care for company this evening, I am more than happy to take my meal in the kitchen.'

Despite the flatness of his tone, and an apparent lack of concern about her decision one way or the other, she sensed an underlying tension. As if he expected her to consign him to dine with the servants. He must think her rude indeed. 'After today's events I would be grateful for your company, Mr Read. And I wish to hear more of Sir Reginald's opinion with regard to the accident.'

His expression lightened, very slightly. He bowed. 'It will be my pleasure. I will let Mrs Lane know you are ready to go up.'

His *pleasure*. Now, why had that word sent shivers skating down her back?

Waiting in the parlour for her return, Blade cursed himself for his weakness, for wanting to spend time in her company. He should not have even thought of having dinner with her, let alone suggesting it in a manner that made it impossible for her to say no. So typical of him, Charlie would say. He'd spent too many years on the strut honing his seductive skills to leave them at the door when in decent company. Too bad. He made no pretence of being more than the guttersnipe he'd been born, the reason why some of the more daring ladies liked him in their beds. A taste of excitement and danger. A bit of rough, one had called him to his face.

Not this one, though. This one was a respectable lady who would not have given him the time of day if he wasn't Charlie's friend. And nor should she.

He still didn't know what to make of her assertion that Garge, or someone, had opened the door, and it was that someone who was worrying him. Who *had* opened the carriage door and looked in? Why would anyone do that and not render assistance?

Old Sir Reginald had seen it as female megrims, but that was too out of character for Mrs Falkner. Could someone have come across the accident, thought to rob the carriage and been deterred by the sound of him coming along the road? Or could it be something more sinister, such as someone hoping to cause Tonbridge harm? Someone who had been surprised by the presence of a woman in his carriage and taken off. Or was it simply a case of the door latch letting go as the carriage twisted and settled on its broken axle as Sir Reginald thought? Blade might have thought so, too, if not for the one unaccounted-for boot print in the mud beside the carriage door.

Nevertheless, whichever it was, Mrs Falkner had been lucky she wasn't more seriously hurt.

Fortunately, like Sir Reginald, she seemed to have no suspicion that it might be anything other than an accident. And since he did not want her frightened out of her wits any more than she had been already, he planned to leave it that way. He still couldn't quite believe she hadn't simply taken to her bed after such a scare.

His unruly mind wandered back to the

scene of her drowsing in the chair when he had come to warn her of Sir Reginald's imminent arrival. Asleep, her face relaxed, she had looked younger, prettier, more like the girl he had been smitten with that long-ago spring. A memory she clearly did not want to acknowledge any more than he did. She was the daughter of a vicar and he was the bastard son of a prostitute who'd kicked him out at the age of ten. *'I don't need you hanging around. You are just another mouth for me to feed.'* The pain of those words stabbed him behind the breastbone. Less sharp than when spoken, but still there. While he hadn't thought so at the time, he'd been fortunate his father had agreed to recognise him as his son or he'd likely have died on the streets of London. Or been hanged for a criminal.

He heard her soft tread on the stairs outside the parlour and opened the door.

She looked startled. 'How did you know it was me?'

'By your step.' He led her to the chair by the hearth. The table was set, but the food had not yet appeared.

He stood at ease, wrist crossed over his forearm behind him. A trick he'd perfected to make the missing hand less noticeable.

'Please, Mr Read,' she said sharply. 'Be seated, before I get a crick in my neck.'

He was tempted to resist what was clearly an order. That had always been his trouble. Rebelling at stupid orders. She suffered from a similar affliction, he recalled, and he wanted to smile.

Her expression carved in stone, her hands folded in her lap, she waited for him to do as she bid.

He picked up the poker, raked around in the fire for a moment or two as a sop to his pride, before he sat in the chair recently occupied by Sir Reginald. 'Why do you pretend we did not meet before?'

Hell, why had that been blurted out of his mouth? Why the devil did it matter?

Her lush lips parted. Her eyes widened in shock before her gaze lowered to her clasped fingers. 'You gave no sign of remembering me either,' she said in a low voice.

At seventeen, and a newly minted ensign, he'd thought her akin to an angel. He'd been far too tongue-tied seeing how pretty she was, how very different from the women he'd known when living with his mother, or those in his adoptive parents' house, to do more than stutter a greeting.

She was also the reason for his first reprimand. He'd gone for Carothers's throat when he'd called her a round-heeled wench in the officers' mess the morning after the local assembly, where they'd been invited to make up the numbers of gentlemen. For that, he'd received a tongue-lashing from his commanding officer and a black mark on his record. Only his father's name had kept him from being thrown out of the regiment.

'It was a long time ago,' he said. Too long ago for it to be of any relevance.

'Yes.' She raised her gaze to meet his, clearly glad to put the recollection behind her. 'Much has occurred since then.'

'Indeed.' She had been married and widowed. He had been as good as discharged from the career he loved.

'I assume Sir Reginald has finished his investigations?' she asked, clearly anxious to change an awkward subject.

He gave a brief nod. 'Apparently it is not the first fatality to occur on that particular corner.'

'I hope he did not blame Josiah Garge. I am sure he did his best.'

'No. No blame.'

'His wife will take some comfort from that, and I know Lord Tonbridge will make a generous settlement. Still, it is a very sad day for the Garge family. What are the next steps?'

'The jury will be called by the coroner tomorrow. They will meet below.'

'Will I need to appear?' She sounded surprisingly anxious. Was there something she knew that she had not told him? Something she wanted to hide? He wanted to question her further, but she looked so pale, so tired, he decided to leave it. For now.

'I believe not. My word and that of the constable will be enough. Once a verdict is reached we can leave for Skepton. Lane will bring the remains there for the appropriate rites and services.'

She nodded slowly. 'Thank you. I appreciate your help and support in this matter.'

If he'd been truly helpful, instead of standing on his dignity, he would have insisted on escorting her and none of this would have happened. He frowned at her. 'You said you were going to hire outriders.'

She made a face. 'There were none available at such short notice.'

He had no way of knowing whether or not that was the truth, but it was water under the bridge. One thing he did know—as soon as he got to Skepton, he would write to Tonbridge and see if he had any thoughts on whether someone might have accosted his carriage and, if so, who.

Then he'd do a bit of investigating of his own. In the meantime, he would enjoy a meal with a pretty woman who, it seemed, was prepared to admit she recalled him.

## Chapter Three

Despite his assurances that all was well in hand, Caro sensed an underlying concern in Mr Read's manner as he gestured to a side table. 'May I offer you a glass of sherry?'

She shook her head. 'Thank you, no.'

His gaze cut longingly to the tray of drinks.

'Please, do not let my abstinence prevent you from partaking.'

He strode to the table and poured himself a brandy. He tossed it off and poured another. Dutch courage? Was she really so formidable to a man who had faced the guns at Waterloo?

An awkward silence ensued, fortunately broken by the entry of Mrs Lane with supper dishes. The young woman with her, a dark-haired lass of about sixteen, eyed Mr Read with obvious interest. Caro narrowed her eyes at the girl, who blushed and giggled before she left the room with a dip of a curtsy.

Mrs Lane, elbows akimbo, gazed from one to the other of them. 'You'll pardon me, sir, if I has this to say no matter what Sir Reginald thinks of the *accident*?'

Mr Read tensed, but his lips formed an encouraging smile. 'I would be glad to hear your opinion, Mrs Lane.'

'I've known Josiah Garge for years. Back and forth he's gone along this road until he knowed it like the back of his hand. He's no Johnny Raw to be taking that corner too fast. Something happened.'

The piercing gaze Mr Read had fixed on the woman's face became more intense. 'What sort of something?'

Mrs Lane deflated, her hands falling to her sides. She shook her head. 'I don't know. But taking a man's good name, talk of drink, fair makes my blood to boil.'

Caro's own indignation rose. 'Is that what Sir Reginald is saying? I have no reason to believe that Josiah Garge was anything but sober. Mr Read, surely—'

'Sir Reginald made no more than a passing comment,' he said. 'One of several possibilities.' His lips flattened. 'But you are right,

Mrs Lane. It is easy for a man's reputation to be blackened by a careless word. I will ensure that no such aspersions on his character will be cast without evidence.'

'His wife will thank you for it, sir,' the landlady said.

'And you may be assured that Lord Tonbridge will see to it that she is properly cared for,' Caro added.

'As he should, or he would hear from me,' Mrs Lane said brusquely. 'Dinner is served.' She nodded for emphasis and left, leaving the door wide open.

'A fierce woman, our Mrs Lane,' Mr Read said. 'Clearly not one to be cowed by the heir to a dukedom. Shall we eat? I told Mrs Lane we could manage to serve ourselves since most of her staff is off on other errands on our behalf. I hope that finds favour with you?'

She certainly didn't want the saucy servant girl waiting on them. And as long as the door remained open… 'Certainly.'

He led her to the table and seated her, managing to slide her chair in with one hand as easily as a man with two. He sat opposite her. 'If you would serve the side dishes, while I serve the beef?'

The beef had been sliced in the kitchen. He

used the large fork provided and placed two slices on her plate. She served him the potatoes, green beans and peas. After spooning gravy on her plate, she passed him the boat.

'Wine?' he asked.

'Thank you.'

He poured a rich red burgundy into their glasses. After a short muttered saying of grace, he lifted his goblet in a toast. 'To those gone but not forgotten.'

The sorrow in his deep voice was not lost on her. This toast meant something more than Josiah Garge. Although there were some people in her life she would prefer to forget, the coachman was not among them. She raised her glass. 'Not forgotten.' She sipped and put the glass down. She usually preferred water.

They addressed their dinner. Or at least she did. She had not expected to feel so hungry, but it had been a long time since breakfast. Something made her look up.

He was watching her, his eyes hooded, his expression something she could not quite read. Was she eating too fast? Did he think that if she was a proper lady she would not be hungry, but should pick at her food? 'Is something wrong?'

He seemed to pull himself back into the

present. 'Nothing.' He picked up his fork and neatly folded a slice of meat into a small parcel before lifting it to his mouth. It was barely noticeable that he had the use of only one hand since he accomplished it with such grace.

'How long do you plan to stay in Skepton?' she asked, more to fill the silence than anything else. There seemed to be a great many silences in Mr Read's company. Perhaps that was what made him so attractive to the ladies. To her. His air of impenetrable darkness.

She mentally shook her head at her foolish thoughts.

He took a sip of his wine. 'Good question.' The pause signified something important. 'After I met you in York yesterday, I received a letter from Lord Tonbridge. He has offered me a position in his employ.'

The way he phrased it, the way he looked at her... Her heart fluttered oddly. 'A position in Skepton?'

'Yes. As house steward at the Haven.'

Her vision tunnelled to a small point. 'The Haven? My Haven?' The place where she thought she and Tommy were finally safe?

He gave a slight grimace. 'I understand that Lady Tonbridge—'

'Yes, of course. She is our patron. Without

her, there would be no refuge. But I thought she trusted— We had an agreement…' She forced herself to stop. 'This is Lord Tonbridge's doing.' She pressed her lips together. What could she say? Her friend was married. Her husband's word was law. And now he would put this man in charge of a house she had managed perfectly well these past many months. Any other man might not be so bad, but what if he recognised Tommy, the way he had recognised her? Fortunately, the lad took more after her than his male parent, who had been almost as dark as she was fair. Only his jaw and his eyes came from his father. The thought of anyone realising she had never been married left her feeling ill. Not for her sake, but for how badly it would reflect on Tommy. On his future prospects. It really was too bad. She did not want to leave a place she had come to think of as her home. Her place in the world.

Like a mask his face revealed none of his thoughts. 'I am sorry if my appointment distresses you, Mrs Falkner. I can assure you, I am not charged with interference in the running of the charity. I am to see to the maintenance and security of the property along with that of the mill until Tonbridge is able to leave his father's bedside and return to his duties.'

'Security?' She stared at him. 'Tonbridge thinks we are in some sort of danger?'

'Tonbridge, like any good soldier, is ensuring his defences cannot be breached. There are rogues everywhere, Mrs Falkner. Thieves as well as malcontents. As I said, the appointment is temporary.'

*Temporary.* She grasped at the word like a straw. But temporary might be a very long time given the apparent severity of the duke's illness. If at all. If Tonbridge's father should die, he would become duke, which would mean he and Merry might never return to Skepton for anything but a brief visit. Oh, why of all men would Tonbridge have chosen this one to stand in his stead?

The answer was obvious. They were friends. Comrades-in-arms. And he was available. 'Then I must congratulate you. No doubt your army experience will stand you in good stead. Things like this—' She stopped herself. She had been about to say 'death', and it would have been such a foolish thing to have said to a man who had spent years of his life in the service of his king and a country at war. If only the sight of the coachman lying there would stop circling through her mind's eye, she might be able to stop thinking about the fragility of life.

'One never gets used to it,' he said softly.

A lump rose in her throat at the pain in his voice and the sympathy.

'Tonbridge told me about the loss of your husband at Badajoz,' he continued. 'I am so very sorry.'

She swallowed her guilt. 'Thank you.'

'Your son is a fine little man. You are doing a good job with him. I have no doubt his father would be proud.'

Her heart caught in her throat at the words. His father had refused to have anything to do with either of them. 'He is a good boy most of the time. Tonbridge advised me to send him away to school where he can be with other boys his age, but I cannot bring myself to do it.' She was terrified someone might see his likeness to his father, though she hadn't dared say so to Tonbridge.

'Boys need their mothers as much as they need a father,' he said. The bitterness in his tone surprised her.

Glad to turn the conversation away from Tommy, she pursued the question he had raised in her mind. 'You lost your mother while you were young?'

He frowned. Darkness filled his eyes. 'Lost?' He took a long pull at his wine. 'Not in the way you mean. But I have not seen her for years.' The words were spoken flatly and discouraged further enquiry.

How the devil had he let the conversation drift to the subject of his mother? He never spoke about the woman who had dumped him when she had found him inconvenient. The woman who had landed him on a father who hadn't really wanted him either.

He eyed the bottle of wine. Thoughts of his mother always fired his anger, and while wine would take the edge off, after an accident that might not be an accident, a dull mind was the last thing he needed. 'May I serve you some of this—' he inspected the steaming dessert '—treacle pudding?'

Mrs Falkner offered him a hesitant smile that struck him deeper than it should have. It made her look pretty and desirable, more like the girl he remembered. Some remnant of his lonely boy's heart remembered the pang of painful and hopeless longing. He shoved the feeling aside and held the knife ready.

'A small slice, if you will,' she said, smiling.

He carefully cut into the sponge and delivered a wedge to one of the small plates provided along with a generous dollop of treacle. The smell evoked memories of childhood dinners alone with his mother. Suppers with his half-siblings in the nursery. Why the devil was he becoming so maudlin? He put down the knife and handed the plate across the table.

Admiration lit her eyes. 'You do that so well with...' She coloured. 'Forgive me. I should not pass comment.'

He chuckled. 'Believe me, it took hours and hours of practice. Thanks to my father's determination, I would not shame him with my lack of manners. And thank you for noticing. Most people look away, uncomfortable at the sight of my difficulties.'

'You are not the slightest bit awkward.' She sounded almost indignant. 'I have seen men with two hands be far less graceful.'

Her outrage on his behalf sent a strange sensation arrowing through him. Painful, yet sweet. 'Graceful is not something usually sought by the male of our species.'

'I do not mean the foppish affectation of a dandy,' she said, her face serious. 'But a manly elegance that cannot help but please the female eye.' Her colour deepened.

Surprised and ridiculously pleased, he

smiled. 'Thank you. I mostly feel horribly clumsy. You instil me with confidence.' Heaven help him, it was the truth. A wave of warmth rushed through him, and to hide it he served himself a far larger portion of pudding than he had intended. Almost miraculously, for the first time in a long time, the sweet treat did not taste of ashes and death.

Clearly he was about to make an idiot of himself, hoping for something that wasn't there, when he'd given up hoping for anything.

Mrs Lane bustled in. She eyed the table with a satisfied nod. 'Will there be anything else for you, sir…ma'am? Shall I bring the tea tray, Mrs Falkner?'

'No, thank you,' Mrs Falkner said, looking becomingly prim and proper. 'It has been a long day. It is time I retired.'

Time to take her prim and proper self away from temptation, no doubt. Because if he wasn't mistaken, she was beginning to thaw to him. The very idea made his blood heat.

'Brandy or port for you, sir?' the landlady asked.

Brandy was not nearly as tempting as Caro Falkner. 'I, too, am ready for my bed.' Or her bed, judging by the embers of desire ready to leap to life at the first sign of encouragement.

Mrs Lane frowned. 'It doesn't seem right, sir, a fine gentleman like you bedding down in the stables with our Freddy when I have a perfectly good room on the third floor you can use.'

Mrs Falkner looked startled.

Blast the landlady. Did he have to explain the proprieties and put Mrs Falkner to the blush? She hadn't wanted his presence on the road. She certainly wouldn't want him beneath the same roof without a chaperone. 'I can assure you I have slept in far worse places. Besides...' he said as he saw Mrs Falkner about to protest, because her stiff manners hid a warm heart. 'I wish to be on hand to keep an eye on his lordship's horses.' Mr Lane had walked them behind the cart he'd used to fetch Garge's remains.

'I understand your caution, sir,' the landlady said, clearly worried by the idea that harm might come to the ducal beasts. 'As soon as you and Mrs Falkner are finished here, then, I'll send t'lass to clear away the dishes.'

'I am finished,' Mrs Falkner said.

She began to rise. He pushed back his chair, helped her to her feet and walked her to the door. 'I wish you a good night, ma'am.' He bowed.

He watched as she mounted the first few stairs and something inside him wished he was going up there with her. That somehow he could have the life the lack of a piece of paper had denied him. Husband. Father. Provider. But if he could not have that, he would at least play the role of protector. On Charlie's behalf, of course, not his own. Guard duty in the rain. It would be like old times.

How pathetic was he, thinking of such discomfort with longing? On the other hand, a few hours in the cold might well help cool his ardour.

Caro put down her book with a sigh, tiredness making the words waver on the page as if they were under water. She rubbed at her sore eyes and squinted at the clock on the mantel. Two in the morning. Exhaustion dragged her towards sleep, but every time she so much as thought about closing her eyes, the memory of poor Josiah Garge floated to the forefront of her vision and she started planning the words she would say to his wife, which brought her wide awake again.

Perhaps a glass of milk would help her sleep as it had in the past when her mind would not settle?

At home, she would not have hesitated to slip down the stairs to the kitchen. But in an inn? Albeit a small one.

If she continued to lie here wide awake, she would be drained tomorrow and she had too much to do to be taking to her bed when she got home. Not to mention that Tommy would be disappointed if all she wanted to do was sleep when she arrived home.

She slipped out of bed, put on her dressing gown, tying the belt tight and making sure her cap was securely fastened. If she did run into the landlady, she was no less decently covered than she was during daylight hours. At least she would not run into Mr Read, since he was sleeping in the stable. She found the man's presence disturbing to her peace of mind. Not only was he far too attractive, he made her want to give in to her weakness and lean on his strength.

Men like him might seem to offer strength and support, but in their wake they left only heartache. A bitter thought, but true nonetheless. Look at the women at the Haven who had been similarly abandoned.

Her chamber door, when she pulled it open, protested with a loud creak. She held her breath, listening for sounds of movement downstairs. All was quiet. She picked up her candle and tiptoed down to the ground-floor kitchen across the hall from the taproom. Hopefully, Mrs Lane would not object to the raiding of her pantry.

She hesitated. Perhaps she really should return to her room and ring the bell for the maid. It just seemed so unfair to rouse the poor girl in the middle of the night. From her own months of working as a chambermaid, she knew only too well what it felt like to be roused from the depths of slumber by some patron with a petty request they could easily see to themselves.

Cautiously, she approached the closed kitchen door and opened it. Fortunately, this one did not make a sound. Candle held before her so she would not trip, she looked around for the door to the pantry. Pots and pans hanging from a ceiling rack reflected back the flickering flame in little points. The dark-red glow of a banked fire cast shadows over a settle beside it. Part of that shadow shifted.

She stifled a gasp.

'Mrs Falkner?' A deep male voice. The shadow loomed upward, blocking the light from the hearth.

Heart thudding, she raised her candle higher to reveal the dark planes of a harsh face and the white linen of a man in his shirtsleeves. 'Mr Read. What are you doing in here? I thought…'

His expression changed from surprise to careful blankness. 'I beg your pardon. I merely availed myself of our landlady's offer of a warm spot by the fire to dry my coats and—' he raised his hand, which held a goblet '—a snifter of brandy before I retire.'

A snifter he'd earlier refused. It was then that she saw his coat hung to dry upon a clothes horse. 'You have been out in the rain?'

'I took a walk. I assume you cannot sleep either?'

'I thought to warm up some milk.'

He gestured with his glass. 'This might serve you better.'

She made a face. 'Horrid stuff. Mrs Lane forced me to drink some earlier.'

No doubt thinking her disgruntlement amusing, he flashed a swift smile. A rather naughty-boy smile that made her breath catch in her throat. 'Come now, it did help, did it not?' He winked.

An answering smile curved her own lips before she could catch it. 'How ungentlemanly of you to remind me of finding me asleep in my chair,' she scolded lightly.

His expression stiffened as if she had said something wrong.

It was all right for him to tease, but not the other way around? How typically male.

'Would you like some brandy or not?' he asked gruffly.

'I suppose it might help,' she admitted.

'Please,' he said. 'Sit, while I fetch another glass.'

He was gone only a moment and returned bearing a lit branch of candles, giving the kitchen a nice warm glow and chasing away most of the shadows.

He placed a chair for her on the opposite side of the hearth, handed her a glass. He sat and, taking up his drink, raised a brow.

She took a sip of the fiery liquid and forced herself not to cough, though there was nothing she could do about the watering of her eyes. She shuddered and swiped the tears away with the back of her hand. 'I'll never get used to it.'

He gave a low ironic chuckle. 'The more you drink the easier it becomes.'

She tried again, but the smell of it set her off coughing. 'I honestly don't think I can.'

'Then I will warm you some milk.'

'I can do it.'

'Please,' he said softly. 'Let someone care

for you for once. Tonbridge tells me how hard you work for what he calls your ladies, as well as your son.'

The gentleness in his tone surprised her as did the thought that he and his friend had made her a topic of their conversation. Was it possible he had told Lord Tonbridge about their previous meeting? Her blood ran cold at the thought. She'd thought she was safe here in the north of England. Must she move again? Leave everything behind once more? Her heart clenched at the thought of so drastic an action.

But it was Tommy she must think of, not herself. If only she could believe she wasn't being utterly selfish. That what she was doing really was in *his* interest. For *his* future.

Even if he eventually hated her for it?

She raised a hand in defeat. 'Thank you, you are very kind.'

It was then that she noticed his muddy boots and the damp patches on his pantaloons below the knees. She spoke without thinking, the way she would have spoken to Tommy. 'Are you mad? You should change out of your wet clothes before you risk contracting lung fever.'

## Chapter Four

Blade felt his jaw drop as a vision formed in his mind of them both naked. Together. He couldn't contain his grin. 'It is not every day a lovely woman asks me to remove my clothes,' he said, lightly, teasingly. The way he might have done with one of his flirts.

She gasped and looked away.

He squeezed his eyes shut briefly. He should never have spoken so crudely to such a gently bred female. What the devil was wrong with him? It should not have even crossed his mind. He wasn't some randy schoolboy without control over his lust. Nor was she the sort of woman who would ever be interested in a dalliance for mutual pleasure.

He softened his tone, kept it devoid of expression. 'It is kind of you to be concerned. As a soldier I am used to being a bit damp around the edges. My greatcoat kept most of me dry.'

She inclined her head as if in acceptance of his clumsy attempt to recoup, but there was pride in that movement, too, and a faint flush high on her cheekbones.

A faint suspicion crossed his mind. Had she, too, had a vision of him naked? Was that why she had averted her gaze? His body hardened. Blast. He really was losing his mind. He strode into the pantry, forcing himself to think of anything but the woman beside the hearth. The stone room was blessedly chilly. He focused on that cold and thoughts of icy rain trickling down his neck during the long hours of guard duty. Finally he got himself under control, found the milk jug, took a deep breath and returned to the warmth of the kitchen. He filled a small pan from the jug and placed it on the hearth to heat. He added the brandy from her glass. 'It won't taste quite so bad this way.'

'I keep thinking of that poor man. Of facing his wife with the news.'

He'd offer to tell the widow for her, but he already knew she would not accept someone else shouldering her burdens no matter how unpleasant the duty. He liked that about her. Her inner strength. Her quiet pride.

And there was no comfort he could offer that would not sound false.

He sat beside her on the settle and placed his hand over hers, lightly. Her hand was small beneath his and, despite the warmth in the kitchen, icy cold. 'You can only do your best.'

To his surprise and pleasure, she did not pull her hand free, though she could easily have done so.

A small sigh escaped her lips. 'It is all anyone can do, I suppose.'

Not anyone. Those with good intentions. There were far too many of the other sort waiting to trap the unwary. He forced himself to rise, before he did something really stupid like putting his arm around her, pulling her close and kissing her soft, pretty lips. Crouching at the hearth, he pressed a palm to the side of the pan. It had warmed up nicely. He filled her glass and handed it to her. 'Try it now.'

She took a sip and made a face. 'Not quite as bad.'

'Drink it quickly and—'

'Get it over with.'

They both chuckled.

'Mrs Lane gave me the same advice, but having experienced it once it seems worse than ever.'

'Everything that does you good tastes bad,' he said. For the first time in a long time he heard his mother's voice in his head. Saying those very same words with a catch in her voice. He frowned at the memory. He could not place where it came from. The circumstances. Or even imagine why he would think of it now when he tried never to think of her at all. Shocked by the direction of his thoughts, he rose to his feet.

Oblivious to his reaction, she lifted her glass in a pretend toast and drank it down quickly. She shuddered from head to toe. He poured the last of the milk into her glass, sans brandy. 'Perhaps this will help take the taste away.'

She drank it down quickly. A residue of the milk clung to her bottom lip. He wanted to lick it away. To taste her. She dabbed at it with the back of her hand, leaving him disappointed.

Bah, he was a fool. He turned away. Went to the window to look out, to get his thoughts into some sort of logical order. 'I informed Lane that we plan to leave for Skepton at first light, if that is all right with you. It will take us a couple of hours given the state of the roads after all this rain.'

He heard the rustle of her clothes as she rose

to her feet behind him. As he had intended, she had taken his words as a dismissal.

To his shock, her hand landed on his arm. His left arm. He swung around to face her and found her looking up at him, a smile on her lips and warmth in her eyes that only a fool would pretend not to understand. Gratitude. Kindness.

If she really knew him, she would not look on him so kindly.

'Thank you,' she murmured. 'I think I will be able to sleep now. I will be up and ready to leave first thing.'

For a moment, he thought she might rise up on her toes and kiss his cheek, like a sister or a friend, but it was his mouth where her gaze lingered. Heat rushed through him. His blood headed south.

The distance between them was so very slight he could feel the graze of her breath against his throat, see into the warmth in the depths of her melting green-flecked soft brown eyes. Could such a kind gentle creature, such a respectable woman, really want a man like him? One who had been to hell and back.

He swallowed the dryness in his throat. Felt the pound of his blood in his veins. And inhaled the scent of brandy on her breath.

The brandy. She wasn't used to it. Was likely unaware of its effects. The numbing of reason. In complete command of her senses, a respectable vicar's daughter would have nothing to do with a man who was only two steps from the gutter.

He stepped back. 'Then I will bid you goodnight.' He gestured to the door.

And cursed himself for a quixotic fool when he saw the disappointment on her face.

The drive back to Skepton was uneventful, though it had bothered Caro greatly that Mr Read had insisted on riding in the rain, instead of joining her in the carriage. She had the feeling that her earlier coldness, her insistence upon the proprieties, had influenced his decision.

She sighed as they pulled up outside the house. Propriety had not been the first thing on her mind the previous evening. It was a good thing he had more of a conscience than most men. She had felt so warm and fuzzy after drinking the brandy she could have sworn she might have kissed him, had he not been too much of a gentleman. If he knew the truth about her, he might not have felt bound by such moralistic sensibilities. Apparently Carothers had said nothing to his friends about the liberties she had allowed in a haze of what she had thought was true love. It eased her mind to know that he had spoken the truth when he had said a gentleman did not kiss, or anything else, and tell, even if he had not kept any of his other promises.

Heat rushed to her cheeks. Shame. Embarrassment at her youthful foolishness.

A footman ran out to open the door and let down the steps. There was nothing she could do about the past. It was the future that mattered. All her focus must be on making sure she did nothing to ruin it for Thomas. She stepped down, pleased to discover that at last it had stopped raining.

Still on horseback, Mr Read was speaking to Lane's driver. He glanced over as if sensing her gaze.

She made a gesture towards the house. 'Will you come in for some refreshment?'

He walked his horse closer. 'Thank you, no. I will have to see to the stabling of Sir Reggie's cattle and arrange some accommodation for myself. Tonbridge said there were decent rooms above the stables.' He paused. 'Would you like me to accompany you to speak with Mrs Garge beforehand?'

Gratitude rushed through her. Some of the tightness left her chest. She ought to say no, but... 'You might be able to answer her questions better than I.' She was such a coward. 'Having spoken with the coroner, I mean.'

He dismounted. 'We should go right away.'

Before gossip ran rife throughout the house, as it would when she was seen returning in a strange coach.

He handed his horse off to a footman. 'Walk him. I will not be more than half an hour.'

Side by side they walked past the kitchen towards the arch into the small courtyard at the side of the house, where a side door allowed entry to the stables and where Mrs Garge would be waiting as usual. Once the horses were settled and the carriage put away, it was usual for her and Josiah to walk to their own small cottage on the edge of town.

The closer they drew to the courtyard the more Caro's stomach tightened.

Mrs Garge rose from the bench the moment they passed beneath the arch, her gaze darting from one face to the other, then past them to see who followed.

Her lined face seemed to collapse. 'Somat's happened.'

'There was an accident,' Caro said, her voice

feeling like sandpaper against her throat. 'Mr Garge was thrown from the box.'

'Josiah? No. Is he all reet? Where is he?' She made to push past them.

'Mrs Garge,' Mr Read said, his voice gentle but firm, 'your husband was killed. Instantly.' He stepped closer and held out his arms. 'I am so very sorry.'

The woman stared at his face for a long moment. 'No.' Tears ran silently down her face. She collapsed against his chest and he held her while she sobbed. The look on his face startled Caro. Most men did not feel comfortable around a woman in tears and this one was sobbing uncontrollably. But his stoic expression held sympathy and sadness, not discomfort or impatience.

Caro put her arm around the woman's shoulders and leaned close. 'I am so sorry. There was nothing we could do for him.'

After a few minutes, Mrs Garge raised her head. 'An accident, you say? What happened? Never in his life has my Josiah found a team that could take him unawares. Not even those dreadful wild creatures Lord Robert used to drive.'

Garge had been with the family since the

twins, Charlie and Robert, had been small children.

'We think something startled the horses,' Mr Read said. 'The wheel struck a rut and shattered. The jolt must have dislodged him from the box.'

Mrs Garge stared at him, eyes wide. 'Dislodged him?'

'There was a rock where he landed. He landed hard. I am sorry, Mrs Garge. It was instant.'

Stepping back, she gazed around wildly. 'I have to go. Tell—' She swallowed loudly. 'Tell my family.'

She rushed past them and was gone.

Caro's knees felt weak. 'Oh, the poor woman.'

Mr Read took her arm and led her to the bench where Mrs Garge had been sitting. Caro sank onto the hard wood and leaned back against the plank wall. 'I didn't even think to tell her we would write to Tonbridge, to ask him to ensure she was cared for. I really meant to do that.'

He put a comforting arm around her shoulders.

'Give her a bit of time,' he murmured. 'I will call round and tell her.'

The sensation of his strength at her side

seemed to seep into her bones. She found her-
self wanting to lean against him. To confide.
Terrified of her reaction, she rose to her feet.
'Thank you, Mr Read.'

She hurried indoors.

## Chapter Five

Courtesy of Lord Tonbridge, the mourners fortified themselves after the funeral on ale, roast beef and meat pies in the taproom of the Lamb and Flag. Blade wasn't surprised at the large turnout of people, despite the rain. The rumour of his lordship's generosity had spread far and wide. The widow, flanked by her daughter and son, held court in one corner of the room, accepting condolences as each new guest arrived in front of the large wing-backed armchair the innkeeper had placed there for the purpose.

Duty done, the guests milled about, conversing and gossiping and tucking into the feast.

Blade did his best to blend in with the mostly working men and their womenfolk who had come to pay their last respects to a man who was clearly well liked in the community.

These were good people and he might well have been one of them had his life turned out differently. As it was, they regarded him with suspicion from the corner of their eyes. The way his fellow officers and members of the *ton* had regarded him at their gatherings, him being neither fish nor fowl. Recognised, but not legitimate. He let go an exasperated sigh. He should be perfectly used to it by now and didn't know why he let it bother him.

The thing that should cause him concern was the group of young men at the back of the room, beside the hearth. Young men were rash, easily roused. The dark glances they cast about them and the intensity of their conversation made him idly draw closer, while appearing to focus on the food laid out on the table running the length of the room.

'We needs to act now,' one of the lads was saying in a mutter as Blade came within earshot. 'Let them know we ain't sheep to the slaughter. Teach *them* a thing or two with the edge of a sword.'

Blade made sure not to look at the group, but had the impression that it was the tallest of them speaking. He seemed to be their leader. The lad had hair the colour of ripe wheat, a lantern jaw and pale-blue eyes.

'Aye,' a couple of the others chorused.

'A few thousand Yorkshiremen riding through their barracks one dark night would make them think again,' another said.

'We need weapons for that.'

'We could steal 'em from the soldiers.'

'And keep 'em where, now they have the right to search our houses and barns when-ever they feel like it? My ma is terrified for Pa because he was at Peterloo. They've already transported half-a-dozen fellows just for being there.'

'I say we ought to pay a few of them nobs what runs Parliament a visit one dark night,' their leader said. 'Throw them out in the cold. Let them know what it's like to be without a roof over their heads.'

A chill ran down Blade's spine. This sort of talk would get these lads transported or hanged. This was the sort of thing Charlie had feared might happen after the mess in Man-chester. The subsequent passing of the Six Acts last December, intended to make it impossible for large crowds to gather and take action or to train with weapons, had added fuel to the smouldering embers of resentment. One group of Yorkshiremen had already planned an attack on a barracks. Fortunately, planning was as far as it went. Blade didn't blame them for their anger, but this sort of talk in a public place was dangerous in the extreme.

Was it possible that one of these men had thought to take some sort of action against Tonbridge's carriage? It was an act of vengeance a person without power might contemplate. He moved away from them before they suspected he was listening in. First he needed to know their names. Then he would discover if any of them might have been involved in the accident. Someone whose boot print matched the one he'd seen in the mud beside the carriage door.

He added a pasty to his plate and almost collided with Mrs Falkner moving down the table in the opposite direction with Beth, one of the ladies from the Haven who served as a general maid of all work, nursemaid and sometimes helped the cook.

Even in her sombre gown and pelisse, with her heart-shaped face set in a stern expression, Caro looked lovely.

Blade realised with shock that despite his interest in the youths in the corner, she was the person whose arrival he'd been most interested in.

'Good day, Mrs Falkner. Beth.'

The ladies curtsied politely 'Mr Read, good afternoon,' Mrs Falkner said.

Beth looked at her mistress. 'Does you mind if I go and talk to Polly Garge, ma'am? She's looking awful sad and her and me are good friends.'

'Go,' Mrs Falkner said, 'give her what comfort you may.' Her eyes looked worried as she watched the girl approach Mrs Garge's daughter. The older woman glared daggers at Beth, but the younger one rose to her feet and the two girls went to the table where a non-alcoholic punch was being served. A moment later, two of the boys he had been watching earlier joined them. Interesting. Perhaps Beth could help him learn a bit more about these young men.

Blade raised a brow. 'It seems all is not well between Beth and the Garges.'

Mrs Falkner sighed. 'No. Mrs Garge knows all about Beth's background, but of course there is little she can say to the friendship, being Tonbridge's pensioner.'

It was an angle he had not thought about.

She glanced over at Beth again. 'I really should go. I left Tommy with Cook and she gets impatient if she has him too long, but I hate to drag Beth away when we have been here such a short while. It is her afternoon off.'

'Why don't I escort you home when you are finished eating and come back for her later.'

'That is an awful lot of trouble for you,' she said. For once, her tone suggested she was not necessarily opposed to the idea.

'No trouble at all. I know no one here and I have eaten my fill. Besides, I think Mrs Garge would be more comfortable with her friends than with representatives of her husband's employer.'

Her smile held gratitude and it warmed him, in spite of knowing he had made the suggestion for his own purposes.

He became aware of a man watching them from across the room. He stared back and the man turned away. 'Do you know that fellow?' Blade asked.

Her glance scanned the room. 'Which one?'

'The man by the window. Middling height, middle-aged fellow with beard and a blue-and-cream-striped waistcoat pulled tight over his paunch.'

She gave a low chuckle that sounded so sensually flirtatious it caused his blood to heat, though he was sure it was quite unintentional. 'Your description is masterful. I have no trouble picking him out, but, no, I have never seen him before. Why?'

Blade's gaze swept the man's person. He was shabbily genteel. A fraction down at heel, but not scruffy. Not the sort of man anyone would notice in a crowd, except for the matter of his gleaming, recently polished boots.

'He seemed to be staring at you.' Blast, that had sounded insulting. Why wouldn't a red-blooded male stare at a beautiful woman?

'More than likely he was looking at the food. He has filled his plate three times.'

'So you did notice him?'

'Only because I was wondering if he'd leave enough of Lord Tonbridge's largesse for the other guests.'

Reason enough for someone as caring of her employer's welfare as Mrs Falkner.

She put down her plate. 'If you are ready, we will say our goodbyes to Mrs Garge.'

He wasn't only ready, he was looking forward to it far more than he should.

'Is something troubling you?' Caro asked after a few minutes of walking along the High Street in what seemed like a brooding silence.

Mr Read glanced down at her with an apologetic smile. 'I beg your pardon. I am wool-gathering when I ought to be paying attention.'

'Is it those young men?'

An arrested expression crossed his face. 'How did you guess?'

'You were watching them very closely, I thought. Without appearing to do so.'

His lips thinned. 'A bunch of young hot-heads. I worry that their idle chatter will lead to something more dangerous.'

He sounded so serious her heart gave a little thump. 'Dangerous, how?'

'With the new law that allows for a search without a warrant, an ambitious man in authority might use it to his advantage, by reporting them. Or they might indeed be guilty of planning something untoward, in which case the authorities should be notified.'

'You think they are?'

'It is hard to tell. I plan to take great care that Tonbridge's interests are secure.'

It all sounded so ominous. 'The ducal family is well regarded in these parts. Merry treats her employees well. With their interest in the Haven well known, surely there is no cause for alarm in that direction?'

'Likely not,' he said more cheerfully. 'I apologise if my ruminations have given you reason for anxiety. I have always been a fellow who likes to plan for the worst and be surprised when it doesn't happen.'

She couldn't help smiling. He sounded much like herself in that regard. 'So you do not think there is imminent danger?'

'I do not.'

She believed him. Trusted him to tell her the truth. Which was a little disconcerting since she trusted so very few people and he, of all those she knew, was in a position to cause her and Tommy the most harm. Again that frightened little clench of her heart. She quelled it firmly. If he had not realised the identity of Tommy's father by now, it was unlikely he would do so in the future. She really must stop jumping at shadows.

With new resolve, she took a deep breath and broached a subject she had been wanting to discuss with him for a couple of days and had not had the courage. 'There is something I have been meaning to ask.'

His eyes crinkled at the corners in a most attractive way as he smiled at her, his head cocked slightly in enquiry. 'And what would that be?'

'There is a dance arranged for Wednesday evening. Tonbridge took out several subscriptions to allow my ladies a supervised opportunity to meet some of the local young men. Since our attendance isn't always looked on with favour by some of the higher sticklers in the community, Tonbridge always acted as our escort and there was little they could say.' Oh, dear, she really was beating around the bush. It was really not done for a woman to invite a gentleman to a dance. 'I was wondering...'

'In no stretch of anyone's imagination do I fall in Tonbridge's noble league. I doubt I will provide that sort of cachet.'

'You are the son of an earl.'

'So my mother would have it.'

'You doubt your mother's claim?' He was accepted as such by society, according to Tonbridge.

He shrugged. 'She believed it.'

'As does your father, I gather.'

'Appearances are trumps. And, yes, I would be delighted to escort you and the ladies, provided *you* promise to dance with me.'

She stiffened. Was he flirting? The thought gave her an odd little flutter low in her stomach. How mortifying that he could elicit such a response. 'I never dance. I am there as chaperone, to lend respectability to the party.'

'You must keep an eye on your charges?'

'Indeed.'

'So they are not really to be trusted in polite company.'

A trickle of unease ran down her spine. She suspected a trap. Indeed, she saw it opening up before her like a very deep hole in the ground. 'That is not what I am saying.'

He patted the hand resting on his sleeve. A kindly, friendly gesture, when they were really not friends. Friends did not lay traps for one another.

'It is,' he said, exceedingly gently, 'what you imply when you watch them with a dragon's eye.'

'I care about their protection.' She was stepping far too close to the edge of the abyss, but... 'Very well, if you advise it necessary to prove they have my trust by dancing, I will do so.'

He beamed at her. A smile of such charm that she knew she'd been handily netted, yet she could not prevent the spurt of joy at the thought of dancing.

'I will ask Ned to join us, too,' he said. 'We'll make the local lads jealous.'

The man could charm a bird out of a tree. She was certainly charmed by the very idea that dancing with her would make anyone jealous. Warmed through and through in the oddest of ways. It was the first time in a very long time that she had even considered herself as a woman. She realised she was looking forward to dancing with him far more than she ought to. The man was indeed dangerous.

She forced herself to remember Tonbridge's warning about his rakish friend. 'One dance only, Mr Read.'

'Yes, ma'am,' he said, clearly chastened by her severe tone, but there was an irrepressible twinkle in his eye that caused a completely different kind of flutter in her foolish heart.

Something she absolutely must not allow.

Rumours spread through a regiment faster than a cholera epidemic. They did the same in a household, apparently. A good officer and a good house steward knew which ones to ignore and which required following up. Such as the one that had been murmured in his ear a few minutes before he headed for Mrs Falkner's domain. This rumour had its feet firmly planted on fact.

He leaned against the door jamb to her office while the lady in question, dressed in cloak and hat, finished doing up the buttons of young Master Tommy's coat.

'Going somewhere?' he enquired mildly, though something of his anger must have coloured his tone, because she glanced up at him

sharply. A needle-sharp look, though she belied it with a cool smile.

He wasn't fooled.

'Tommy and I needed some fresh air,' she
said calmly, wrapping a bright red scarf around
the boy's scrawny little neck.

'Unescorted?' he said pointedly.

A crease formed over her pretty nose, bringing her finely arched brows closer together.
'We are not going far and Beth is busy in the
kitchen. Cook is feeling her rheumatism today.'

And the other girls were at their place of employment. Dressmaking or some such.

'We are going to feed the ducks,' Tommy
piped up, his face beaming with excitement.
'Would you like to come with us, sir? It is
splendid fun.'

Blade had no trouble reading the desperate
hope in the little boy's eyes or the worry in his
mother's. She didn't want him to go. In the cold
light of day, she was no doubt regretting her
weakness in giving in to his importuning. The
rejection stung, but it wasn't unexpected. He'd
applied his skills of seduction into wheedling
her to dance. He didn't even know why he had
done such a thing, except he had the feeling
the woman had very little pleasure in her life.
And that she was lonely. If there was one thing

he'd learned to recognise, it was loneliness.
And there was nothing like a little flirting to
lift the spirits of a lonely widow. Hopefully, the
woman had too much pride to cry off.

'I would love to come with you,' he said to
the boy. 'It is a long time since I had reason to
communicate with such fine worthy fellows
as a paddle of ducks.'

Tommy giggled.

And thus he would keep his promise to himself that while things were so unsettled he
would not let her go anywhere without an escort and unfortunately, or perhaps fortunately,
Ned was off on an errand.

Her lips pinched a little. 'If you have nothing better to do, then by all means come along.'

Her way of telling him he was neglecting his
duties. But she was part of his duties whether
she liked it or not. And, if he was honest with
himself, a very pleasurable part of his duties.

'There is nothing more important than filling the stomachs of Skepton's waterfowl.'

'Nonsense,' Mrs Falkner said, but still, he
caught a flash of a smile that said she was
amused rather than angry. Pleased, he crouched
down to bring his face on a level with Tommy's. 'And what are these ducks to eat?'

'Stale bread.' The boy held up a linen bag

pulled tight at the neck. 'It's hard as a rock. I tried some.' He made a face. 'But Mama says the ducks will like it.'

'I am sure they will. I will get my hat and coat and meet you on the front step.'

He found them there a few minutes later, Tommy hopping from foot to foot.

Blade offered his arm to Mrs Falkner and his hand to the boy and they strolled towards the High Street. Every now and then the lad would skip a step or two, clearly delighted with the way the afternoon had transpired.

The brisk April wind blowing down from the moors quickly reddened Mrs Falkner's cheeks. The flush made her more tempting than usual. It was the kind of colour he'd like to see on her skin after a night of—

He cut the thought off. He was not the sort of man a woman like her would ever want in her life. Not in that way, at least. It was wrong to even give it a thought. He had nothing to offer other than a casual dalliance. Less than nothing now he'd left the army. Although the woman could do with a bit more pleasure in her life. A bit more splendid fun that did not involve small boys and ducks.

It did not take them long to reach the village green and they were not the only ones enjoying the air. There was an elderly couple doddering across the grass arm in arm. A couple of young men idling on one corner, smoking clay pipes and trying to look as if they were beaux on the strut. On another corner, a young lass was selling posies of dried lavender. He thought about purchasing one for Mrs Falkner, but decided it might be misinterpreted and send her back into her shell.

The moment his feet touched the grass, Tommy galloped straight for the pond that had a sloping weedy bank. The ducks squawked and shot away as he teetered on the muddy edge. Blade sprinted after him, grabbing the belt on his coat before he could tumble into the frigid water.

'Steady now, lad,' Blade said. 'We are feeding bread to the ducks, not small boys.'

Tommy giggled.

His mother arrived, her face panicked, a scold ready to deliver on her tongue.

He shot her a warning look and spoke gently. 'All is well.' He turned to Tommy. 'A soldier never leaves his post without permission, young man, and you were on escort duty, were you not?'

Tommy looked astonished. 'I was?'

'Indeed. You were tasked with escorting your mother and you left her side.'

Tommy glanced up at his mother, whose face held concern.

'You won't be doing that again, will you, Mr Thomas Falkner?'

'No, sir. I am sorry, sir.'

Blade gave him an encouraging smile. 'Perhaps it is your mother to whom you should be making your apology. She is, after all, our general on this expedition.'

He gave his mother a brilliant smile. 'I am sorry, Mama.'

'Then there is the matter of punishment,' Blade continued, keeping his smile in check.

Apparently, not well enough, since the lad looked more intrigued than scared. Most likely his mama usually scolded him to death. But a lad needed more than berating. There needed to be consequences.

He glanced down at his feet, the high shine of his Hessians destroyed by mud that had been enhanced by deposits from the ducks. 'It will be your job to clean our boots upon our return to headquarters.'

Tommy followed Blade's gaze, took in first his large pair of boots and then his own smaller but far muddier pair. He wrinkled his nose, but straightened smartly. 'Yes, sir.' His voice was a little less enthusiastic than usual.

'Excellent,' Blade said warmly and meant it. The little lad needed a male hand in his life, but he was all in all a good boy. 'Let us find a seat for our general, then see about leading a well-considered attack on the stomachs of our feathered friends.'

Tommy laughed, his spirits instantly restored. 'There's a bench over there.' He held out his arm like a proper escort. 'Come along, Mama. We need to get you settled.'

His mother smiled fondly. At them both.

Blade felt an odd pang in the region of his chest.

*Idiot.*

# Chapter Six

The day was crisp, and while clouds were scudding across the sky, occasionally blocking what little warmth the sun gave off, they did not threaten rain. A sense of peace invaded Caro's being. Birds tweeted and fluttered about in the shrubs around the pond. The ducks quacked and splashed around Tommy and Blade. And nearby a group of boys were calling back and forth as they played cricket.

Watching Blade teach Tommy to aim his bread to a specific duck made Caro's heart sing. Their boots were getting muddier by the minute and neither of them seemed to care. Blade had been right. Where Caro would have scolded and fussed and ended up with a sullen boy who no longer wanted to feed the ducks, he had discovered a fitting punishment, a manly punishment, and both of them were as happy as grigs.

The boy needed a male role model. One he could look up to. One who would take him in hand. A doting mother was not enough. Her joy dimmed at the thought of someone else being important in her boy's life. Selfish. Wrong.

Tonbridge must have seen the lack, too. It was why he had suggested school. Still, she could not bear the idea of letting Tommy go. He was all the family she had. But if she loved him, she had to think of what was best for him.

*'You would not have to send him off quite yet if you married again.'* Merry's sly suggestion.

Ach, how could she even let such a thought enter her mind? She could not marry. That ship had sailed years ago. A husband would expect to know the details of his wife's past and, unlike expectations for young men, wild oats sowed by a woman were looked on askance by decent people. A lump rose in her throat. Tears she would not shed, though they were never for herself. They were for the harm she had caused an innocent child.

She blinked and discovered Tommy standing in front of her looking worried. Mr Read was almost upon her, too.

She'd been so involved in her own selfish thoughts, she hadn't realised they were on their way back.

Tommy, his face pink from exertion, put a hand on her arm. 'Is something wrong, Mama?' He glanced down at his filthy boots and rubbed one on the back of the stocking on the other leg. 'I promise I will clean them.'

She managed a smile. 'Nothing is wrong, my son. Nothing at all.'

Blade gave her a sharp-eyed glance. 'Getting cold, are you? The air is chilly. Time for a brisk walk. Once around the pond, ma'am.'

Grateful he had not challenged her about her self-indulgent moment, she rose to her feet. 'The wind is slightly cool.' She took his proffered arm and they began a steady perambulation with Tommy skipping along beside them.

'Were the ducks suitably pleased with their lunch?' she asked her son.

'They have no manners,' Tommy observed. 'Sometime the bread sank to the bottom and they never even got it, because they were fighting.'

A salutary lesson. 'Much like people sometimes,' Caro said. One of the reasons she had always dreaded sending her boy to school. She had heard such stories of cruelty. And they would be cruel if his schoolmates ever learned of his background.

Tommy frowned and she realised her words had been a little sharper than she'd intended. Her son was becoming far too sensitive to her moods, for he took her hand. She gave it an encouraging squeeze to let him know everything was all right.

Tommy looked up at Blade. 'Why don't you wear your uniform any more?'

Blade's expression shuttered. His jaw flickered as if he was restraining words he knew ought not to be spoken. 'I am no longer a soldier.'

'Tommy,' she admonished. 'That's—'

'It is a perfectly valid question,' Blade said quietly, stopping to face the boy and crouching down to bring himself to Tommy's eye level. 'The war is over and I resigned my commission. I hope that does not mean we cannot be friends any longer.'

The twinkle in his eyes, his gentleness, warmed Caro to her toes, even though it was directed at Tommy. Only because he was being kind to her son. It had nothing to do with how the warmth transformed his face from stern and fierce to something utterly charmingly devastating. And the clench in her lower abdomen was all to do with her appreciation of his kindness.

Read stuck out his hand.

Tommy shook it with all the aplomb of the gentleman she was trying to bring him up to be. 'Oh, no, sir,' the lad said. 'We can still be friends.' He frowned. 'Don't you want to be a soldier any more?'

'I do not,' Mr Read said firmly but kindly, rising to stand.

'Well, I am going to join up the moment I am old enough. Just like my papa. He was very brave. Mama said so.' His gaze dropped to Mr Read's pinned left sleeve. 'Did it hurt?'

Mr Read's expression froze for a second.

Caro drew in a sharp breath, but before she could speak an admonition, Mr Read answered calmly, 'It hurt a great deal.'

Tommy grimaced in sympathy. His gaze dropped to the floor. 'It hurt when I fell and scraped my knee. Mother said I was brave when I let Beth clean it and put a bandage on.' He glanced up with a look of misery on his face. 'But I wasn't. I cried.'

'There is nothing wrong with a man shedding a few tears when he is in pain,' Mr Read said, lifting an eyebrow.

Tommy's eyes rounded. 'Did you cry, too?'

'I did.'

Caro felt a terrible pang in her heart at his words. But she also felt admiration at his honesty. Not too many men would admit to such a thing to another male, even if he was a little boy.

'Beth gave me one of her bullseyes and kissed it better,' Tommy said cheerfully, clearly not realising the importance of this manly conversation.

Mr Read gave a low chuckle and something deep in Caro's abdomen tightened when his gaze, full of wicked amusement, met hers over Tommy's head. 'Nothing like a bullseye and a kiss from a pretty nurse to take away a fellow's pain.'

The man was incorrigible. He was flirting with her. Again. She should be shocked. But she wasn't. She felt breathless and hot.

They arrived back at the bench. Tommy looked around. 'What shall we do now?'

'Do you know how to play cricket?' Mr Read asked.

Tommy shook his head.

'Then it is likely time you learned. Go and

watch the other boys over there for a while and see if they will let you join their game. But be honest with them. Tell them you've never played before.'

Tommy looked worried. 'You won't go anywhere?'

'We'll stay right here, I promise,' Caro said, sitting down.

Her boy wandered diffidently across the grass and stood watching for several minutes.

One of the lads approached him and said something and the next moment Tommy was part of the game. The lesson Mr Read had taught him while throwing the bread suddenly made sense.

She glanced at him in surprise. 'You meant that to happen.'

He leaned back against the bench, a small smile turning up the corner of his mouth. 'I did nothing. It was all up to your son.'

Who right now looked extremely pleased with himself, half-crouching in imitation of the other boys.

'You would make a wonderful father,' she said, thinking out loud.

He looked startled. Opened his mouth to reply, thought better of it and closed it again. When he finally spoke his voice was casual.

'He needs the company of other fellows his age, that's all.'

'So Tonbridge has been saying.'

'And what is worrying you this fine day?' he asked. 'Apart from your son.'

Her shoulders stiffened. 'What makes you say that?'

'Beth. She mentioned that Cook being ill was one more trouble you did not need.'

Inwardly, Caro let go a sigh of relief. He wasn't talking about her biggest worry. 'Katy and Flo have been offered permanent employment. They will be leaving us soon.'

'Surely that is a good thing?'

'Of course it is, but when they leave at the end of the month the Haven will be empty. Despite our success with these girls, no new ones have come to seek our aid. I thought once others saw how well these girls were doing, more would seek our aid.' She'd even approached some of the girls on the street. 'This was my idea. It will be difficult to ask Tonbridge to continue to support the venture if there is no need for it. Perhaps we should have located it in a larger town.'

He looked thoughtful. 'How many women do you have room for?'

'Up to five, but it depends on whether they

have children or not. The more children the fewer places.'

'Children?' He sounded startled.

'When women who do not have the support of family have children, they are most often forced to give them up. The children go to orphanages or workhouses. It is very hard for them.'

She glanced at his face and his expression was grim, but when he said nothing she continued. 'I am not saying that these places are bad, but if a way could be found for the women to support themselves and their children, if that is what they want, I believe it would be...better.'

'You speak from experience, of course.'

She swallowed a gasp.

'It must have been difficult when your husband died and left you to struggle alone with a child to bring up.'

She felt weak with relief, but managed to gather her thoughts. 'If not for Merry's help, I might not have managed.'

'I think it is one of the best ideas I have ever heard.' Something in his tone made her look at his expression more closely. Beneath the grimness was pain. Had he suffered something similar? She knew little about his circumstances other than he was an earl's natural son. Also that perhaps he harboured some bitterness towards his mother. She opened her mouth to question him and thought better of it.

'Perhaps if you spoke to the vicar,' he continued as if unaware of her curiosity, 'he might know of women who are desperate for the sort of help the Haven offers.'

'I have. Merry has. As has Tonbridge. The Haven is accepted but not well liked among the notables of Skepton. They see it as encouraging wickedness rather than helping those in need. And yet I know there are women out there who are desperate for the sort of help we can offer.'

'Let me put the word out around the local inns and such, places you cannot go.'

Surprised, she stared at him. 'You would do that?'

'Of course.' He gave her a self-deprecating grin. 'After all, my livelihood depends on the success of the Haven.'

A pragmatic answer, but she sensed it was not entirely the truth, that there was some other emotion beneath the smile. A deeper caring that she might not have suspected if it wasn't for his kindness to Tommy. Beneath the rakish charmer. Beneath the efficient soldier. Beneath the person he showed to the world, there resided a good and kindly man. One she could respect without reservation.

Her heart gave a happy little hop.

As they walked home and he purchased a sprig of lavender to pin on her coat, she knew she was falling for him. Something she had sworn she would never do again.

But this time it was different. He was different.

Or was she seeing only what she wanted to see?

Her son's future relied on her being a respectable woman. Respectable women, even if they were widows, did not engage in flirtations with handsome soldiers.

'You did what?' Ned ceased his combing of Apollo's mane, much to the horse's disgruntlement, expressed by the impatient stamp of a hoof.

The well-trained Ned returned to his task, but his expression didn't look any less grim.

'I said you would join me and Mrs Falkner and the other ladies of the house at the assembly two days hence. You like dancing.'

'I liked to be asked,' Ned said in his irascible way.

'I am asking now.'

Ned fumbled in his pocket and came up empty. Blade handed him a lump of sugar.

A grunt was all the thanks he got, but Apollo crunched happily on the offered treat.

'What are you about, Captain?' Ned glowered at him. 'She's a decent woman. Not your usual sort at all.'

So that was the problem. 'I am doing my job, Ned. Mrs Falkner wants to go to the blasted assembly with the other women in the house and it is my job, whether I will it or no, to accompany her.' His very great pleasure to accompany her, he acknowledged to himself. Not something he needed to tell Ned, however. 'Knowing how much you like to show off your manly attributes to the ladies, I...er...offered your services also. What other motive would I have?' Not a question he should be asking of Ned, who knew him all too well.

'I see the way you look at her. Like you'd like to gobble her up.'

'You, my old friend, have bats in your belfry.'

Another grunt.

'Well, will you do it, or do I have to tell Mrs Falkner what a disobliging fellow you are?'

'You haven't been to a ball or an assembly

since…' His gaze dropped to Blade's mangled appendage. 'They'll notice.'

'I have a plan for that. Ned, stop havering and tell me one way or the other.'

'Yes, damn you. I'll come to your benighted dance as long as that wench Beth is going, too.'

Blade did not admonish him for the use of the word *wench*. Ned was impossibly shy and his gruffness was a form of self-defence. 'You must dance with all the lasses from this house, not just Beth.'

'If'n she'll dance with me at all.'

Another male seeking comfort where it would never be offered. 'She'll dance with you. Mrs Falkner will see to it.'

'Not the same.' Ned exited Apollo's stall and latched the gate. 'And another thing.' He sat down on the bench beside Blade. 'Someone's been asking questions about your Mrs Falkner.'

If only she could be his. Blast, where had that stray thought come from? 'Who? And who has been giving him answers?'

'It seems he knew better than to ask them of me, but he collared that varmint of a grocer's boy.'

'The grocer's boy who stands at the back door flirting with Beth, you mean?' An unnecessarily cruel dig, but Ned needed a bit of a push sometimes.

Ned shot him a glower that said he knew what Blade was up to. 'Him. The gent who's been asking questions is a middle-aged codger with a large belly and a niggardly purse.'

There was a familiarity to that description. He'd seen a man like that somewhere. Recently. 'What sort of questions?'

'Who lives in the house? Where they came from and such like.'

'And what did this rival of yours tell him?'

Ned's eyes narrowed, promising retribution. 'Whatever he knew.'

'Which is what?'

'Not much, I'm thinking. The names at least. The connection to Tonbridge and his missus.'

'Countess.'

'Ah, well, he weren't having no countess when he was playing at being Lord Robert, were 'e?'

'What else?'

'That Mrs Falkner has no family to speak of. Turns out he delivers the letters from the post office to save Beth trekking to the post office every day. Happy to do her a favour, he is.' His expression soured. 'And Mrs Falkner don't get no letters except those franked by Tonbridge.'

'Blasted observant, this grocer's boy.'

'T'were more about the skill of the questioner, I'm thinking.'

'Do you have a name for me, Ned?'

'Butterworth. And fat as butter he is. Staying at the Green Man.'

'Horse? Carriage?'

'Arrived by stage two weeks ago. The tapster there thought he might be in trade, but he's not been seen at any of the markets. He did rent a horse three days ago. Brought it back wet and covered in mud. Said he went for a ride in the country. Took ill with the ague and was in bed for a couple of days.'

Might he have been the fellow who had opened the carriage door? If so, why would he not have offered assistance? And why was he asking questions?

'Thank you, old chap.'

Ned hunched a shoulder. 'Don't thank me, thank the grocer's boy.'

Blade grinned, despite his consternation. 'Have I or have I not provided the opportunity for you to dance with Miss Beth?'

Ned shuffled some wisps of straw around with the toe of his boot.

'Anything on the other front?' Blade asked.

'Hothead talk. Rumours of an uprising in

Scotland. Gossip about men practising up on the moors with pitchforks and ancient rifles.'

Could things be getting so serious? 'See if you can find a name or a way in. Even a meeting place.'

'Just so long as it don't get me arrested under this new Act of theirs.'

'It won't. Tonbridge will see to it.'

Ned wandered off to fetch oats for the horses.

Clearly at some point this Butterworth fellow merited a closer look.

A great deal of excitement rippled through the house. Flo and Katy had been granted a half-day holiday from their employment in order to ready themselves for the evening's festivities. Not that the time had been granted purely for their sakes. Their employer had a hopeful daughter of her own and intended to spend the afternoon at home ensuring she was turned out in prime style.

Skepton's marriage mart relied on these events, just as London's beau monde relied on Almack's.

Caro looked at her ladies with a critical eye. Modesty was the watchword of the evening. Though these country affairs were not nearly as formal as those of high society, it was important that they represent the Haven creditably. Beth looked lovely in a pale-blue muslin that showed off her dark hair. Flo and Katy were in Pomona green and lemon respectively. Katy twitched at her skirt. 'Ellen Fitch has three rows of lace at her hem.'

Whereas Katy and Flo had only one.

'All the lace in the world won't make Miss Fitch look any prettier,' Mr Read said, coming into the hallway from the kitchen. He must have entered the house through the back door. He looked absolutely gorgeous in his crisp white linen and black evening clothes. Better than he had ever looked in his regimentals, though he had looked exceedingly handsome in those, too. Not that Caro should have been noticing, then or now.

Flo sniggered. 'He's right. Her looks aren't a patch on yours, Katy. No one's going to look at her hem when they can look at your face.'

'You both look perfect,' Caro said firmly. 'Please remember that the reputation of the Haven rests on your behaviour. If things go badly, the committee will likely refuse Lord Tonbridge another subscription on our behalf.'

'That would be a crying shame,' Beth said.

Everyone nodded.

'We'll be on our best behaviour, Mrs F.,' Flo said. 'Don't you worry.'

Mr Read opened the front door with a flourish. 'After you, ladies.' Another round of giggles ensued.

Outside on the footpath stood Ned Wright, his face shiny from a recent very close shave.

'Why, Mr Wright,' Flo cooed, 'don't you look a proper handsome gent.'

He did, too. In his dark-blue coat and shockingly bright blue waistcoat, he looked more dandy than groom.

Beth shot Flo a glower.

Female rivalry while Blade Read was a study in innocence. He knew about this budding relationship. Caro narrowed her eyes. The Haven could not afford any sort of scandal.

With what Caro could only describe as a wicked twinkle in his eye, Mr Read offered one arm to her and one to Beth, causing Ned Wright to glower for a very brief instant, before he turned to Flo and Katy and did the same for them.

Now it was Beth's turn to look less than happy while they walked to the Assembly Room in the middle of the town. Those were the joys of youth Caro didn't miss. The tortured state of uncertainty and longing.

The role of devoted widow and mother suited her far more.

It hadn't taken the six of them long to walk the half-mile to their destination. The rooms hired for the assembly were on the first floor of the largest inn in Skepton and were reached by way of a side door, so attendees did not have to run the gauntlet of the inn's regular customers. They handed their wraps to the staff waiting in the entrance hall and changed into their dancing slippers, before they mounted the stairs to the first-floor ballroom. A mama could not have been prouder of her children than Caro was of her protégées as they swept into a gallery that had been decorated with flowers and bunting and lit by several large chandeliers. Only if one looked hard could one tell that the room's usual use was for billiards and other male indoor sports.

'May I fetch you some punch?' Mr Read asked, once he had found them all chairs in a spot out of any draughts and with a good view of the dance floor.

'Ratafia,' she said with a smile of thanks. It was too easy to be enchanted by a man when under the influence of strong drink, as she knew to her cost. Enchanted and seduced and humiliated. Of course, she had also been too inexperienced to taste the rum that had spiked the punch that evening. Her father never imbibed strong drink. Nor had he accepted her excuse that she had not known.

Carothers had known, though, of that she was positive.

Spilt milk and far too long ago for tears.

She had made a good life for herself and her son and she must do nothing to jeopardise all she had fought so hard for. No matter how attractive Mr Read, she must keep him at a distance.

Something deep inside her ached.

Flo and Katy were soon absorbed into a group of young women, some of whom were also employed by Mrs Fitch, while Beth took Ned off to meet some of her acquaintances, one of whom Caro recognised as the grocer's delivery boy, a lanky youth in the first flush of awkward adulthood.

Idly she watched the ladies in charge of the evening's entertainments instructing the leader of the small band, no doubt ensuring there would be nothing so disgraceful as a waltz played at their event. She had offered her services to their committee when she had first taken up her post at the Haven, but while they were forced to accept Merry into their cir-

cle at their husbands' insistence, they looked
down their noses at Caro and her *institution*,
as they called it.

She didn't care.

With Merry as her friend and her work, she
had no need to involve herself in the affairs of
the community. She just wished they would
find it in their hearts to send her more troubled
girls and women, instead of pushing them off
to the workhouse. Or worse.

Feeling as proud as a mother hen, she
watched Beth and Ned take their places in a set
beside Flo and Katy, who both had respectable-
looking partners. By the time the set ended,
their faces were flushed from the energy the
dance required and their eyes were bright with
enjoyment.

'It is good to see them enjoying themselves,'
she murmured. Good to see them having fun
as young women, young respectable women,
should.

Mr Read glanced down at her, a smile in
his eyes. 'It is good to see you enjoying yourself as well.'

'Thank you.' She tried to sound stiff and
stern, but he was right—she was enjoying herself.

He smiled a rather cocky smile. 'Then may

I ask you to honour me with the next dance? A Scottish reel, I believe.'

The dance she had promised him, he meant. It was then that she realised she'd been tapping her toes in time to the music.

'I would be pleased to dance with you.' It was the honest truth.

As he led her out onto the dance floor, she noticed his left hand encased in a glove of what looked like white kidskin.

He must have seen her surprise. 'My father insisted upon presenting me with several...' He paused for a second. 'I suppose you would call them "attachments". I rarely use them, but since I will be exchanging partners I thought it might be less disconcerting.' He sounded hesitant. Uncomfortable. She could only imagine how some ladies might have reacted to his missing extremity. 'Would you prefer I remove it?'

'Certainly not. I was surprised, that was all. I think it is an excellent idea.'

A flash of relief crossed his expression. Clearly the man was not as confident as he appeared, and in a way that helped her feel a little less unsure, as if they were facing an ordeal together.

As they danced, she was pleased to see that

while some of the ladies noticed the oddness of his touch, not one of them refused to hold his hand or commented. She also noticed there was more than one gentleman dancing who was missing a limb or sported some other injury. The war with France had asked a heavy price.

As was proper, Mr Read asked several other ladies to dance, ladies, she noticed, who had lacked for partners for most of the evening. When asked, she also danced with other gentlemen who were known to her through Merry or Tonbridge. Mill owners mostly, who wanted to question her about Tonbridge's whereabouts and his stand on various issues. None of which she answered except in the most general of terms.

The Tonbridges were her friends and they deserved her loyalty and discretion. If they wanted these men to know things, then they would ensure that they did.

One of her partners even went so far as to guarantee positions for any of the girls she helped who were willing to work hard, if she would put in a good word for him with her noble friend. As if she could be bribed. And added insult to injury by asking her not to mention his offer to his wife.

'I doubt your lady wife will be asking me to tea any time soon,' she had replied and walked away at the end of the dance with her head throbbing from the tension of watching out for these political traps. The next time she was asked to stand up, she excused herself as needing refreshment and found a quiet corner where she could watch over her charges in peace.

She'd been sitting there for about fifteen minutes when she became aware of someone standing behind her.

'Would I be addressing a Miss Caro Lennox?' a hoarse voice murmured in her ear.

Her heart leaped into her throat. She gasped, desperately trying to maintain her composure at the sound of her maiden name. She turned her head to meet the questioning gaze of a florid stranger. Or was he? Had she not seen him before?

Ah, yes, at the wake for poor Mr Garge. 'You are mistaken, sir, and I do not believe we have been introduced.' Heart thudding painfully, she turned her face away.

'Is there a problem?' Mr Read asked, appearing at her side and glaring at the man, who seemed to shrivel inside his coat.

'I beg your pardon, ma'am. It was only that

you looked familiar.' He bowed with an apologetic smile, turned and left.

Blade's gaze hardened as he followed the man's progress to the other side of the room. He turned that hard gaze on Caro. '*Do* you know him?'

She felt ill. 'I— No, I have never seen him before in my life.' She coloured. 'That is not quite true. He is the man we noted at the wake. The one intent on eating all the food.'

'I remember.' He frowned. 'Are you all right? You look very pale. Did he offer you some insult?'

By speaking her real name, he had destroyed her world. 'It was, as he said, a case of mistaken identity.'

Now what was she supposed to do? Her mind whirled. The man seemed to accept her word that he was mistaken. Perhaps he was someone she had met in her youth. Her father, seeking news from town, had entertained many visitors at the house. Surely if he'd been certain of her identity, he would have argued his case or said something to Mr Read.

'Are you sure you are all right?' Mr Read asked.

'I have a touch of the headache, that is all.'

'Do you want to leave?'

Dashing off right after meeting the man might only serve to make him suspicious, though right now he seemed uninterested in anything apart from the dainties laid out on a table at the end of the room.

'I can't leave without Beth and the other girls.'

'Don't worry. I'll have Ned round them up.'

'I couldn't possibly. It would be wrong to spoil their fun.'

He looked about him, his expression a little grim. 'You know, it is past midnight and, if I am not mistaken, the most respectable of to-night's attendees are also taking their leave. What will be left are the riff-raff.'

He was right. Several of the well-to-do families were bidding farewell to friends; others had already gone.

She breathed a sigh of relief. It would behove her to leave, too.

With the skill of a general, he marshalled their party and had them down the stairs in minutes. As they left the inn, he placed her wrap around her shoulders. She looked up into his handsome face and felt a rush of traitorous warmth at the solicitous expression she saw on his face.

'Thank you,' she said as he walked her out into the street.

'The pleasure was all mine,' he said softly.

And her foolish heart wanted to believe him.

## Chapter Seven

At just before midnight, Blade walked the perimeter of the house and stables. Something he'd been doing at irregular intervals throughout all the nights he'd been here. Ned looked after most things around the property during the day, leaving Blade free in the afternoons to roam the local inns with an eye to picking up any gossip that might be of interest to Tonbridge, such as men forming a citizens' army intent on wrecking property.

Before escorting the ladies to the assembly he'd spent the afternoon in the taproom of the Lamb and Flag, making friends and acting the disaffected soldier without learning anything of use. Nevertheless, he'd been disturbed by how many of his countrymen had expressed similar disaffected feelings, particularly when they discussed the circumstances of the Peterloo massacre and the Six Acts intended to quash any further rebellion. In his opinion, the north was ripe for revolution. All it needed was a leader.

Yet he'd learned of nothing specific. Nor was he surprised. While the men might talk to a stranger in general terms, Yorkshiremen were a closed-mouthed lot when it came to naming names or getting a fellow Yorkshireman into trouble with the authorities. He had a long way to go before they trusted him with those sorts of secrets. And so he patrolled the house just in case.

He paused in the shadows of the stables wall, looking up at the windows across the back of the main house.

As he expected, there were no lights to indicate the occupants were anywhere but where they should be. In their beds. He pictured Caro Falkner in her bed. Likely in a nightgown of flannel that covered her from neck to toe. The image was so erotic as to make his breeches feel uncomfortably tight. More fool him.

She was a lovely lonely widow and she was lovely and dreadfully lonely for all she tried to hide it beneath her prim and proper ways. It showed in the shadows in her eyes. And lovely lonely widows were his speciality among the ladies of the *ton*. Caro Falkner, however, was not of their ilk. She deserved a man who could give her so much more than a brief affair, no matter how pleasurable.

And so he continued his perambulations, making plenty of noise as he went. He wanted anyone interested to know the place was well guarded. He circled around to the front of the house. Nothing amiss here. He bit back a yawn, half-wishing something would happen to ease the boredom. He returned to the back of the house and took up position in the shadows.

A faint grinding noise caught his attention. A light flickered in the kitchen window.

Hell, had somebody found a way past him and into the house? He pulled his pistol from his waistband and checked it was primed and ready before moving towards the back door.

As he reached it, it swung wide.

'Let me see your hands,' he whispered.

The figure gasped. 'Is that you, Mr Read?'

'Mrs Falkner?' Wearing, if he was not mistaken, nothing but a dressing gown over her nightclothes. 'What in the devil's name are you doing out here?'

'I brought you a cup of coffee. I thought you might be cold.'

Not when he had his trusty flask of brandy. A soldier's best friend on a long cold night.

'I could have killed you,' he said in a low mutter. 'What can you be thinking, sneaking around in the dark?'

'I wasn't sneaking,' she said indignantly. Then surprised him with a soft chuckle. 'Well, only a little. I didn't want to wake anyone. I am sorry if I scared you.'

'Hardly,' he scoffed, uncocking his pistol and tucking it back in his waistband.

He took the coffee mug from her hand and led her to a wooden seat outside the kitchen door. He sat down beside her. 'What are you doing up at this time of night?'

She let go of a soft sigh that sent his blood heading south to a part of him that had no brain at all, though it knew what it wanted. 'A sound woke me and then I couldn't go back to sleep.'

'What sort of sound?'

'That is the trouble. Creaks I never used to care about now have me leaping from my bed. All this talk of insurrection is making me nervous, I suppose. Even Cook was going on about it this evening. Talking about the need for good Yorkshiremen to rise up to take back their rights.'

The whole thing was a mess. Parliament, it seemed, had lost touch with the people it was supposed to represent. Hopefully, sensible men like Tonbridge could convince the government to use their heads for once.

'I'm sorry you are distressed. Be assured, I will not let anything untoward happen to the occupants of this house. Word of significant male presences on duty will be enough of a deterrent.'

He sipped at his coffee. It was strong and sweet. Just how he liked it. Had she enquired of the cook as to his preference? Not something he could ask without looking a fool. But it gave him a strangely warm feeling inside to think she had cared enough to ask. Who was he fooling? Likely it was simply a lucky guess.

He took a deep breath. 'There is one thing. Young Beth—'

Her shoulders tensed. 'What about her?'

'Did you know she went out shortly after dark? Not long after nine. She has a key.'

With a groan, Mrs Falkner pressed her palm to her forehead. 'She asked me if she could visit Polly Garge. I told her I wanted her to remain indoors with the other two ladies. Are you saying she went and hasn't yet returned?'

'She has not.'

'Now what do I do?' She put down her mug and closed her eyes for a brief moment. 'After all she has been through you would think she would know better. She will put the reputation of this house at risk.'

She sounded so defeated, so bewildered, he couldn't stand it. 'I sent Ned to follow her. He'll watch out for her.'

She turned her face away, swallowed loudly, then sniffed.

A feeling of horror went through him. Was she crying? He rummaged for a handkerchief and handed it over.

'Thank you,' she whispered, her voice thick. She dabbed at her cheeks and blew her nose.

The little snort was the sweetest sound he had ever heard for all that it made her seem so terribly vulnerable when he had hoped to make her feel safe.

He felt like the worst cur imaginable, telling her about Beth. Yet she had to know what was going on under her roof. He had no doubt she would have been angry had she discovered it later and learned he had known. He put an arm along the back of the seat, an offer of comfort without touching. 'She will be all right, Mrs Falkner. I promise you. She likely wanted to gossip with her friend.' Hopefully, she wasn't off seeing the grocer's boy.

'Caro,' she said. 'Please, call me Caro, just as Charlie does. Since it seems we are to be thrown together in this enterprise at least for the next few weeks, we might as well observe the courtesy of being friends. At least in private.'

Did that mean she was afraid to be his friend in public? He cursed himself for his defensive reaction. He'd become too jaded, too ready to sense rejection, and yet he did want her friendship. At the very least.

He forced a note of cheerfulness into his voice. 'My friends call me Blade.'

Caro could not believe how having him close could offer such comfort. This was what she had dreamed of as a girl. Her own personal knight in shining armour. A foolish dream, as she had learned the hard way. Men only wanted what they wanted, and if you were fool enough to succumb to their charm they would walk away. And yet she trusted Blade in a way she had not trusted for a very long time.

She'd been calling him Blade in her mind since the afternoon at the pond.

A shiver went down her spine. The harsh

unforgiving sobriquet suited him. A soldier. A man who dealt in death. As hard as steel and honed to cut through whatever was in his way. If he knew the truth about her past, he might not be so kind as to offer friendship. And who would blame him? While he might be illegitimate, *his* father—an earl, no less—recognised him as his son. *Her* father had told her exactly what he thought of her and turfed her out of his house when he learned of her sin.

He'd been ashamed. Disgusted. If her mother hadn't come after her and silently pressed money into her hand before running back into the house, things might well have gone very differently for her and Tommy.

She would never have been able to afford a midwife without those funds. Nor would she have been able to support herself until she found work. And even that had not been going too well after Tommy's birth. Trying to work and keep a child had been nigh impossible. And then she'd received the letter from Carothers's parents telling her of his death. They wanted their grandson. And only their grandson. It was what had made her leave Bath and run north. If Merry had not come along when she had, she might have been forced to give Tommy up. The thought of it made her blood run cold.

It was the fear that kept her awake at night and the reason why she was letting a man she barely knew sit with his arm almost around her shoulders in the dark. Not let. She was leaning into him. Cuddling closer.

'I should go in,' she said, trying to force herself to sit upright. To move away.

'Yes,' he said.

Neither of them moved.

He took another sip of his coffee.

They sat in companionable silence.

There was something she wanted to ask him. Had wanted to ask for quite some time. 'You were at St Peter's Field that day. Did you see what happened?'

'I saw.'

'I hear such conflicting reports. Was there a riot?'

'There was not. It was a peaceful gathering of people who wanted to hear Hunt speak and to make those in power understand their problems.' His voice was full of regret. 'The newspapers reported correctly. The militia struck the first blow. They rode down innocent men, women and children without a second thought.'

'Some people are saying the newspapers made it all up to make the soldiers look bad.'

He shook his head. 'I was among those men.' His lips twisted bitterly. 'It was a massacre.' Clearly distressed, he got up, leaving her feeling chilled. 'It is time you went inside, Mrs Falkner.' His voice was friendly but distant, as if talking about that day was not something he could ever do with ease. 'I thank you for the coffee. It was most welcome.'

She took his coffee cup and looked up at him. He looked so lonely, so alone, she went up on tiptoes and kissed his cheek. 'Thank you, Blade, for looking after us all so well.'

He turned his head and his lips met hers, gently, tenderly.

Heat lit up her blood. Warmth spread out from low in her abdomen.

After blissful seconds—no, even less, merely moments—he leaned back to regard her face, the light from the lantern beside the door clearly showing puzzlement and a question in his expression.

*Are you sure?*

A fair and honest question given her frequent claims of respectability. From a man who had been kind and generous to her little son. A man also, Merry had told her, whose skills as a lover were greatly sought after by the naughty ladies of the *ton* and who could be trusted for his discretion as well as his expertise. An embarrassing sharing between a married lady to a widow Merry had often said ought to take a husband or a lover. Merry had no idea she had never been married or that her one experience with a man had been so miserably unpleasant, she had never wanted a repetition.

Where had been *her* enjoyment the bolder married women teased about? Was she not owed some pleasure? Provided no one learned of it. Especially not members of Tommy's family, whom she had not seen or heard from for the past three years.

She liked this man. Was drawn to him in a way she had never been drawn to anyone else. She trusted him. Mostly.

In answer to his question, she put her free hand around his neck, drew him down and kissed him back. Felt his lips soften beneath hers, become pliant and wooing. He traced the seam of her lips with his tongue and tingles drizzled across her shoulders and down her spine. She gasped at the strange sensation of the tip of his tongue touching, licking at, the tip of hers.

A small sound startled her. A little moan

of approval. Hers. And flutters where no flutters ought to be. And heaven help her, she could scarcely breathe for the feelings rioting through her body. Amazing, wonderful, terrifying out-of-control feelings.

Shuddering, gasping for breath, she stepped back, so unsteady on her feet, if he had not kept a hand beneath her elbow, she might have stumbled. He led her to the bench against the wall, seating her and taking the mug and setting it down. He sat beside her, his thigh close enough to feel its warmth.

With a care that permitted her to object, he settled an arm around her shoulders.

She leaned against his solid form. 'That was…' She did not know how to express what she was feeling.

'A surprise?' he offered. 'Too much? Not enough?'

The teasing note in his voice dispelled her tension.

'It was lovely.' The loveliest thing she had experienced since holding her child in her arms for the first time and perhaps anything before that, too.

'Lovely is good,' he said, skimming warm soft lips across her temple. 'My next question is, where do we go from here?'

Heat rushed to her face. 'I thought I...that is you...'

What on earth did one say?

Lavender-scented warmth bloomed against Blade's cheek. The prim and proper widowed Mrs Falkner—Caro—was blushing? And the moment his brain realised the import of that blush, desire, up to now a low murmur, roared to life behind his falls.

The hound that resided inside every red-blooded male perked up its ears, while the remaining human part of his mind recommended caution. To this point there had been nothing in her demeanour, not a flirtatious glance or innuendo in her words, to hint at prurient interest. 'Are you suggesting that we engage in some sort of intimate relationship? Hmm?' Hardly tactful.

A nod of assent accompanied by intensifying warmth against his skin had the hound sitting up and panting. 'Of the carnal sort?' he added, for clarity for all concerned, still not quite believing his meaning was clear.

She lifted her head from his shoulder and looked him in the eye with a determined bravery. 'Yes.'

The hound bounded around in joyful circles. The man was not entirely convinced.

'You do understand that I have no interest in marriage?' So what was he doing? Trying to talk her out of it?

A look of horror crossed her face. 'Oh, no. I assure you that is not my intent.'

Why did he feel slightly disappointed, when this was all the assurance he needed? Marriage would ultimately result in progeny, randy bugger that he was, and no child of his would be put through the misery of knowing what it was to be considered less than his peers, because it was born to a bastard. Nor would he be able to stand back and watch his wife suffer the slights he had endured and see her resentment grow.

'And if we were to consider such…intimacies, you understand the need for precautions to prevent any unwanted consequences?' he enquired. Like bastard children. That he would never permit, even if he had to marry the woman and suffer the consequences.

'I understand this perfectly well, Mr Read… I mean, Blade. I know all about such precautions. Merry and I decided early on that we would make sure our ladies understood how they might take control of their lives. We provide them both instruction and items.'

The devil they did. Did Charlie know this about his wife? The hound was now whining in protest at the delay. He quelled its enthusiasm. 'You have these necessary items to hand?'

'I do. In my room.'

What more could a man ask? Or a hound. And yet doubts abounded. 'Is there some reason you chose me for this particular adventure?'

She averted her face. 'It has been a long time since I enjoyed male company. I find you attractive and in your person attentive to cleanliness, and I believe we have come to like each other.'

She could have been ticking off a list of requirements. A list very much like his own. Not that liking was usually all that important. She continued with her logical recitation.

'Merry said that you enjoyed the company of widowed ladies who were not actively seeking a husband and suggested I could do worse.'

What? 'Charlie will be interested to learn his wife is acting my procurer.' He could not keep the dryness from his tone.

Umbrage stiffened her shoulders. 'Mr Read, if this suggestion does not appeal, I beg you will not give it another thought.'

Was he mad, when he finally had what

he wanted? Her in his arms and in his bed. Would he throw such a lovely offer away for the sake of a few inconvenient scruples? Had he not been taught never to deny a lady what she wanted?

'It more than appeals, dear one. It appeals greatly.' The hound was sitting up and begging, it appealed so greatly. He bent, took her lips and allowed the cur to rule over the proceedings, while the man shook his head in regret at his weakness.

Her lips were soft and plush. Her scent delicious. He teased at her mouth with his tongue and her little gasps and moans of pleasure were an utter delight. Strangely and most enticingly, she lacked the artifice and skill of a woman versed in sensual matters, but swiftly followed his lead until he wasn't sure who kissed whom and lust was a roar in his ears.

He eased her onto his lap for better access to her mouth and to enjoy the torture of her soft derrière against his arousal. And this time when he kissed her he coaxed her to open her lips and delved into the hot sweetness of her mouth. The silken slide of her tongue against his drove his desire to the limits of control. What they needed was a bed and privacy, preferably before one of the household staff arose from sleep to peer out of the window. Or Tommy.

He gathered her in his arms and carried her inside.

A soft palm touched his cheek. 'Where are we going?' she murmured, her voice husky.

'Your room.' At least, that was his intent. His was above the stables, where he slept with Ned next door, to preserve the proprieties of a widowed lady. Hah!

When he heard no objection, he climbed the stairs to the landing. 'Second door on the right,' she whispered, her face tucked against his neck, her breath sending shivers over his skin. 'Tommy is at the end of the corridor.'

Far enough away. He hoped.

The bedroom was lit by one candle beside the bed and a banked fire in the hearth. The bed was mounded with embroidered pillows that tempted him to lay her down and have at her. He set her on her feet and gazed into her face, trying not to show too much of the hunger that gripped him to the point of pain. He stripped off his redingote and the coat beneath it, tossing them on the floor, leaving him in only his shirtsleeves, his gaze never leaving her face. She was so lovely. He cupped her face in his palm, took her lips and kissed her until he felt her once more leaning into him, melting and kissing him back. Forcing himself to leave her, he set about lighting more candles.

She blinked at him as he returned to take one of her hands in his. Puzzled by? 'You would prefer the anonymity of darkness?' he asked, trying not to feel disappointed or like a thief in the night taking something to which he was not entitled.

Her gaze skittered away and came back to rest on his face. She licked her lips. 'Whatever is usual is fine.'

'Usual,' he mused. And though her eyes were hazed with the passion of their kisses, they also showed a hint of dread. Did she fear he would find her lacking in some aspect? Women were notoriously sensitive with regard to their appearance. 'It is usual for a couple contemplating intimacy to get to know each other. Likes and dislikes and so forth.' He did so by watching his partner's reactions. 'We can proceed in darkness if you prefer.' Though he would be sorry, touch and hearing would tell him almost as much.

She swallowed. 'I don't know.'

He needed to put her at ease. 'Let us not decide yet, then.' He took her hand and led her to the dressing table, gesturing for her to sit on the stool before it. 'I would love to see your hair down around your shoulders.' A pleasure only ever afforded a husband or a lover.

'My hair?' She touched a hand to the plait she must have pinned up before coming down to make him coffee.

'Allow me.' He freed it from its pins and tugged free the small blue ribbon at its end. He combed his fingers through the twisted silky strands, starting at the bottom and slowly unravelling the braid. He picked up her hairbrush and began to brush through the shiny luxurious chestnut tresses in long slow strokes. A glance in the mirror showed her gradually relaxing, her eyes growing slumberous, her lips a sensual curve.

'You are very good at this,' she said dreamily, watching him.

'My mother used to allow it sometimes.' When she wasn't entertaining callers of an evening.

'I am surprised at how good it feels. Nothing like when my maid does it.'

'To your maid it is work. To me it is a pleasure.' He bent and kissed the vulnerable delicate skin of her nape. Inhaled her lavender scent. The velvety softness of her skin against his mouth tasted delectable and it took great effort to ignore the demands of his arousal. He arranged her hair so it fell over her breasts and down her back in a vision of femininity. 'Beautiful,' he murmured softly in her ear and felt her shiver. He touched her earlobe with his tongue, tasted the rapid pulse in her throat and kissed the angle of her jaw.

She turned her face to catch his next kiss on her lips and the pure pleasure of it had his breath catching in his throat and his body aching as she rose to twine her arms around his neck, her hand winnowing through his hair as he drew her close.

He drew back to look at her, their hips pressed tight together, where she must feel the evidence of his lust. He stroked her hair back from her face and looked into her eyes. 'Are you sure this is what you want?'

Here he went again, giving her the opportunity to change her mind like some besotted schoolboy instead of a man to whom seduction came as second nature. He almost groaned out loud at his stupidity, for in her eyes the wariness, the fear, remained in evidence.

Her eyelids fluttered shut and the breath she took brought her soft full breasts in delicious contact with his chest. He readied himself to move away, to leave, even as he toyed with chestnut strands of hair.

'I am certain,' she said softly. 'Though I am unsure of how to go about this.' She waved a vague hand that encompassed them, the bed, the room and the universe in equal measure.

Thank all the stars in heaven. He slowly undid the tie of her robe and let it fall open, revealing a nightgown with little tucks across the bodice and trimmed with lace high at the neck. Marching down the front, where buttons held the bodice together, were little yellow ducks.

They brought a smile to his lips. 'Ducklings?'

She smiled back. 'I know. They are quite silly.'

'I adore them.' They showed a side to her only hinted at before. Sweetness. Kindness. Gentleness. But most of all those little ducks told him the playful side he'd admired long ago had not been entirely extinguished by life. For all her widowed state, her marriage, her child, this woman was also strangely innocent. And no matter what he got out of this encounter, he would happily devote himself to her pleasure.

He put an arm around her waist and led her to the *chaise* angled towards the fire. He seated her and settled alongside. There were certain things a man with one hand had trouble doing for himself. He cursed his choice of footwear this evening. He didn't have to take them off, but he wanted this first time to be perfect, for her.

'Caro, have you ever helped a man remove his boots?'

She popped up off the seat. 'Not that I recall, but I have seen it done.'

Practical sensible Mrs Falkner had his boots off in minutes. She eyed the rest of his clothing like a cat eyeing a mouse.

He pulled her down to sit beside him and kissed her cheek. 'Thank you.' He shifted to settle her more comfortably within his arm, so his back was to the armrest. 'Relax,' he murmured. 'No need to rush matters. We have lots of time.' Days if need be. Even if the waiting drove him to madness. He shifted lower, his left arm resting on her hip, his right hand guiding her chin to give him access to her lips, and plundered her soft luscious mouth. She responded eagerly and he allowed himself the privilege of gently sifting his fingers through her lovely lavender-scented hair.

As she turned into him to meet his kiss,

her leg draped over his hip and pressed into his groin.

Lust scorched through his veins.

The restlessness inside Caro needed more than a kiss to appease its demand. The tension centred low in her abdomen ached for something far more substantial than his fingers winnowing through her hair and his tongue invading her mouth. Those were lovely, but they only served to make the ache stronger. Nor was his reserve, his gentleness, what she had expected from this strong silent man. She'd expected him to be more demanding. Overpowering.

Though his kisses overpowered her and left her weak with longing.

She shifted until she lay along the length of him on the sofa, her breast pressing against the wall of his hard chest. The scent of him, something spicy and woody, filled her nostrils and she drifted her fingers through his silky hair, down his cheek, across his jaw where a day's worth of stubble rasped against her skin. With what felt like great daring, she stroked her hand over his waistcoat. It fit so snugly, she was certain she could feel the definition of the muscle beneath. And the warmth of him. Her hand trailed lower.

His breathing hitched when she passed across the flat of his stomach.

When his tongue teased hers and withdrew, she followed it, learning the contours and softness of his mouth. So enticing. He made a soft sound in his throat, which she interpreted as longing. Was it possible he could want her as much as she wanted him? If so, why was he being so dashed gentlemanly? She arched against his body, seeking relief from the terrible tension within her, feeling as if she wanted to crawl inside his skin. She needed to be so close, and yet all this clothing— She attacked the buttons on his waistcoat. In moments he had helped her to get it undone and pull it off his shoulders and down his arms.

Better, but not nearly good enough. She tugged at his cravat.

Without breaking their kiss, he rose up on his elbow and wrestled her around, so she now lay beneath him, his thigh pressing between hers and against her sex. The tension ratcheted up and she moaned and tilted her hips. She felt dizzy and aching and— 'Blade,' she demanded.

His hand cupped her breast through her

nightgown, his palm heavy and warm, his thumb brushing against her nipple, back and forth, until she thought she would go mad with the pleasurable sensations rippling across her skin. And the throb deep in her core.

'I want…more,' she muttered, knowing not what 'more' meant and yet knowing it was there, not far from her reach.

He let go a long breath and got up, leaving her feeling cold and bereft. The sensual heavy-lidded expression as he stared down at her caused her insides to flutter.

'What is it?' she asked.

He tugged her to her feet and pulled her close. 'If you want us to stop,' he murmured, his voice harsh amid his ragged breathing, 'tell me now, Caro.' A warning. A lovely warning that he was almost as undone as she.

'Stop…' she said, hanging on to his shoulders for dear life. He froze. '…and I *will* kill you,' she managed to finish on a sigh.

He threw back his head and laughed.

It was the first time she had really heard him laugh or seen such a boyish look on his face. Happiness. She stood on her tiptoes and kissed his smiling lips. Sunshine and hope and affection met her questing tongue. And she loved the flavour.

Slowly, tenderly, he drew back, his eyes blazing with desire. 'And now we must take those precautions we spoke of.'

Heavens, yes. In the heat of passion she had almost forgotten. 'Give me a moment.' She went behind the privacy screen and used the system of sponges she and Merry had discussed with all of their ladies and tried for themselves so as to understand the whole business fully.

Feeling wanton, sinful to the point of shame, she emerged from behind the screen to find him flipping through the pages of a book as if she had merely gone to fetch a handkerchief or a shawl. He turned with a smile and put the book away. 'Now, where were we?'

'Kissing.'

He pulled her into his arms and kissed her silly, again, before swooping her up and carrying her to the bed.

'Candles out?' he asked tersely, sweeping back the quilt and laying her down.

'Oh, no,' she said, feeling wicked and bold. 'I want to see every inch of you.' A blush rushed up from her belly and she hid her face with her forearm, still managing to sneak a peek at his expression. Because it would mean he would see every inch of her, too.

He raised a brow, but he did not seem at all dismayed. Or disgusted by her boldness, yet there were shadows in his eyes. 'A lady always gets what she wants.' He unbuttoned his shirt and drew it off over his head.

Her breasts tingled at the sight of the hard sculpted muscles across his chest and down his arms, his left tucked slightly behind his back, she noted vaguely. A light smattering of tightly curling brown hair dusted the expanse of his chest and curled around the tight buds of his nipples. It trailed in a line down a flat-ridged belly to disappear into his waistband. She reached out to touch the crisp curls, running her fingers through them lightly and scraping her nails across the tightly furled buds, watching them pucker at her touch.

A hiss of indrawn breath made her jump, and she would have withdrawn her hand if he had not covered it with his. 'I like it,' he said.

He touched her nipple through her nightgown, rolling it between his thumb and finger. She moaned at the pleasure of the way it made her feel boneless.

She smiled at him shyly. 'I like it, too.' She glanced down at his breeches, wondering if he would remove those, too. Hoped. She drew in

As her first experience had been anything but...

'Saints above but you are beautiful,' he whispered, looking at her with what she could only describe as awe.

Blade had lost his mind. What should be a simple sexual gratification between two consenting adults, an exchange of sensual intimacies on an admittedly grand scale, was turning into something far more dangerous. He was pleasuring a woman he had been desiring for days, weeks—all right, nigh on a decade, though he might have forgotten her during the intervening years—and 'casual' did not describe what he was feeling.

Instinct screamed that no matter how mutually pleasurable this dalliance, or how casual or how fleeting, someone, perhaps both of them, was going to get hurt. And there was nothing he could or would do about it, except ensure it never happened again. Because if it did he had the sense he would lose some things he valued. Friendship and trust. Things she did not hand out with gay abandon. Something he might already have lost.

He smiled wryly at himself. *He'd* already gone well past that point of no return. The

hound whimpered. He quelled it with a glare.
Once only, he promised himself. After that he
would keep a proper distance.

He savoured her sweet lips and the taste
of her skin, the flush of her skin beneath his
palm, her encouraging cries as he fondled the
lush fullness of each breast. He eased over her,
until he was cradled by her hips. The blunt heat
of his erection nudged against the folds of her
sex. Slowly she relaxed, surrendering to the
pleasure of touch in that most intimate part.
He stroked himself against her slick wet heat,
his weight on his forearm while he kissed her
lips and caressed her breast. His balls pulled
up tight to his body, creating a blissful tingle
at the base of his spine. *Not yet.*

He licked at the delicate skin of first one
breast then the other until her hips undulated
in a silent request for more. Then he suckled.

She bucked. Opening to him. Letting the
head of his shaft slide a mere fraction into her
hot silken sheath. Bliss beckoned. He focused
on the drill for cleaning a musket and not on
the sensations rocketing through his body, demanding he take her.

Beneath him, she froze. He raised himself
up, to see her eyes wide, her lips pressed tight
as if holding back a cry of distress. He was not

a small man, and though he had as yet barely penetrated her body, he could feel her fear. 'Caro,' he murmured, stroking the riot of her hair back from her face, 'am I hurting you?'

Her eyes went distant as if her mind was taking inventory. Then her gaze fixed on his face in a kind of wonder. 'No.' She sounded surprised and he wanted to curse. Had her husband's attentions been painful?

If so, her trust was doubly humbling.

'I will not hurt you,' he said, making his words a solemn oath. 'If you want me to stop at any time, say so. I will stop.' Even if it killed him to do so. 'I will do nothing you do not wish me to do.'

Never had he needed to give such assurances in the past, but he prayed she'd believe him. 'Tell me what you want.'

A shy smile touched her lips. 'Kiss me?'

His lips roved her jaw, her throat, her lips, paying careful attention to her sighs and her little breaths. She shifted impatiently. He repressed his smile. 'Where?' he whispered. 'Where do you want me to kiss you?'

In the sweetest moment of his life, and the most erotic, she cupped her breast. 'Here.' She looked adorably confused and worried. When he didn't move, she arched upward, presenting her nipple to his mouth. 'Please. Do that again.'

Something filled his chest—it was warm and soft and painfully sweet. He pushed it aside, unwilling to examine its meaning. 'It will be my greatest pleasure.' And he meant that honestly.' Open-mouthed, he tended to each of her breasts in turn, then to each nipple, building desire in her and him to a pitch where he certainly could not see straight, and then he suckled first one breast then the other.

With a moan, she wrapped her legs tight around his waist, locked her ankles at the small of his back and drew him deeper into her body. And with each slow gliding thrust she sighed her pleasure until he was seated to the hilt and the urge to move ever faster had him in torment. To keep the driving urges at bay, he kissed and licked and suckled every inch of her skin he could reach without breaking his rhythm. She picked up the tempo, her inner muscles clenching him tight, her hand kneading his buttocks, her nails digging into his flesh.

'Darling,' he murmured. 'Let it happen. Let go.' *Please.*

And still she hung between agony and bliss.

He reached down and found the centre of her

pleasure in a desperate bid to give her what she clearly needed, yet did not know how to claim, while he drove harder and faster, meeting each arching lift of her hips until she cried out her desperate need. He watched the sheer wonder on her expression when her body seized, her inner muscles fisting around his shaft, pulsing around his sensitive flesh. The haze of bliss filled her eyes and softened her features. Paroxysms of pleasure shuddered through her. He followed her over the edge. Pulse after pulse of wild heat thundered through his veins—her pleasure or his, he wasn't sure. He collapsed to one side of her and pulled her into his embrace.

Nothing in his past had led him to expect something quite so cataclysmic. An orgy of delight. In shock he gazed down at her. 'Are you all right?' he managed around the pounding of his heart.

'Lovely,' she said dreamily. 'You?'

'Lovely, too.' And so much more, which he did not want to mention, given their understanding of things.

But really, once? How could he have even thought he could keep such a promise? The only good thing was that he had not made his vow out loud. Hades. He was already beginning to want her again.

One thing he would not do, however, was put her to shame.

He forced himself out of bed and cleaned them both up without causing her to do more than stir and smile. He tucked her in, got dressed, picked up his boots and left. It wouldn't do for the servants to find him in situ. Whatever had happened here tonight needed careful thought. Perhaps even a new vision of the future.

## Chapter Eight

'You sent for me?' Blade stood in the doorway to her office, his handsome face expressing caution and his eyes wary.

No doubt he was worrying that she might throw herself into his arms this morning demanding marriage, despite her declaration that she had no interest in anything but one night of pleasure. Yet *pleasure* was far too weak a word for what she had experienced last night. Nothing she had imagined had led her to expect such an extraordinary sensation of bliss. Nor had she anticipated the very real longing to experience it again. She must not give him the least hint of her desires or she might well lose any hope of keeping him at a distance. For it really must not happen again. Not if she was to be the kind of mother her son deserved.

While it would be difficult for them to return to what had been a growing friendship, that was the most she could allow from now on, unless she wanted to lose what remained of her self-respect. A pang of sorrow in her chest made her breath catch in her throat.

She let none of her emotions show on her face. He would no doubt take it as a sign of weakness, as an invitation to indulge yet again. Oh, but she did wish she could.

*Stop!*

'I have an errand to run today, Mr Read,' she said coolly, calmly, despite the rapid beat of her heart.

He flinched slightly at the formal address, but she continued before he could say something he might regret. 'With Beth busy in the kitchen, I wondered if you would accompany me.'

His expression cleared, as if he was relieved. Perhaps having seduced her, he was no longer interested. Like Carothers, once was enough. Thank goodness she had retained enough of her sanity to resist the temptation he presented to her newly heightened senses.

'I can, of course, go alone,' she said with studied indifference, 'but you did insist I not leave the house without an escort.' He had insisted very sweetly. Charmed her, in fact.

Made her feel cared for, perhaps even treasured, when it was simply another task on behalf of his employer. The man was skilled at seduction and she would do well to remember it.

'I beg your pardon,' he said. 'I can easily put off my own plans. Certainly, I will go with you. I'll fetch my coat and hat.'

Out in the street, a cold wind was blowing off the moors and he glanced at the sky. 'No rain today, I think.'

He held out his arm. She took it, because that was what a lady did, but she didn't have to like the little thrill of pleasure that ran through her, or revel in the comfort of his warmth at her side or the sense of protection provided by his bulk. Those things were foolish nonsense. He was not going to be happy when he realised where they were going.

He might even try to stop her, but she would deal with remonstrations when they arrived at their destination.

They walked in silence for some little distance, but when she turned onto a road that led to one of the poorer parts of town, the area occupied by Skepton's most unsavoury citizens, she sensed his reluctance and unease.

'Where are you leading me, Mrs Falkner?'

'You will see.'

He muttered something under his breath she assumed was a curse and, like any respectable lady, she ignored it. They entered a narrow alleyway, at the end of which sat what in an earlier century had been the home of a wool merchant. It was larger and less run-down than most of the buildings around it.

He pulled her to a halt.

'You aren't serious.'

The anger in his face, in the tension of his shoulders, was palpable. She lifted her chin. 'With you or without you, Mr Read.'

'Charlie warned me about this. He also told me you had promised never to do this again.'

'The matter is urgent.'

Dreadfully urgent. Even now she might be too late to save the child. A shudder ran through her at the thought of what might have already happened within this house of ill repute. She only had her informant's assurance that the auction would be tonight. The woman had been half-drunk and frightened and had run away before Caro could obtain any details, but she had no doubt the girl was at this house. She could only hope she would be in time.

'If you want my help, Mrs Falkner, you will tell me what is going on,' he said sternly.

She didn't want his help, but she needed it. The last time she had been here, she'd been lucky. She'd taken them by surprise. They had laughed at her, but hadn't expected any of the girls to take her up on her offer. Flo had jumped at the chance to leave and they had let her go. She'd received a message the following day that the house harboured another girl Caro might like at three times the price.

An innocent young woman who had been snatched off the street for the purpose of getting more of her coin. Tonbridge had been furious when he'd learned what had happened. He had dealt with the abbess himself and made Caro promise never to go there again. If the townspeople ever learned of it, Caro would have ended up in prison or worse.

After that she had only approached the girls on the street while the abbess's minions had jeered at her. Katy had been the only other girl to seize the opportunity the Haven offered. The rest of them had been either too apathetic or too sure they could do better in their trade. Or too afraid. But she had let them know her door was always open. That if they needed help, they would find it at the Haven. This morning there had been a real cry for help.

'I am told they have taken a child from her

father in payment of debt,' she said baldly. 'There is to be an auction where she will be sold to the highest bidder—'

His face paled. 'Let me deal with this.'

She wished she could. 'The mistress of the house said she would deal with no one but me. Tonbridge scared her badly. I was told to come alone, but I am not such a fool. You will do exactly as I say, is that clear?'

His expression darkened, his lips flattened, but he nodded once.

'Good.' Not that she thought he would obey her orders if he decided on some other course of action, but then, that might be just as well.

Arm on his, she walked down the alley to stand at the foot of the steps leading up to the porticoed front door. It was painted in garishly bright red in advertisement of what went on beneath its roof.

A doorman in red livery sat on a chair in front of the door. He stood at their approach.

'I believe your mistress is expecting me,' Caro said firmly, aware of the unsteady beating of her heart.

The doorman's eyes, however, were fixed on her escort. 'Well, if ain't Mr Read. I don't think she expected you, sir.'

'Likely not,' he said calmly.

Only one reason made a man's name known here. Betrayal was a foolish hollow ache in her chest. For the sake of the child held somewhere inside, she ignored it and mounted the steps.

The look of disgust in Caro's eyes hurt. No doubt she thought he had come here to make use of the girls, when he had come here seeking information at the card tables. Let her think what she would. Clearly she was like all the rest of the women who enjoyed his services. She wanted nothing else from him. Not that he had much to offer.

And while this was not the way he had planned to spend his afternoon, since he had wanted to assure himself Butterworth really had left town, keeping Caro safe was more important. *Try to stop her from going off half-cocked* had been Tonbridge's exact words in his letter. A helpful warning that had made him think to bring along his pistol. A habit left over from the war. A soldier never knew when he might need his firearm, even on the most peaceful of days.

If he had been able to get to the pistol the night he lost his hand, things might have turned out very differently. For one thing, he would not have been alive to tell the tale. He pushed back the darkness of the memory.

The porter opened the door and Caro swept inside with Blade bringing up a very close rear.

In the daylight, the hall looked tawdry and garish, like the outside, but at night when the candles flickered and nubile females wandered around in scanty clothing, the male guests didn't notice the furnishings. Blade knew exactly how a brothel worked; he'd spent the first few years of his life as an occupant. He'd been lucky he'd been permitted to stay there with his mother.

The doorman gestured to an open door with his thumb. 'Missus is in there. She's expecting you.'

Caro marched into the room with her chin up. Blade stayed close at her shoulder.

The voluptuous henna-haired woman sprawled on the sofa in a gauzy robe didn't get up. The man behind her, a rough-looking fellow, narrowed his gaze on Blade.

'Nice to see you again, Mrs Falkner,' the woman said in a husky voice some men would have found attractive when she was younger. Now she merely looked raddled in her elaborately curled wig and a robe cut so low across her bosom it left nothing to the imagination.

'Brought your bully boy with you this time, did you?' The irony in the woman's voice grated on Blade's ear, but he said nothing.

'This is Mr Read,' Caro said calmly. 'Late of the Twenty-Fifth Hussars.'

'I know who he is,' the woman said, smiling at him coyly. He tried not to show his distaste. There was no sense in insulting the woman. At least, not yet.

Mrs Falkner removed her gloves in the manner of a pugilist removing his coat. 'I am told you plan to auction a girl of fourteen this evening. I will give you fifty pounds for her.'

The woman glanced up at the man behind her. 'I told you.'

Fifty pounds? Blade reeled at the princely sum.

'That is what you expect to realise at the auction, is it not?'

'Perhaps more,' the abbess said.

'Or perhaps not as much,' Caro replied. 'A bird in the hand, madam?'

The woman appeared to be considering the offer.

'If you don't take it,' Blade said, 'I'll have you closed down by the end of the afternoon.'

'On whose authority?'

'The Duke of Stantford. While his son is out of town I am acting as his representative.'

Caro looked startled, but didn't speak.

The woman's eyes narrowed. 'I don't believe you.'

He pulled out his letter of commission with the ducal seal. 'I can assure you it is true. Now, shall I have you closed down or will you co-operate?' It was no idle threat and the woman knew it. Oh, she would start up again—they always did—but in the meantime she would have no income and her girls would scatter far and wide.

'What Mrs Falkner is offering is more than fair,' he added with a hard smile. Far more than fair. And if Tonbridge wouldn't pay it, Blade would raise the money himself. Somehow.

'I'll need the money in my hand before I hands the lass over,' the abbess said, her voice more a whine than a demand.

Caro plucked fifty pounds from her reticule and held it up.

The woman hesitated, but the sight of the money was too much. The sum equalled what she'd likely make in profit in six months.

'All right, I'll take it.' She sat up and reached for the bills.

Caro whipped them out of her reach. 'In addition,' she said, with twin spots of colour high on her cheeks, 'you will promise me you will not take in any more children. You will swear that they are off limits from now on.'

A look of greed came over the woman's face. 'What about the rest of my ladies?'

Caro shook her head sadly. 'They are adults, and if they come to me seeking refuge of their own free will, I will offer them a chance at a new life, but you must promise me you will never again permit a child through your doors.'

Astonished at her courage, Blade shifted closer. He needed to be ready, because the man behind the abbess looked as if at any moment he might leap into the fray. He must have caught Blade's movement because his gaze flickered from Caro to him and back again.

'Do you want me to teach them who is in charge here?' the man growled.

The woman laughed and waved a languid hand. 'Fetch the girl.' She looked at Caro and there was an odd look on her face. If it weren't impossible, Blade would have thought it was sympathy. 'And tell me,' she said as the man left the room with a last threatening glance at Blade, 'what will this lass be doing at this Haven of yours?'

'She will learn to read and write, if need be,

and be assisted to enter a respectable trade.'
She pulled a pamphlet from her reticule. 'This
outlines our mission. Our main aim is to keep
mothers and children together. But all women
are welcome within our doors.'

The woman reached out and took the pamphlet.

Blade could barely prevent his jaw from
dropping. He'd seen generals with less panache
and authority than Caro Falkner. And in that
moment, he knew he not only liked her, that
not only did he find her an attractive sensual
woman, he knew he was feeling something far
stronger. Something she had made perfectly
clear that she would not welcome from any
man. He wanted to make her his.

The man dragged a girl into the room. She
was so small, he wondered if she was even as
old as fourteen. Her glance took him in and
her large blue eyes opened wide with consternation. And then he wondered if she wasn't far
older than she looked at first glance.

The girl spotted Caro and a look of intense
relief passed over her face. Blade realised that,
standing as he was between Caro and the door,
the girl had seen only him at first.

'Linny, you are to go with this lady and do

as she says,' the abbess said, eyeing the fifty pounds in Caro's hand.

Caro handed over the money and held out a hand to Linny. 'Come, child, we are going to find you a nicer place to stay.'

The girl looked Blade up and down. 'With this gentleman, mum?'

Her voice was from the country, somewhere to the west, Blade thought.

'No. With me,' Caro said firmly. 'What is your name?'

'Linny. Linette Sanders, I was baptised,' the girl said. She glanced over at the abbess and pouted. 'You promised me a pretty dress with red ribbons.'

'This lady will give you all the red ribbons you want,' the abbess said. 'Won't you, ma'am?'

'I am sure we can find some,' Caro said. 'Come along, Linny.'

The girl took her hand and they walked out.

Blade lingered a moment and addressed himself to the abbess, while keeping a watchful eye on her man. 'I'll be dropping by from time to time to make sure you keep your word to the lady.'

The ruffian made a move in his direction. Blade put his hand in his pocket, closing his fingers around the pistol grip.

The abbess put up a hand. She gave Blade a knowing look. 'I'll wager the loss of your hand don't hamper you much, does it, Mr Read?'

'Not much,' he acknowledged.

'Any time you fancy to sample the wares here, sir, you'll be welcome. Girls love a soldier in or out of uniform.'

He bowed. 'Unlikely, ma'am. But I will keep it in mind.'

The woman grinned. Her man smirked.

Blade strode out on Caro's heels relieved nothing had happened, but also with the disquieting sense it had all been much too easy.

'It's a lovely dress,' Caro said, trying to keep her voice calm and soothing so as not to distress the newest occupant of the Haven.

Linny looked far from certain about the sprig muslin Caro had found among the gowns she had purchased in the market for just such an event. Respectable clothes, usually cast-offs given to ladies' maids and then sold on.

'You said I'd have red ribbons,' the girl said sadly. 'Everyone keeps promising me red ribbons and then never gives me them.'

'I'm sorry,' Caro said with as much patience as she could muster. 'I will go to the market first thing in the morning and purchase you some.'

'Can you not go now?'

'Sadly, no. The market is closed.'

A sharp knock heralded Mr Read's entrance.

Caro tried not to bristle. It was none of her business that both the doorman and the abbess had recognised him. He was a man. And men did as they wished, but she was disappointed.

In fact, her stomach had sunk and her heart had ached at the knowledge he was known at that place. She had no right to feel disappointed. He was a single gentleman who would take his pleasures where he could find them. And the fact that she had been weak enough to let him find them with her was her own stupid fault.

At least there would be no unfortunate results this time. Yet she could not think of Tommy that way. Not for a minute.

Mr Read's gaze took in the tea tray. 'It seems I am just in time.'

'Apparently so,' Caro said in a slightly sharper tone than she had intended.

She just wished he didn't look so handsome and charming with his wickedly sensual smile.

He looked over at Linette. 'May I compliment you on your appearance, Miss Linette?

The colour of that gown shows your eyes to advantage.'

Far too charming. 'What did I tell you, Linette?'

The girl tossed her head. 'It doesn't have red ribbons.'

Mr Read reached into his inside breast pocket and withdrew a small packet wrapped in brown paper. 'I stopped at Mrs Fitch's after I left you here.' He winked at Caro.

Winked! How had she fallen to the level of being winked at? No gentleman winked at a respectable woman. But then, she wasn't respectable, was she? Hadn't been for a very long time. It had all been an act. One he'd now seen right through. How very lowering.

Eagerly, Linette took the package and tore open the paper. A tumble of red ribbons fell into her lap. She gazed at Mr Read with a huge smile. 'Now you are what I calls a proper gent.'

A stab of jealousy pierced Caro's breast, causing a hitch in her breathing. She could not be jealous, not of this child and not when, as she had repeatedly told herself, what they had enjoyed was merely physical.

'Mrs Falkner asked me to purchase them for you,' he said.

An out-and-out lie for which Caro felt stupidly grateful.

The girl gave Blade a considering look before she smiled at Caro. 'Thank you, ma'am.'

'You are welcome,' Caro said primly, deciding that arguing the point in front of the girl would be senseless. As well as undermining to her authority. 'I was not sure Mr Read would find any given the lateness of the hour.'

'Can I wear them?' the girl asked.

'You may. Go and ask Beth to help put one in your hair. Then she will take you up to join Tommy in the schoolroom. We can decide what to do with the rest of the ribbons later.'

The girl got up, bobbed a curtsy and left.

'May I pour you some tea?' Caro asked Blade.

'Thank you.' He cast her his seductive smile and she tried to ignore the melting going on inside her. And the longing.

'You don't know how grateful I am at this moment,' she said. 'I was at my wits' end. All she could think about were red ribbons.'

She passed him his tea. He took the cup and set it on the table beside his right hand, which must be why he'd chosen that particular chair in the first place. He'd assessed the room and taken the only chair where it would be easy for him to manage the teacup, like a soldier assessing the position of his enemy on a battlefield. He was a very intelligent man. Clever.

And that was why he, and not she, had thought of buying the ribbons.

He sipped at his tea. 'So, what will you do with her?'

'She says she wants to be a nursemaid.'

He frowned. 'Do you think she's old enough to be given the care of a nursery?'

'One thing is certain—for all her simple ways and small stature, she is a good deal older than fourteen.' She heaved a sigh. 'It seems once more I have been gulled by that woman. Still, I do feel Linny does not belong in that place. I have asked her to keep Thomas amused while Beth is standing in for Cook. It will give me an opportunity to judge how she handles responsibility. Once I feel she is ready, I will look around for a position with a family with young children.'

'She cannot return to her own home?'

A spurt of anger rose in her breast at how easily she'd fallen for their tales. 'All that talk of a father selling her to pay his debts was a tarradiddle, apparently. She says she's an orphan and was put out to service. She left her last employer because they treated her badly and ended up at the bordello a few months ago. They lured her in with the promise of lots of red ribbons. They've been teaching her to act the child.'

'You believe this story?'

How did he know she wasn't quite satisfied with what the girl had told her? 'I think she is hiding something.' She winced. 'But she seems sincere in her wish for a new start.'

He frowned. 'You want me to talk to the abbess?'

'What, so that I can ask for my money back?' She shook her head. 'No, I won't do that. And my mistake won't cost Lord Tonbridge a penny. I used my own money.'

'A great deal of money.'

She sighed. It was the money she was setting aside for Thomas's schooling. She would just have to be more careful in future. 'I could not let her stay in that place.'

He looked grim, but said nothing and took another sip of his tea.

Caro looked exhausted, Blade thought. And worried. Deep inside he knew it was his duty—no, his very great pleasure—to take that worry from her shoulders. If only she would allow it. But how to do it when the woman was set about with defences that even Wellington could not breach?

'You were extraordinary today,' he said.

She stiffened. 'I apologise if you consider my behaviour inappropriate.'

Was that what she believed he thought? Her lack of trust ran bone deep. Once more he wondered who had made her so suspicious of the motives of others. He took a sip of tea and considered how best to allay her fears. 'You misunderstand me,' he finally said. 'You were reckless. Foolhardy in the extreme.' Her face became a rigid mask of indifference. 'And also marvellously brave. I am in awe of your courage.'

Her posture relaxed, somewhat. A crease formed between her brows, as if she did not quite understand what he was trying to tell her. He wanted to kiss away that little frown, but knew she would not be pleased at such a gesture of affection. Not yet.

'It is not the sort of thing a respectable woman should be about,' she said. 'But with the information I had, I could see no alternative course of action.'

She would have come to him and asked him to handle it, *if* he'd had her trust. He ignored the pang of disappointment. It would require a great deal of effort to earn this woman's trust. It would be like fighting the French on the Iberian Peninsula, moving forward inch by inch, until a last final rush carried the day.

Or defeat stared him in the face. What was it they had used to say before battle? The risk was worth the prize. And he had won an inch of ground—she had asked for his escort.

'If respectable women would help their troubled sisters more often, as you did today, then perhaps—' Hell, he had not meant to think of his mother. Of her downward spiral. Had someone like Caro come along things might have been different. He might have been different.

'Perhaps?' she asked, breaking into his unwanted memories.

'Perhaps the world would be a better place for all.'

For a moment he thought she would question him further, but she did not. She would not pry, because she did not feel she had the right. In one way he was glad of it; in another, the past seemed to weigh him down more than usual. He almost opened his mouth to speak of it. To share the guilt of it. Almost.

She breathed deep. An inward sigh.

'You are upset,' he divined.

Surprise filled her eyes. She stretched her neck as if it was stiff. 'A little.'

More than a little. He got up and went around behind her. He put his hand on her shoulder, felt the tension. He rubbed a slow circle with his thumb. Then another and felt some of the tension leave her. But not all. 'You are also angry.'

She sighed. 'I am angry that a young woman was taken advantage of for the sake of a few red ribbons. I am angry that another woman would actually condone the ruination of so young a girl.'

He dug deeper with his fingers and she groaned. Her shoulders drooped; her head fell forward. 'How do you know how to do that?'

'My mother taught me.' His fingers moved over her nape, caressing, massaging the knot of muscle at the base of her neck.

When had he ever mentioned his mother to anyone?

'That is blissful.' She made a soft sound of pleasure that went straight to his groin.

Not nearly blissful enough.

'And you are angry at yourself,' he suggested gently.

She shot a glance over her shoulder like a warning volley, then slumped back against the cushions. 'I was so terrified about going into that place I could scarcely speak for the way my heart rose in my throat. Then, once I was there, it was as if I was watching things happen from a long way off. Watching myself speak so calmly, so determinedly and wondering who that woman could possibly be.' She smiled. 'Now I feel as if I have not an ounce of strength left.'

'The same thing happens to soldiers facing a battle,' he said. 'The initial fear and excitement of what is to come. Then the attack. Fear is gone, pain is gone, and everything comes down to one slow minute after another of fighting for your life.'

He ceased his massaging, but left his hand on her shoulder, knowing the warmth would also help. 'Better?'

'Much better.' In a gesture of gratitude, she covered his hand with one of hers. A gentle giving touch. The delicacy of her small white hand against the brown of his blunt-fingered paw a stark contrast. Unable to resist, he kissed her fingers, then the vulnerable place where feather-light tendrils of hair skimmed her nape.

She exhaled a breath. 'We must not. Someone might come in.'

His groin tightened at the unspoken promise. He strode to the door and turned the key.

'Blade,' she said, her voice attempting scandalised but sounding breathy with longing, her eyelids heavy with sensual need. 'It is the middle of the day.'

'All the better to see you, my lady.'

'You would play the wolf?'

The hound panted its agreement. He gave her a look that told her given the chance he would gobble her up and she smiled. A beautiful welcoming smile.

In a few swift strides, he returned to stand behind her again. Began the gentle massage of her neck and shoulders all over again, though this time she was already soft and pliant beneath his fingers. With a sigh she gave herself up to the pleasure.

A surrender that caused him to harden to iron in his breeches.

For all her outward primness, she was a creature of sensuality. Of great passion. She lowered her head, leaned forward, to give him better access to the muscles across her shoulders. To rouse her to new heights of pleasure, to show her what pleasure a man should give his woman, when her husband had not, was an imperative he could not afford to give in to. He wanted her for himself. Wanted to sink into her heat. Lose himself to the wonders of her lovely warmth and never give her up when a dalliance was all this could ever be. Because in the end, she would give him up and he didn't need the pain of any more losses.

He leaned down and brushed his lips across her shoulder. She shivered.

He kissed the side of her neck, nibbling with his lips, teasing the shell of her ear with his tongue, nipping at her earlobe with his teeth while his hand continued to ease the tension across her shoulders. He rubbed circles with his thumb and massaged with his fingers. With two hands he had been so much more adept, but she did not seem to care.

His lips explored her jawline. She turned her head so their lips met.

Without breaking from the lovely feeling of her mouth on his, he came around to the front of the sofa and leaned over her, the better to access the bounty she offered. She pulled him down, her mouth opening to welcome his tongue.

Leaning his left forearm on the sofa for balance, he skimmed his hand down her arm and then across her breast. Felt the peak of the hard nipple, felt her arch into his hand, filling it with the plump flesh hidden beneath her chemise and stays.

'You undo me,' he murmured softly, cradling her face in his one good hand, the skin soft and silky beneath it.

She sighed, looking deep into his eyes. 'I promised myself this would not happen again.'

The words wounded even as he recognised the sense of defeat she suffered. He had no desire to cause her pain. He, too, had promised.

It cost him, but he uttered the words he knew he must say. 'Shall I go?'

The second of hesitation felt like a lifetime. She shook her head. 'I want you to stay.'

He took her in his arms and kissed her, slowly, lingeringly. Feeling her melt against him was the sweetest thing he had ever known. The most precious gift he had ever been given. Until these past two days she'd been true to her husband's memory, and for all that man's lack of skill, she must have loved him to have remained alone. Thus this gift was precious beyond words.

His heart seemed too large for his chest. Words he should not speak hovered on his tongue. Love. Marriage. Foolish things that only a man of honour should offer a woman. A man of honour would not be doing this. Instead he'd be courting her properly. Offering her a future.

So he kissed her. Hot. Deeply. Pressed her back against the sofa, shifting her bodily, so she lay along its length. He raised his head to look down into her eyes, seeking permission.

The half-smile on her lips was pure invitation.

'Caro,' he murmured.

'Hush,' she whispered, pressing a fingertip to his lips. He nipped at it and she laughed low in her throat. 'I need you.'

As he needed her. He would never have enough of her. Even drunk as he was on her scent, her touch, the thought sobered. What was he doing? He should leave before this thing between them got out of hand yet again. Then he felt her hand burrow between them and her fingers curl around him and gently squeeze.

The pleasure was almost too much.

Awkwardly balancing himself on his forearm, he reached down, captured her small hand in his and brought it up over her head and pinned it there. 'Not so fast,' he growled.

'We certainly don't want that to go to waste.' Her eyes glinted with mischief. She looked like the girl he remembered all those years ago, bright, happy, then on the cusp of womanhood, now a woman full grown. Except shadows remained in those dancing eyes that had never been there when she was a girl.

The sadness of loss.

He rocked his groin against her soft thigh and the pleasure of it rippled across his skin. Not quite so intense. Manageable, at least, and he nuzzled his lips against the rise of her soft full breasts. 'Give me your other hand,' he rasped.

She complied, lifting it languidly above her head so he could enclose her wrist beside the other one. 'No moving.' He let her go and worked her skirts up her thighs until he had her bared to his view.

She was lovely. The chestnut curls invited his touch and he petted and stroked. He slid a finger along her pink feminine flesh and closed his eyes in pleasure at the heat and the wet he found waiting for him.

He lowered his head.

## Chapter Nine

⚬⚭⚬⚭⚬

Caro gazed down the length of her torso to where her skirts were rucked at her waist in a sensual haze. All she could see were the crisp waves of Blade's light-brown hair, where he knelt between her open thighs, and a glimpse of the pale skin of one of those thighs pressed against the cushion of the sofa.

He shifted downward and her heart skipped a beat. Surely he wasn't going to—? She lifted one hand to— What? Push him away?

'Hush,' he murmured and pressed hot open-mouthed kisses against the little hollow of her naked hip. It felt wonderful. Delicious. Tormenting. She let her hand drop beside the other above her head and felt…worshipped as his mouth trailed kisses across her stomach.

And lower.

And lower still.

His tongue licked a path along her and she swallowed a cry of pleasure. Yet she could not stop herself from raising her hips to give him better access. He licked again and she melted, her body feeling loose and disjointed, yet unbearably tense. It was heavenly. And extraordinary. And not at all respectable, she was sure.

She looked down again and he was looking at her, his gaze hot and wild, with a smile on his lips so devastatingly boyish she wanted to kiss him. Badly. He raised an eyebrow in question. *Did she like this?* She nodded, letting her head fall back, resigning herself with great joy to the next round of delicious torture.

She was not disappointed.

His lips and tongue and fingers did things to her she could never have imagined any man doing, and she moaned and writhed and sighed until she was dizzy with a passion so vast it hurt to contain it.

'Blade,' she said, finally giving in to his demand and begging for what she knew she needed.

'Caro,' he said softly, and he used his fingers and tongue on that little point hidden deep in her folds to send her over the edge into mindless bliss. Before the shudders and ripples of pleasure had subsided, he came over her, supporting himself each side of her shoulders on the cushions.

'Hold on,' he grated as he unerringly entered her body and thrust himself into her to the hilt.

She'd been wrong to think he had brought her to the peak of pleasure, for now it built again to a height that left her panting and answering his thrusts with undulations of her hips as he drove deeper and harder. She cradled his face in her hands and saw the strain in his expression, the utter concentration as he brought them so close to the brink she couldn't think. Seared by heat and driven by need, she forced herself up on her elbows and kissed him. He thrust his tongue into her mouth and she suckled.

He drew back, panting, his lips drawn back in the agony of denial. 'I can't— Now, Caro,' he demanded. 'My darling. Now. Come with me.'

Her insides tightened at the harshness of his voice and the utter pleasure on his face, and her vision darkened as with one last drive of his hips he pushed her over the edge into heart-stopping bliss. He withdrew from her body, and with one last pump of his hips, he groaned

and went still, collapsing against her, careful
not to crush her beneath him, his arm around
her shoulders as he stroked her cheek, her jaw,
her throat, the rise of her breast.

She drifted into warm darkness.

When she came awake he was lying on his
side.

'I fell asleep,' she said, wondering.

'You did.' He smiled at her, his eyes warm.

'I should—I mean we should—get up.'

He twined a strand of her hair that had come
loose around one finger. 'Caro, sweetheart,
will you—?' He hesitated. 'I think—'

She froze. Panic rocketed through her mind
at what he might be trying to say. She shook
her head. 'There is nothing to be said.'

His lips smiled, but his eyes filled with an
emotion she could not read. 'As you say, but
still—' he lightly brushed her lips with his '—I
do thank you.'

He got up, straightened his clothes and left.

Full of regret, for herself, for him, she rose
and locked the door behind him.

An hour later, after making some pretence
at working on her correspondence while she
settled her nerves and let cold fresh air from

the window clear the air in her parlour, she rang for Beth to take the tray.

The woman had tried the door earlier but, finding it locked, had gone away. Caro had recognised her step, though for one painful moment had wondered if it was Blade returning.

He would not return now.

She did not know what he had been going to say, but she did know she'd hurt him by refusing to listen. Perhaps that was an end to it. That would be a good thing surely, even if the thought of him turning his back on her made her stomach churn and her heart feel heavy. He presented far too much temptation for her wanton desires. Too much allure, for he was what she had always dreamed of as a girl. A handsome noble knight who would leave his life of service to his king and serve only his lady.

Foolish nonsense, of course, brought on by reading too much romance, her father would have said. As he had always predicted, it had led her astray. And yet wasn't life a little more pleasant with a dash of romance? Her mother's life would have been, she was sure. Where were her family now? she wondered. Still in that little village not far from Worthing?

Was her sister married? With children? There was no way to know, not without bringing the wrath of her father down on their heads.

She once more checked her hair in the mirror as well as ensured her gown showed no signs of disarray and seated herself at her writing table.

Barely in time, too.

'You are finished with the tray?' Beth asked.

Caro smiled her assent.

She glanced at the clock, a little surprised Thomas hadn't made his afternoon foray to find her.

'Where is Tommy?'

'Went for a walk, mum,' Beth said, giving her a little curtsy. 'To the duck pond with the new girl.' Beth glanced at the clock and frowned. 'I told them not to be more than an hour.'

'When did they leave?'

'Not long after I took her up to the nursery. Two hours ago that be.'

It seemed their new addition to the house had no idea of the passage of time. 'I expect Tommy has found some playmates and she may be having trouble convincing him to leave. I'll go and find them.'

'Reet you are, ma'am.' Her eyes held worry.

'I did tell the lad I'd skelp him good, did he not behave. He promised me.'

'Then his punishment will be all the more severe for breaking his word,' she said, heading for the corridor to the back door, where she kept her warm woollen cloak and an old black bonnet for her forays in the streets. One did not go to the poorer parts of town dressed in Sunday finery.

'Should I let Mr Read know you are going out?' Beth asked. 'Made it very clear you was not to go unescorted by him or Ned.'

'I'm only going as far as the green,' she said. 'And Linette and Tommy will escort me back.'

Beth looked dubious, but said nothing more.

Blade morosely watched Ned grooming Apollo. He'd ridden out after he'd left Caro, needing to clear his head. To think about what he was doing with a woman, another woman, who wanted him merely for a little dalliance. Why had he thought her different? Or that he could persuade her that perhaps he was worth more? He wasn't. He'd ruined himself for any chance of a career. His erstwhile commanding officer would see to that. He had no stable income. Not even a name worth the mention. Not to mention those other declarations women wanted. Love and devotion. All that claptrap that faded over time. He'd seen it time and time again or why would married women seek to dally with the likes of him? Even his mother's love had died a death when it no longer suited her to have him around. He was not such a hypocrite to speak words he did not believe.

Why had he even let her tempt him? He was the one supposed to be the seducer, yet he found himself thoroughly seduced. By a woman who didn't want him.

His excuse to leave the house had been his need to track down Butterworth. Or rather, to ensure that his suspicions were unfounded and that the unpleasant fellow had left the neighbourhood permanently.

And so he had. There had been no sign of him at any of the other three inns in town, leaving Blade exactly where he'd started. Wondering who might have meant Caro harm up on the moors.

He rose as the person at the centre of his thoughts entered the barn in haste. Her pallor and anxious expression caused his gut to tighten. 'Is something wrong?'

She cast him a look of anguish. 'Tommy's gone.'

'Gone where?'

'I don't know.' Tears welled. Impatiently she blinked them away. 'He went with Linette to feed the ducks while we...while we—'

A glance out of the stable door showed dusk rapidly approaching. He pulled her into one of the empty loose boxes, out of Ned's earshot before she said something he knew she would regret.

'We will go and fetch them home since they are late,' he said.

'I went. They aren't there.'

Anger rushed up from his belly. 'You went? Alone? Have you no care—?'

She brushed his words aside with an impatient hand. 'The duck pond, Blade. Two streets from here. And I am safely back, but Tommy isn't there.' Panic filled her voice.

He kept his own voice calm, matter-of-fact. 'You are sure you did not miss them on your way? That he is not safely in his room?'

'If he was do you think I would be here?' she hissed. 'I am not a fool.'

He put his hand on her shoulder. 'No, you are not. Does Tommy know his way back from the duck pond?'

'I don't know. He has been there many of times, but he's barely eight years old. He could easily have got turned around, and as far as I know, Linette has never been there before.'

'Do we even know they arrived there?'

She stared at him, shook her head and swallowed. 'No,' she whispered.

'Then we search from both ends. Ned will follow all possible routes to the pond and we will go to the green and work our way outwards.'

She licked her lips. 'Do you think Linette...?'

'I don't think anything but that they have missed their way. Wait here.'

She clutched at his sleeve. 'Where are you going?'

'I need a moment to prepare.'

'There's no time.'

'Five minutes,' he said. 'It is getting dark. I need my pistol.'

She winced, then nodded, releasing him.

He raised his voice. 'Ned, with me.' Up in his room in the loft, he armed himself, while he told his man what he knew.

His worry, that the young hotheads who talked of taking action might have seen this as their chance to wreak havoc on the government they hated, didn't make sense. All the talk he'd heard in the inns had been of marching against the barracks, against the soldiers and militia involved in Peterloo. He could not see them kidnapping a child who was only peripherally connected to Tonbridge.

If the lad wasn't simply lost, then it was more likely the abbess and her minions out for revenge. Out to take the girl back. She was a very pretty girl and he would not put it past the woman's greed to want her cake and eat it too. If so, Tommy was simply collateral damage. Cold filled his gut at the thought of what that might mean for the boy. It could mean his death, or it could mean something worse. Young boys were as valuable as pretty young girls, perhaps more so, to some. Or they might simply return him or abandon him, fearing Tonbridge's wrath. How he hoped it was the latter.

He ran down the wooden ladder with Ned close on his heels.

Caro looked ready to tear his throat out. 'What took you so long?'

'Ned, scour the streets close by,' he ordered. 'Work your way towards the green. If you come across street sweepers or vendors, ask them about the girl with a little boy. Especially ask the men. She's a beauty.'

Ned nodded and ran off.

'We will take the route you usually use with Tommy,' he said.

'I searched that way already.'

'This time we will ask if anyone saw them. We must discover if they arrived or not.'

She closed her eyes briefly and took his arm.

Inwardly he cursed. So many hours had elapsed since the boy had left home, it might be impossible to find anyone who had been on the street at that time.

The sweeper on the corner, an old man with rheumy eyes and clawed hands, stared at them blankly. They moved on, but no one had seen either the girl or the child and they reached the green no further ahead.

Two boys were throwing pebbles in the pond. He strode towards them.

'They were not here when I came a few minutes ago,' Caro said.

'Lads come and go and return betimes.'

On his approach the boys dropped their pebbles, which they had been clearly skimming at the ducks that were racing about in a mad flutter. He glared at them.

'We weren't hitting them,' the bigger boy said defiantly.

'You were one of the lads playing cricket last time we were here,' Blade said.

The lad nodded.

'The little boy who was with us, he joined you for a while. Have you seen him this afternoon?'

Both boys shook their heads.

'You do remember him, though?' Caro asked.

'Right gradely lad,' the younger boy said. 'Fetched the ball for us.'

'He's lost. He was supposed to come here with his nursemaid, but they didn't come home. We think they might have missed the way. If you see him, will you bring him to Sixty-Five Bleaker Street, please?'

Her voice was heartbreakingly steady. She was barely holding on.

'The whore haven for sluts and their bastards?' the older boy said, curling his lip.

Caro winced.

'Watch your language, lad,' Blade growled at him, angry for Caro and for the maligned women.

'That's what my ma calls it,' the boy said, shrugging.

Blade glared at him. 'Never mind that. It is the boy we are concerned about. Your mother wouldn't see an innocent child left to come to harm, would she?'

'If I sees him, I'll bring him,' he said sullenly.

'There will be a reward for whoever finds him,' Caro said.

The lad visibly cheered. 'How much?'

'A pound,' Blade said.

'We'll find him for you, mister, don't you worry.' The two boys shot off, planning how they would spend their money, no doubt.

With night getting closer, Blade felt his own sense of panic rise. Skepton wasn't a huge place, but it had its dark corners and unsavoury characters. Where to look next? As he stared around him, he had the feeling of something missing. Something that ought to be here, but was not.

Something or someone.

'Where do you think we should look next?' Caro asked, her voice full of misery and fading hope. 'Perhaps they got turned around and instead of going south, towards home, they went north.'

'It is possible.'

He just wished he could think of what it was that was sitting at the edge of his vision and refusing to come into focus. 'Who else was here the day we came together?'

She stared at him blankly, then frowned. 'The boys playing cricket. An older couple out for a stroll. A nursemaid with a little girl.'

None of those were what he was seeking. He stared at Caro, trying to think. The tiny dried sprig pinned to her coat caught his gaze.

'The flower girl,' they said in unison.

'She is always here,' Caro said. 'Every time we came, she was standing on that corner.'

'Likely she leaves before it gets dark, but she might have seen them.'

'Blast, those boys probably know where she lives, too.'

Blade pointed to the inn on the corner adjacent to where the flower girl sold her little posies. 'Someone there will know.'

Caro didn't hesitate when they reached the door into the small inn beside the green. Blade did not know about her past, but she had spent more time inside similar taverns before she had been rescued by Merry than she cared to remember. He gave her an odd look as he held the door open for her to enter the taproom where a young man was polishing a pewter mug.

'What can I do for you, sir?' the lad said in a broad Yorkshire accent. He glanced at Caro with a frown. 'Miss,' he added.

'We are looking for the flower girl who sells lavender on the other corner,' Blade said.

The lad's expression became less friendly. 'What do you want with her?'

'We need to talk to her,' Caro said. 'Nothing else.'

'What's she done?'

'She has done nothing, as far as we know,' Blade answered. 'But she might have seen something. We have lost a girl and a small boy, and we are hoping she might have seen which way they went.'

'I don't suppose you saw them?' Caro asked, glancing at the small window facing the green. 'She was wearing a blue cloak and he is about this high.' She gestured with her hand. 'They would have been on the green at about three o'clock.'

The young man shook his head. 'I was working out back then,' he said. 'Sweeping the yard.'

'But the flower girl might have seen them,' Caro said.

'She might have.'

'Do you know where we might find her?' Blade said, tossing a shilling in the air.

'That I do, seeing as how she's my sister. You'll find her at home helping Ma get me da's tea ready for when he's finished at t'mill. I used to work there, too.' He held up a mangled hand. 'Got me fingers caught, so now I do this.'

Blade pulled his wrist from his pocket and revealed a wicked-looking hook. 'You have my sympathy, lad.'

The boy stared at the implement. 'Stap me, it might almost be worth…' He glanced down at the twisted fingers clutching the rag.

'It isn't,' Blade said. 'Now tell us where we can find this sister of yours.'

Instead of giving them directions, the lad went in search of his employer and came back without his apron, saying he would take them to his dwelling. 'It's a bit rough,' he explained. 'They doesn't like strangers. They especially doesn't like soldiers.'

'I am no longer a soldier,' Blade said stiffly, clearly not happy his calling had been instantly recognised.

'Ah, but they wouldn't ask, like, would they?' The lad flashed a grin and led them out of the inn and into the part of town where Caro had found Linette the day before. Once

again the panic in her chest, the tightness, the
difficulty breathing. Would the girl have gone
back to the abbess and taken Tommy with her
if she was lost? Or was there some far more
sinister reason she had taken Tommy? He must
be terrified by now. He was a brave little man,
but he would not understand what was happen-
ing. Would be asking for his mama. Wondering
why she did not come to fetch him.

Guilt swamped her. If she had not let her
wanton desires run rampant, this would never
have happened. Heaven help her, if they found
him she would never neglect her duty again.
She promised. *Please.*

They stopped at a small tenement near the
edge of the town. 'Wait here,' the tap boy, Bert,
said. He went inside and they heard the clatter
of his boots climbing the stairs.

Caro looked at Blade, who was looking very
stern and very fierce. 'Let me talk to the girl.'
She didn't want her frightened into silence.

He nodded tersely. 'Caro, I am sorry this
happened.' He grimaced. 'I feel as if this is my
fault. I should have been on duty—'

'I am equally to blame. I put her in charge
of my son, when I knew nothing about her.'

They both subsided into silence. No doubt
he had as many regrets as she did, and yet, no

matter what happened, she would always treasure the memory of their time together. Wicked as it was, she knew she would. Because inside she really was the shameless hussy her father had named her.

Bert returned in a clatter of boots followed by the girl from whom they had bought lavender a few days before.

She looked worried and dipped a little curtsy. 'Bert says you are wishin' to see me, ma'am…sir.'

'You remember us?' Caro asked.

The smile the girl directed at Blade lit up her face and made her almost pretty despite her wind-chapped cheeks and a missing front tooth. 'I do. Most generous the gentleman was.'

'Do you recall the little boy with us?' Caro asked, forcing herself to speak calmly.

'Oh, yes. Sweet little chap. Bert says you've lost him. He was at the green today.'

'You saw him?' Caro's head spun. Blade caught her by the elbow, held her steady.

'Oh, yes. Happy as anything he was, getting to drive such a grand carriage.' She looked at Blade. 'Was it yours, sir?'

'Drive a carriage?' Caro said, astonished. 'Are you sure it was Tommy?'

'Well, as to that, ma'am, I don't rightly know his name, but it was the lad who was with you when your man bought the lavender. Light hair. Blue eyes. Fair jumping up and down he was to get up on the box with the coachman.' She frowned. 'I wondered at the girl letting him get up there, but she didn't seem to take no never mind about it, so—' She shrugged.

'The girl with him,' Blade said quietly, clearly wanting to make sure he did not scare the young woman. 'Did she go in the carriage also?'

'Climbed right in, sir. A gentlemum opened t'door to her.'

'Did you see the gentleman?'

'No, sir. Just his arm when he opened the door.' She frowned. 'He had on a black coat and yellow gloves.'

Just about every man in Yorkshire would fit that description.

Caro looked at Blade. 'What do we do now?'

'I don't suppose you recognised the carriage, did you?' Blade asked.

The girl gave him another winsome smile and Caro felt a squeezing pang behind her breastbone. Really? She was jealous? After her promise? She took a deep breath, quelling such a stupid sensation.

'It looked like a hired carriage,' the girl said.

'Did it? What makes you say that?'

'Has a sign on it. Words.'

'What did it say?' Caro asked.

'I'm sorry, mum. I don't know. But it was green. The Green Man rents out a coach what's green.'

'It do,' Bert said.

Blade looked thoughtful, then pulled out a shilling. 'You've been very helpful, Miss…'

'Daisy,' the girl said, shaking her head. 'I don't want your money, sir. Not for helping a little lad find his way home.'

'Then take it as an advanced payment for lavender sprigs. I'll have one every time I see you,' Blade said.

'Go on with you, sir,' the girl said, refusing the coin. 'You pays when you sees me.' The girl spun around and went back indoors.

'Us Mullhollands are good people,' the boy said proudly. 'Pleased to help, sir.'

'Thank you,' Blade said with a bow.

The boy tipped his hat and ran off.

'I suppose now we go to the Green Man,' Caro said.

'We do,' Blade replied, his tone grim.

'Who do you think was in that carriage?'

Caro asked, racking her brains trying to understand what was going on.

'A man by the name of Butterworth,' Blade said.

Caro's mouth dropped open in astonishment.

'Come on,' Blade said. 'I'll explain as we go. We need to hurry.'

## *Chapter Ten*

Blade was furious. At himself, but more importantly at the innkeeper, who had told him that Butterworth had left two days before, but had neglected to mention the hire of a carriage.

While he fervently wished Caro safe at the Haven, he didn't bother to suggest he take her home first. She wouldn't have listened. To tell himself the truth, in her position he would not have listened either. Who was this Butterworth character and why had he chosen to abduct Tommy? Did he plan to use the lad to bleed Tonbridge?

'Do you think he's seeking a ransom?' Caro asked, so in tune with his own thoughts it struck him as eerie. And there was hope in her tone, which was strange to say the least.

'If so, a note might have arrived after we left,' he said. 'We'll have to go back and see, but I think we should at least find out what the innkeeper knows before we do.'

She nodded her agreement.

As they arrived at the Green Man, Ned came running up. 'He left town on the box of a carriage rented from here,' he gasped. 'Tommy was trying to take a turn at the reins and nearly ran an old fellow down at the crossroads. Still blaspheming he was, when I found him sitting on his—' He turned bright red. 'Sorry, Mrs Falkner.' He bent over, winded. 'When I didn't find you back at the house, I thought to come here and see if the landlord knew where he was going.'

'Good plan, Ned. Please remain here with Mrs Falkner while I see to matters inside.'

'I'm coming with you,' she said.

'It would be better—'

Her glare stopped him cold. 'Very well, but please do not interfere. This time I am asking the questions.'

He marched in. As luck would have it, the landlord was coming down the stairs into the dark panelled entrance hall. 'Mr Read,' the landlord said. While his lips smiled, his eyes darted about looking for escape.

Blade let him get two steps towards the kitchen, then trapped him against the wall.

'Tell me again about how Butterworth left two days ago and never said where he was going.'

'Mr Read, how dare you, sir?' the greasy fellow protested, his foul breath making Blade want to gag.

Blade lifted his left hand and placed the point of his hook very close to the landlord's eye. 'I dare because I am stronger than you and better armed. Not to mention that Butterworth has abducted a child and when he is caught, and he will be, you will be an accessory.'

The man shrivelled like a punctured pig's bladder. He swallowed noisily. 'He never said nothing about no abduction. Him nor his doxy.'

Blade's gut knotted. 'His doxy?'

'Well, she weren't his wife. Proper slut she was, pretending to be all innocent like. Proper took me in till my missus figured out her game.'

Blade swallowed a curse. The landlord was not the only one who had been gulled.

He released the man. 'So they rented your carriage. Where were they going?'

'York.'

Caro's face blanched. And yet for once she said nothing. She was simply staring, her expression one of pure terror.

'You didn't object to him taking your carriage such a distance?' Blade asked.

'The landlord at the Bull will send it back with his driver and a few bottles I ordered,' he said sullenly. 'Do it all the time, I does.'

'And where did they say they were going once they reached York?'

The man shrugged. 'He paid me well enough not to ask questions.'

'Ned,' Blade said.

'On my way, sir.'

Ned would ask all the people who worked at the inn and anyone else who might possibly have information.

'I must go to York,' Caro said, already making for the door. 'I must catch up with them before they—' She stopped herself.

He caught her arm to slow her down. 'First we return to the Haven.'

She nodded. 'Of course. I need a conveyance. Merry's phaeton would be the fastest, but I have never driven such a vehicle. I will take the gig.'

His jaw dropped. 'You don't think you are going alone.'

Her shoulders straightened. 'This is none of your concern, Mr Read.'

Of course it wasn't. And naturally they were back to the formalities.

Her worst nightmare had happened. All because she had let down her guard. Let her desire for this man, her wantonness, scramble her wits.

She hurried along the street, Blade easily keeping pace with her, though thankfully not insisting she take his arm. The slightest kindness from him and she might burst into tears. She did not have time for tears. She must find Tommy. Get him back. It had been late in the afternoon when Tommy got into the carriage, so surely this Butterworth would be forced to stop somewhere on the road. But what would she do then? Most likely he'd want money. And heaven help her, what a fool she'd been, she'd used almost every penny she had to pay the madam at the brothel.

She broke into a run.

Blade grabbed her arm and swung her around. 'Stop!' he said in a low harsh voice. 'What the devil is going on here?'

She tugged at her arm, but he did not let her go. She glared at him. 'You know perfectly well what is going on.' She turned her glare on a couple who had stopped to watch them. They hurried away. She lowered her voice. 'Tommy has been abducted and I have to get him back.'

'I know that,' he said bitterly. 'Here I was worrying about radicals out to do Tonbridge harm and all the time this was about you and Tommy. You should have told me you were in trouble.'

'I wasn't in trouble until you came along,' she muttered. 'And what do you mean by *this*?'

He flinched, but didn't let her go. 'I believe it was Butterworth you heard open the door to the carriage up on the moors.'

Her stomach fell away. 'You think he caused the accident?' A shudder went through her. 'He killed Mr Garge?'

'I doubt if that was deliberate, but I think he intended to stop the carriage. Had you planned to take Tommy with you to York?'

It was beginning to come clear to her, too, now. 'Yes. At the last moment, he had a touch of gripe and I decided to leave him behind with Beth.'

'Somehow Butterworth learned he was to go with you. It must have come as a shock to discover you alone in the carriage. Why does he want the child? You are hardly a wealthy woman.'

He would despise her if he knew the truth. 'I don't know.'

He cursed softly. 'I'm not letting you take another step until you tell me what is going on.' He edged her against the wall of a building to allow other people to pass by them. He frowned at her. 'Is your husband still alive? Have you run to keep Tommy from him?'

The disgust in his voice cut like a whip. The truth formed on her tongue. She couldn't tell him. She just couldn't. All these years she'd managed to keep the facade intact. If they reached Tommy in time there would be no need for him or anyone else to know. Tears welled up and almost choked her, but she had to tell him something. 'Tommy's father is dead. I swear it. Now, can we please go after him?'

Relief showed on his face, but he shook his head. 'Tell me, Caro. When you learned he had been abducted, you were not surprised. You were shocked. You were frightened. But not in the least surprised. Why?'

She sagged against the wall. The man was not going to let her go until she told him. 'Tommy's father died before Tommy was born. I don't know for certain, but I am guessing Tommy's grandparents have employed Butterworth to take him from me.'

'His grandparents?' To her relief, he tucked her hand in the crook of his elbow and started walking. 'You can tell me the rest as we go.'

She quickened her pace to keep up with his long stride. 'There is nothing else to tell. They want Tommy.'

'Is it such a bad thing?'

'They want him, but not me.'

'I see.' His tone was as grim. 'Who are they?'

If he hadn't figured it out, she saw no reason to tell him. 'It doesn't matter. I will not see my son brought up without me. I cannot do it.'

'I agree. All children need their mothers.'

She looked up at him, at the hard look on his face, and wanted to hug him for that small bit of comfort, but right then he looked far from huggable. He was glaring at the pavement.

'Surely the settlements should have dealt with this issue,' he finally said. 'Or your father can convince them it would be better for all if you stayed with Tommy…' His voice trailed off. 'There is something you aren't telling me.'

Bile rose in her throat. 'All that matters is that I find Tommy. Then we will move on. Find somewhere to live where they will not find us. I should never have stayed here this long.'

'Who is Tommy's father?'

Dare she trust him? If he took sides with Carothers's parents, she would likely never see her son again.

'If you don't tell me, I will find out. Butterworth will tell me.'

Since he would not allow her to search for Tommy by herself. What was it that she had thought about him? That he was the knight in shining armour she had dreamed of as a girl? And hadn't she once thought the same about Carothers? But Blade was different. Like a knight of old, he would not let a woman go on a quest alone. If at all.

'Let him tell you, then.' Once she had Tommy back, she did not care what Butterworth said, because she'd run. Start again. The thought of it made her feel weak at the knees. Made the back of her nose burn with angry tears.

He let go a sigh. When he spoke again his voice was weary, pained. 'Fine. Keep your secrets. It really is none of my business, but I will help you get Tommy back.'

She had hurt him. She hadn't wanted to, but she had. And that made something inside her ache. But her feelings did not matter. What mattered was her son. He would be wondering where she was. Why she had not come to fetch him. Why, oh, why had she ever let him out of her sight? She knew why and the knowledge was bitter.

At the Haven's front door he stopped her with a hand on her sleeve. 'I promise you, we will find him.'

The determination in his eyes lifted her spirits. He was a man who would always do his best to keep his promises. She trusted him, when she trusted so very few people any more.

But she did not dare trust him with her heart.

'Then we need to hurry,' she said briskly.

Heartsick for Caro and for her son, Blade watched her disappear through the front door. The woman was blaming herself for what had happened. Blaming herself for indulging in a few moments of stolen pleasure and leaving her son unguarded.

But usually a child did not need to be guarded, not an ordinary child of an ordinary woman. He wished she would trust him with her secrets. It might make the task of finding her son a great deal easier. Did Charlie know? Or Merry? There was no time to ask.

Tommy was alone with strangers and likely terrified. Blade could remember like yesterday the anguish of abandonment. The sheer terror of being alone with people he did not know.

Who were these grandparents who wanted the child? He believed her when she said it was not the father... Then whose parents? Her parents? The father's? And why did she not want to tell him? Well, there would be no hiding it once they caught up to the boy. Hopefully, they would be in time to stop Butterworth from handing the child over before some agreement was worked out.

Blade couldn't help feeling sympathy for the grandparents' predicament if Caro was refusing to grant them any access to their grandson. It wasn't right that the child should not know other members of his family, but it was the wrong way to solve the problem, as he knew only too well.

He entered the stables and found Ned readying Tonbridge's now-repaired carriage.

'What did you learn from the stable lads at the Green Man?'

'Not much. The carriage was hired to go to York. Butterworth rented it to visit friends on his way to York, where he planned to hire a post-chaise for London.'

And they were at least three hours ahead. 'When you are done there, saddle Apollo for me, would you?' Mrs Falkner wouldn't want to be seen closed up in the carriage with a single gentleman. She guarded her reputation very carefully and rightly so. And he'd been a blackguard to take advantage of her loneliness. No doubt part of her reluctance to trust him.

Leaving Ned to finish up, he ran up to his room and packed a valise.

When he returned downstairs, the coach was already waiting in the courtyard with Ned on the box and Caro ensconced inside— alone. He frowned. That he had not expected. 'Where is Beth?'

'I cannot leave the Haven unattended,' she said calmly. 'Our door is always open to women in need.' She took a deep breath. 'And the fewer people who know about this the better.'

A woman had her pride, in other words. And he was not about to rob her of that.

'Will you dither about all day or will you get in?' she said.

'I'm riding.'

She looked surprised and relieved. He tried not to feel hurt. She was, after all, a lady and he was not really a gentleman. He never had been.

He got up on the box and had Ned help him on with his riding coat while he issued instructions. 'My guess is he will drive through the night. He is supposed to go to the Bull, but I'm not banking on it. The man is as slippery as a bucket full of eels.'

This Butterworth chap had done this sort of thing before. He'd hidden his intentions well or Blade might have tumbled to what he was about more quickly. The man hadn't fitted any of Blade's theories about the radical element in Skepton because he wasn't part of it.

Blade should have realised that his interest was not Tonbridge, but Mrs Falkner. He only appeared when she was about. Not surprisingly, it had never occurred to him that such a respectable woman would have enemies.

Ned grinned at him. 'Like old times, Captain. Glad of it, too. I was getting right bored.'

Gads, it was a bit. Oddly, this time, the stakes seemed higher. He clapped his old friend on the shoulder, jumped down and mounted up.

They turned out of the courtyard and took

the road to York. As soon as they were clear
of the residential streets, Ned whipped up the
horses. Tonbridge's cattle were fine beasts.
Even with a three-hour start, they might well
catch up to their quarry before he reached
York.

Fortunately, it wasn't raining, so while the
evening was chill, he and Ned would not have
to endure a soaking. And that was a good
thing.

Their luck did not hold. A quick enquiry
at the Crossed Keys and they learned Butterworth had also made good time and was still
more than three hours ahead of them. Mrs
Lane, bless her heart, handed over a batch of
freshly made sandwiches and a flask of brandy,
which she had prepared while Caro made use
of the facilities. Caro refused the brandy, but
did swallow a hot cup of tea.

Butterworth had not stopped.

But then, he had likely prepared for the journey.

'There was no boy riding on the box as they
went by,' Mrs Lane said to his enquiry. 'I heard
them coming and came outside to see if they
would come in. They never spared us a glance

as they passed. Looked to be in a hurry. The horses looked nigh worn to the bone.'

Perhaps the fool would end up in a ditch.

He scotched that thought the moment it formed. He didn't want Tommy coming to harm. The only hope now was that in fear of pursuit, he would spring his horses on the flat and be forced to walk them up hills. Blade would not make such a greenhorn mistake, for all that Caro urged Ned to go faster.

'Thank you for your help,' he said, touching his hat as he closed the carriage door on Caro, and then they were off again. It was now pitch dark and the lanterns each side of the driver's box were not much help.

'Take care, Ned,' Blade called out. 'Tonbridge won't be pleased by another accident to his coach.' And he certainly didn't want any harm coming to Caro.

## Chapter Eleven

By dusk the next evening, they were miles along the road to London, with no sign of their quarry. They'd changed horses at one of York's livery stables in the middle of the night and were now travelling from one posting house to the next. Their hopes of catching the fugitives quickly had been cut to ribbons in York. It had taken more than an hour to find where Butterworth had left the first carriage and to discover that he was definitely continuing on to London by post-chaise. The delay put them more than four hours behind the fugitives, forcing them to be content with following in his footsteps rather than trying to cut him off.

Caro's eyes burned from lack of sleep and worry, but she continued to stare out of the window at the passing countryside while willing the carriage to greater speed.

Wedged into the far corner of the carriage, Blade dozed. His horse had been tethered to the back of the carriage. Seeing his exhaustion at one of their recent stops, she had encouraged him to rest his horse, which meant he could also rest himself. She could not resist the occasional glance at his face, though soon the darkness would make it impossible to see much at all. At rest, he seemed a great deal younger and less stern than he did when ordering people about and worrying over their safety.

The Carothers family had a town house in London. It was where she had gone to beg for help. They also had a couple of country estates, though. Wherever they were going, once they had Tommy behind their walls, she would have little chance of getting him back.

She leaned back against the squabs and closed her eyes. Opened them again. Shifted on the seat. She could not rest, not until she had Tommy safe. Panic hit hard. There would be no fighting Carothers's parents. Not once they had her child. Possession was always nine-tenths of the law. Especially if the possessors were noble and moneyed.

'We'll find him.'

Blade's voice was little more than a comforting murmur and his eyes remained closed. He must have sensed her anxiety.

'I am sorry if I disturbed you.'

He opened his eyes. 'Not at all. A soldier snatches his rest when and where he can.'

'Tommy will be terrified.'

'He's a brave little man. And he knows you will come for him.'

Yes. He would know. But if she did not succeed? What then?

The horses slowed.

Blade sat up and leaned so he could see ahead. 'A posting inn. We will get news of them here. They will have changed horses here, but we have been making excellent time. We will stop to eat.'

'No.'

'He must also stop to eat,' Blade said gravely. 'And while I am prepared to travel through the night, I need my sustenance. And so do you or we will be stopping because you are ill.'

She heaved a sigh. But in truth she was grateful for his thoughtfulness. The fact that he was willing to accompany her on this wild chase was something of a miracle.

The carriage swung into the coach yard and there, having its team changed, was a yellow bounder. A post-chaise very much like the one they were following.

'It can't be,' she said, her heart racing so hard she thought it might leap from her chest.

Their carriage had barely drawn to a halt when Blade jumped down and ran for the other coach. He yanked open the door.

Hiking up her skirts to make the leap, Caro followed him out of the door and across the cobbles. The chaise was empty.

'This way,' Blade said. He strode into the inn and there in the parlour sat Butterworth with a substantial dinner set before him, and no sign of Tommy or his female accomplice.

'Where's Tommy?' she practically shrieked across the room.

Butterworth looked up. 'Madam, are you addressing me?'

'Leave this to me.' Blade stalked up to Butterworth much in the way Caro might imagine a tiger stalking up to its prey. He yanked the table clear of the fat man, grabbed him by the front of his shirt and stroked Butterworth's cheek with the point of the hook on his left wrist. 'No games, Butterworth. You were seen leaving Skepton with the lad.'

Gasping and coughing, Butterworth shrank

back from the wicked implement so close to his eye. 'All right. No need for violence.'

Blade shoved him backwards so hard the chair rocked on its legs. 'Where is the boy?'

Butterworth fussily brushed at the front of his coats. 'I left him in York.' He looked over at Caro. 'With his doting grandparents.'

They were too late. Legs trembling, Caro sank into the nearest chair.

'Where were they headed?' Blade asked. 'If you lie to me, I will come and find you.'

Butterworth shrugged. 'I have no idea. I am not party to their plans. I met the old gentleman in London, but it didn't seem as if they planned to go any great distance.'

'They have a house near Lincoln,' Caro said, her heart plummeting to the soles of her shoes and perhaps lower.

'Then we have overshot badly,' Blade said. He was looking at her with sympathy.

A dreadful weight descended upon her chest. She was going to have to tell Blade the truth. And Merry and Tonbridge. She felt ill. They would despise her as much as she despised herself.

Blade glared at Butterworth. 'Bait and switch. Very clever.'

Butterworth grinned proudly. 'My idea, that.

I know how you feel, lad. I was tricked the same way more than once when I worked for Bow Street.'

'You are a Runner?'

'Was. I find private work for the nobs a deal more lucrative.'

'Tonbridge's carriage? Was that you?' Blade asked.

Butterworth made a face of disgust. 'I made out my horse was lame, expecting the carriage to stop. The blasted coachman whipped up the horses instead. Nigh on ran me down. Then he went off the road. All for naught.'

Caro gasped.

'Idiot,' Blade said. 'What did you expect in such troublesome times?'

The man blew out a breath. 'I expected a bit of courtesy.'

'The girl, Linette, was working for you?' Caro asked.

'Linny? She'd been working at the brothel for weeks. Saw my offer as a way out.' He glanced over at Caro. 'Seems you made some enemies in Skepton with your do-gooding ways.'

'The madam at the brothel was also in on your plan,' Blade said, sounding disgusted.

Caro cringed inside. She knew she'd made

enemies, but never imagined they would harm her child. But people were cruel. They did not care whom they hurt.

'For a generous payment. The lad's family are anxious to get him back.'

'Back?' Caro almost spat the word. 'They never wanted him.'

Blade gave her a sharp look and she bit her lip. If she wasn't careful, he would guess everything and she still hadn't decided what was best for Tommy.

'Where is Linette now?' Blade asked.

Butterworth made a face. 'By the time we got to York, the little lad was clinging to her like a life raft. The old gentry mort offered her a position as nursemaid. Seems as how Linette preferred that to her former occupation. Naturally, I didn't tell them what that was.'

'I should have guessed there was something not right about that girl,' Blade said, clearly blaming himself.

'If she's giving Tommy comfort, then I am glad of it,' Caro said. But inside she felt as if her heart was breaking. Worse was the sense, the almost certain knowledge, that perhaps her son really would be better off without her. These past few weeks had proved her father right. She wasn't fit to bring up a child. *Slut*.

*Wanton.* The words echoed in her ears. If she had not been so easily seduced, so driven by her passions, Tommy would not have gone alone to the green with Linette, would he?

All these years she had tried so hard to be good, to be a respectable woman, to be what she should have been from the first, but the moment temptation had come her way, she'd succumbed.

Blade took one look at Caro's face, read defeat in her expression and the slump of her shoulders, and he wanted to commit murder.

'Leave,' he said, leaning down to glare into Butterworth's face.

'Now see here,' the man said. 'I've as much right to my dinner as the next man.'

'If you don't go now,' Blade said, lowering his voice to little more than a murmur, pressing the point of his hook between the rolls of fat below Butterworth's jaw, 'you will not have a gullet to take the food from your mouth to your belly.'

The fat man raised his hands in surrender and Blade stepped back.

Butterworth snatched the napkin from around his neck and flung it down. He lumbered to his feet. 'I'll leave you to settle my shot, then.'

Blade nodded. 'It is a bargain, just to be rid of your company, but one thing you will not do is run to your employer.'

'Why would I? I've kept my part of the bargain and been paid. Besides—' he gave Blade a rather triumphant grin '—you will discover you are expected. Good day to you, sir.'

He stomped out with a venomous glance at Caro and a few minutes later could be heard shouting for the postilion so he could be on his way.

To Blade's consternation, Caro didn't move. She simply remained staring at her hands in her lap.

He stuck his head outside the door and found a waiter hanging about in the hallway looking confused. He stepped out to speak to him. 'Do you have two chambers with a private parlour?'

The man nodded.

'The lady and I will take them if you will be so good as to show us the way. Please arrange for dinner to be sent up as soon as possible.'

The landlord came along right at that moment. 'Is something wrong?'

'This gentleman is asking to bespeak rooms

for him and the lady. A parlour and two chambers for the night.'

The landlord gave him a suspicious look. 'The gentleman who just left told my stableman you was to pay his shot.'

Blade nodded. 'I will.'

His expression looked a little less sour. 'Whom do I have the pleasure of entertaining in my humble establishment, sir?'

'Mr Bladen Read and Mrs Falkner.'

The frown reappeared. 'This is a respectable house—'

Of all the self-righteous... 'Mrs Falkner is my sister. My widowed sister.'

The man's face relaxed into something resembling a smile. 'Then welcome to the Blue Anchor, sir. I will have dinner sent up to the private parlour directly. If you would care to freshen up beforehand, William here will show you to your rooms. The two rooms at the front of the house, William, with the parlour between. Our best rooms, sir.'

And his most expensive, no doubt. But that was the price one paid for dissembling.

He returned to the dining room and found Caro sitting where he'd left her, her face white and set. Her eyes were cold as she looked at him.

Inwardly he winced. He shouldn't have been

quite so brutal with Butterworth. Not in front of a lady. Shame filled him at the realisation that he'd exposed her to the real him. The guttersnipe who hid beneath the guise of civility. Barely. Any gently bred woman would be horrified by what she had witnessed. 'I apologise for shocking you. I would not have done what I threatened.'

She stared at him and said nothing. Damn it all, she thought him the worst of curs. He straightened his shoulders. Let her think what she would. 'We will stay here tonight and turn back in the morning. I have booked rooms and a meal.'

At the widening of her eyes, the lips parting to object, he wanted to hit something. 'Separate rooms. I told them you were my sister.'

The nod she gave him was of the numb variety. She heard him, clearly comprehended the words, but she had withdrawn into herself.

'Let us freshen up, have dinner and then talk about our next steps,' he said gently.

The footman escorted her upstairs while Blade went off to arrange for her bag to be brought up, as well as request the services of a maid. He also stopped by the stables to let Ned know what was going on and have the carriage put up for the night.

As he sat in his bath in his chamber, he pondered their next steps while carefully forcing his thoughts away from the expression of disgust he had seen in Caro's eyes.

Apart from the normal requirements of eating a meal, Blade had left Caro alone with her thoughts until they had finished dining. Not that she was hungry. The heavy lump in the centre of her chest was not conducive to the consumption of food.

At the start of the meal she had refused Blade's offer of a glass of wine, despite his suggestion that it might help her sleep.

No matter which way she viewed what had happened, she could not see any way for things to return to the way they had been. It seemed very likely Tommy was lost to her. Under normal circumstances, the courts might favour a mother's claim to a child over that of the grandparents, but in her case there really was no hope. Everyone at the Haven would have known about her and Blade. A clever lawyer would be quick to exploit any further fall from grace in order to shore up the bad character she'd already demonstrated by having a son in the first place. No doubt Butterworth had passed all he knew along to his employer. The courts could easily deem her morally unfit to care for her child.

She knew all this because she had spent part of the precious hoard of coins she'd saved when she'd first started her employment with Merry to discover what rights she had under the law. She had been shocked at how easily the rich and powerful could override the rights of the rest of society. She had also known she must maintain a spotless reputation if she wanted to stand even a small chance of keeping Tommy if his grandparents ever ran them to earth.

She wanted to scream.

But most of all, she wanted to cry.

Crying got one nowhere. She had cried when her father threw her out and when Carothers's family refused their aid. It hadn't helped then and it would not help now. What was important was Tommy. For years, she'd denied her selfishness. Convinced herself Tommy was better with her. But what if she was wrong?

With his grandparents, Tommy would lack for nothing. Oh, but how she would miss him if she let him go. She wished she knew for certain what would be the best course to take. For his sake.

'Perhaps we should return to Skepton in the morning,' she said, breaking the silence once the waiter had cleared away the dishes and left Blade with a decanter of port and her the tea tray. Just saying the words caused a stab of pain behind her breastbone.

He sat up in his chair, looking bewildered. 'You cannot mean to abandon your son now?'

If he said any more, she might well cry. 'It is not a question of abandoning him. I am thinking logically. His grandparents can provide so much more than I.'

His expression darkened. Filled with disgust. 'Is it logical to leave him with people I presume are strangers while you merrily go on your sanctimonious way saving girls from iniquitous choices?'

She flinched at the anger and scorn in his voice. 'I am thinking of what is best for my son. If you don't mind, I would like to retire now. I will inform you of my decision in the morning.'

She crossed the room to enter her chamber, back straight, head held high while inside she shattered into a thousand pieces. He didn't even know the full truth and thought the worst of her. So much for him being a friend.

He came up behind her, his fury a wild storm breaking at her back. 'I won't let you do it to that poor little chap. You are his mother. He needs you.'

Anger rose up, swallowing her grief in hot waves. She swung around to face him. 'He needs more than I can give him. The Haven is not a good place for a boy to grow up. Surrounded by women who—' she took a breath '—who are no better than they should be. Already he sees things he should not. Hears things. Soon those things will mean something. You saw him at the duck pond. He needs to play with other boys. Decent boys. Do you think those boys will be permitted his company? You heard what that boy said yesterday.' And perhaps one day, he'd understand exactly what sort of woman his mother was and be ashamed. The thought was almost more than she could bear. 'His grandparents can give him the life he deserves. The sort of life his father—' oh, it was such a lie, but she had to say it, had to make him believe her, had to make herself believe it '—the sort of life his father would have wanted for him. Am I not being selfish, wanting to keep him with me and denying him that life?'

She collapsed in the nearest chair and buried her face in her hands, lest she disgrace herself and weep on his shoulder. She felt so torn apart.

He remained standing, towering over her. 'Who are they, these grandparents who can give him everything and want him so badly and yet who hold their daughter-in-law in such aversion that they would steal her child?'

The emptiness of impending loss in the place where her heart should be spread outwards. She could prevaricate no longer. Once he knew the truth, he, too, would hold her in contempt. As would Tonbridge. And Merry. They would revile her for her wickedness and for her deceit. 'Lord and Lady Thornton,' she whispered.

She had the dubious pleasure of hearing him draw in a hiss of breath. He spun away, his booted feet carrying him to the other side of the room. 'Harry Carothers's parents?'

The pity in his voice said he had grasped the whole of the sordid story. After all, Carothers had been his friend, had he not?

'Tommy was born out of wedlock,' he said softly.

A kind way to describe it. 'Yes.'

'The bastard.' He flushed. 'I beg your pardon. I am referring to Carothers. How…? It is none of my business.' He clenched his fist.

She swallowed the dryness in her throat. 'It happened the night of the assembly.'

His voice was flat. Hard. 'I presume he promised marriage before…' He made a sound of exasperation.

All the old shame came rushing back. The bewilderment. 'He made a number of promises.' That he loved her and that if she loved him, she would prove it. 'Your regiment left for foreign parts shortly afterwards.'

'Did he know about Tommy?'

'I have no way of knowing if he received my letter before he died. When I read of his death in the newspapers, it mentioned his parents' house in London. I went there, hoping for help. They refused to believe my story, thinking I was some fortune hunter trying to get money. Apparently I was not the first woman claiming Carothers had left them in trouble. They turned me away. At the time, they had no need of an illegitimate as-yet-unborn grandchild.' And certainly wanted nothing to do with his whore of a mother. The earl's vicious words still stung. But the earl had been grieving the loss of his youngest child and she'd had no proof of her claim. 'His older brother was still alive then. It was only when *he* was dying that they sought me out. I had left the address of a friend with them and she sent their letter on. It was clear from what they wrote that it was Tommy they wanted. I would be required to disappear from his life.'

His frown deepened. 'Tommy cannot be their heir.'

'No. They also made that clear. But he is something, when they have nothing. I wondered if perhaps the countess might have persuaded the earl of this.'

'They have decided to believe your story, then?'

'Apparently so.' She wasn't quite sure why, but there had been no doubt in the letter they had written. When she saw what they proposed, she had left Bath and gone to York, where she had hoped to remain undiscovered. Clearly Lord Thornton was far more determined than she would have suspected.

'And you are giving Tommy up without a fight.' The scorn was back in his voice. 'Did you love him?' he asked. 'Carothers?'

Inside, she froze. Outside she hoped none of her roiling emotions showed. 'I scarcely knew him.'

'But—' He stared at her. He came to kneel at her side, took her hand in his as he gazed at her face, looking suddenly terribly dear and kind. A sweet pang tightened her chest.

He would weaken her, if she let him. She snatched back her hand.

He did not try to take it again, but he did not get up. 'Caro,' he said softly, carefully. 'Did he force you against your will?'

A lump formed in her throat at the horrid recollections. Her giggles. At first. Her feverish excitement at his kisses. The roughness of the tree at her back. The groping hands at her skirts. The sound of his harsh breathing and grunting in her ear. The pain. The humiliation when he signified his dissatisfaction with her as a woman. She turned her face away, aware of the welling of hot tears. She swallowed them down. 'No, he did not force me. I encouraged his attentions.' The heady sensations rushing through her blood she had thought were love had been nothing but lust.

'Is that what you think?' he asked, sounding disgusted. 'Oh, my dear Caro,' he said, stroking her hand where it lay on her lap. 'Do you think a man cannot control his base urges when confronted by a female he wants?'

He was trying to make her feel better. 'It is what he said.' What he had said as he leaned against her, breathing hard from his exertions while she had sobbed. *'It is your own fault. You should have said you didn't want it.'* Such an odd way to put it, she'd thought. 'It is the woman's responsibility to keep herself pure. It was what my father said, when I realised that there was no way to hide what had happened.'

'Because you were enceinte.'

She nodded, breathing around the tears in her throat that made it impossible to speak. Tears of shame. And of pity for the innocent girl she had been. She forced down the tears, lifted her chin and turned to face him. 'My father had forbidden me to go to the assembly.'

'And Carothers convinced you otherwise.'

She risked a glance at his face and there was none of the condemnation in his expression that had been there before, that she knew she deserved. 'I knew better than to disobey my father. And he was right, wasn't he?'

'I thought you were to attend with your mother. It was your first real dance, you had said.'

'You remember?' There had been a group of young officers with Carothers when they had discussed the coming assembly. He had been one of them.

He gave her a rather shamefaced grin. 'I was rather taken with you myself. Not that you ever gave me a second glance. Carothers was older and far more charming. But I did go to the assembly that night in hopes of one dance with the pretty Miss Lennox. Not a *great* deal of hope. I hadn't had my growth spurt and was half a head shorter than you. *Why* did your father forbid you to go?'

'I had been rude to him earlier in the day. He said it was because I was overexcited about the dance and perhaps I wasn't ready. He forbade Mother to bring me.' She wiped away her tears. 'I was so angry. And disappointed. And I felt like a fool, for I had told Carothers I would be there. I shouted at Father and he sent me to my room.' She shook her head at the memory of her hot anger and wicked excitement as she had dressed herself in the dark. 'I slipped out of my window and climbed down a tree.' She'd felt so daring and clever.

'All the old biddies were talking behind their fans about my lack of a chaperone, of course. But I didn't care. Father was mortified when it got back to him the next day. I wasn't permitted to leave my room for days. And then—'

'And then Tommy.'

'Yes.' She hung her head. 'Father threw me out. He was so ashamed that a daughter of his…'

'I can imagine at least one of my sisters doing the same thing under the circumstances as you describe.'

'You have sisters?' She hadn't known that about him. Indeed, come to think of it, she knew very little about him at all, except that he was Tonbridge's very good friend and that he had been instrumental in helping Merry when her cousin had tried to kill her. He had also been Carothers's friend. And while she'd been warned about his rakish ways, just like when she was a girl, the warnings had done her not one bit of good. His kindness to Tommy, and to her, had sent her wits begging. Again.

'I have three half-sisters. All younger.' A strange expression passed across his face. Regret? 'I have barely seen them since Waterloo.'

Where he had lost his hand. She shivered.

He rose. 'Come, sit by the fire where it is warmer.'

She let him lead her to the sofa. He sat down beside her, a large warm bulwark against the world, and stared into the flames. 'How on earth did you manage without ending up in a workhouse or...?' He grimaced. 'Or worse?'

The night she had been thrown out of the house was so vivid in her mind it might have been yesterday. So terrifying, she still had nightmares. 'Mother came after me. Catching me up on the road without my father's knowledge. In his rage, he refused me anything but the clothes on my back. Mother brought a small bag with clothes and some money she had somehow tucked away. She directed me to a woman in Worthing who helps...' Her voice caught. 'Girls like me get rid of an unwanted child.' She shuddered. 'I couldn't do it. She was dirty and mean and...' She shuddered. 'I used the money to live on until I found work.'

She lifted her head. 'I swore if I ever got the chance I would help other women in my situation. Merry gave me that chance. But I never told her about Carothers. I told her I was a soldier's widow. I lied to her. I was too ashamed to tell her the truth after she was so kind to me.' The tears let go and she buried her face in her hands.

He put his arm around her shoulders and pulled her close. 'It is all right, Caro.' The hook on his left hand lay just above her breast, glinting evilly in the firelight.

Somehow it made her feel safe. And treasured.

## Chapter Twelve

⟨⟨⟨⟩⟩⟩

The desire to murder a dead man, while irrational, was satisfying to imagine. God, she wasn't the one who should be ashamed. The blame belonged to Carothers. She'd been an innocent whereas he had been a man of the world. He'd also been a bit of a bully. Blade had more than once suffered the lash of his wicked tongue and his fists, until he'd grown large enough to defend himself.

No wonder she had seemed so blatantly innocent. And so wonderfully enthusiastic when she realised the pleasures there were to be had of a partner in bed. It had just never occurred to him that such a prim and proper woman with a child had never been married.

Yet all the signs had been there. The maidenly blushes. The modesty. The anxiety. He'd not seen them because he hadn't wanted to see them. He'd wanted her to be like his usual fare. A widow happy to enjoy a bit of pleasure with no expectations of or desire for anything lasting.

A ripple of disgust wormed its way through him.

Disgust at his behaviour, not just with Caro but with the other women who had come his way, even if they hadn't seemed to mind.

And there was another recollection about Carothers teasing the back of his mind. Gossip when he'd last been in town on furlough. Something about him having had a fiancée before he died. Though why anyone had cared, he couldn't imagine, unless it was because the title was headed for escheat when the current earl cocked up his toes. No doubt the Crown was rubbing its hands together at the thought of the Thorntons' estates dropping into its greedy fist. What an irony that both sons had died without issue and yet the youngest was a father. A fate that would have any noble family sweating in regard to the succession.

He drew her closer, felt a slight resistance and was about to let go, when, to his inordinate relief, she relaxed.

She turned her head to look up at him, her eyes inexpressibly sad. Indecision rampaged across her face. 'I want what is best for Tommy.'

Unlike *his* mother, who had merely discarded him like last year's fashion in slippers when his presence had become an inconvenience.

Caro was different. She'd stuck by her son when it must have been extraordinarily difficult. The thought of this separation was clearly nigh on killing her. 'Perhaps at the least, you can come to some sort of understanding with them. Annual visits, letters once a month, anything so he knows you care.' He hesitated. 'Butterworth said they were expecting you.'

Caro stared at her hands, wiped them down her skirts, her gaze far away. 'If I don't go after Tommy, will he think I don't love him?'

Love. Was there really such a thing? 'Possibly. I was ten when my father took me from my mother at her request.' He spoke calmly, but his voice was thicker than usual. He cleared his throat and blinked to clear the sting caused by smoke from the fire. He'd felt so out of place in his father's house, where there were legitimate sons and daughters not much younger than he was, who stared at him in puzzlement, and a woman who asked him to call her Mother, but who had looked at him with a dreadful sadness in her eyes. For days, he had stood by the front door, expecting his mother to come for him. He'd refused to believe what she'd said when she forced him to leave with his father. *Can you not see? You are in the way here.*

'He might feel abandoned,' he said, recalling that dreadful sensation in the pit of his stomach when he realised she'd disappeared from London without leaving an address. 'Perhaps if you explain your reasons…I don't know. It might help.'

She nodded slowly. 'I will think about it some more.'

He cupped her cheek in his hand and kissed her, feather light, on the lips. A fleetingly gentle kiss, when what he wanted to do was ravage her mouth. But he was not what she needed right now. 'Think and get some rest, for tomorrow will be another long and trying day, whatever you decide.'

He helped her rise and escorted her to the door leading to her chamber. And against all his baser urges, all his desires, he let her in and shut the door, from the outside.

Once the maid had helped her with the tapes of her gown and stays, Caro smiled at her. 'I can manage the rest, thank you.' Growing up, she and her sister and her mother had helped each other with laces and ties and hair. Since coming to live with Merry and more recently at the Haven, she'd missed the closeness such intimate assistance entailed. Talking over the day's events, laughing at silly things. But as one must, she'd adapted to being helped by a stranger.

She eyed the steaming bath that Blade had ordered. The man was unbelievably thoughtful. And kind.

She touched her fingertips to her lips. Though his kiss as they parted had been so brief as to be chaste, it left her in a state of longing. Which was not kind of him. Nor was it sensible of her to feel so needful. The man enjoyed seduction, but was not, as Merry had carefully explained and he—equally as carefully—had confirmed, the marrying sort. But then, neither was she. Not because of inclination, but because honour would have required her to admit to any man willing to marry her that she had been living a lie and never been married. Inevitably, Tommy would have learned of it, too. Her biggest fear was that her son would turn from her in disgust when he knew the truth of her fall from grace. When he realised what he had lost because of her recklessness. The world was not kind to those born out of wedlock.

Blade had been surprisingly accepting of her situation. Or perhaps it wasn't so surprising, given his own illegitimacy.

She stepped into the tub and sank down into the water, not too hot, but warm enough to feel thoroughly luxurious. Her body relaxed in physical contentment, but her mind kept going back to their conversation. His concern that Tommy not feel abandoned. Her worry that she, in her own selfish need to keep him close, had ruined his chances at a decent life. The thought made her feel chilled inside and out.

She washed, got out of the tub, put on her nightdress and robe, then rang the bell for them to take the tub away. After the footmen left, she climbed into bed.

Go back to Skepton or go on to Lincolnshire and insist on being part of Tommy's life? Those were her choices.

She punched at her pillow. She had already decided it was better for Tommy to know his grandparents, so why make herself suffer more than she already was by having their door slammed in her face? They had made their position perfectly clear, both when she'd gone to tell them she was expecting a child and in the letter they had written, when their son and heir was dying.

She flopped onto her back. Then there was Blade. What would he think of her if she turned her back on her son, the way *his* mother had turned her back on him? He'd been so insistent she try to come to some sort of agreement with the Thorntons. As if it mattered deeply.

Why would he have revealed his story unless he'd been hurt by his mother's actions? She'd been so wrapped up in her own agonising decision, she hadn't realised that beneath the matter-of-fact telling he was also in pain. The hurt of wondering what he had done wrong to make his mother send him away.

Her heart ached for the confused little boy he must have been.

Blast it all. She was going to continue on to Thornton Manor and get her son back. Somehow. Blade needed to know this. He needed to know it, because right now he must be thinking she was as heartless as he thought his mother. While he hadn't said it in so many words, she had heard it in his voice. She didn't want him to think she could be so cruel.

She got up, put on her robe and crossed through the parlour to the door on his side. Heart racing, she hesitated.

Never once in her life had she visited a man in his room. Only once had a man ever visited her in hers. Him. Blade. She took a deep breath and tapped, barely making a sound. No answer. No sounds in the room beyond the door. If he was sleeping she had no wish to disturb him. He, too, had dealt with a long and trying day.

Oh, and wasn't she a coward?

Breath held, she tried the handle. The door opened and she peeked inside. He was sitting in a chair, in a silken robe, a drink in his hand, staring into the dying fire. It and three candles beside the bed across the other side of the room were the only source of light. Not wishing to interrupt, she backed away. The door squeaked. He looked up and their gazes locked.

He rose.

Seeing the surprise on his face, she felt utterly foolish. If it wasn't for the memory of his tender kiss on her lips… 'I have made up my mind.'

He blinked as if he was only now believing what he was seeing. 'Come in. Sit down.' He helped her to the chair where he'd been sitting and brought another from beside the bed and placed it on the other side of the hearth.

The warm glow from the fire softened his features, though his expression was haunted.

'Tell me this decision that cannot wait until morning,' he said, making an effort to smile.

He looked so careworn and dear her heart ached. She swallowed, clasping her hand in her lap so she wouldn't reach out to him. That was not why she had come. 'I thought about what you said.' She stared at her hands instead of his handsome face. 'I will not give up Tommy without a fight. At the very least, I want to be part of his life, those visits and so forth you spoke of. More if it can be arranged. I would be grateful if you would accompany me.'

She hadn't planned that last sentence, but as she spoke she knew it was true. Without him at her side, without his support, she might lose her courage.

He nodded slowly. 'It would be my very great honour to escort you.' He took a deep breath. 'I think I should write to Tonbridge, however.'

Her stomach gave an unpleasant lurch. 'To tell him about me.'

'To tell him I have escorted you to meet

Tommy's grandparents at your request and ask that he have his man of business to find someone to keep an eye on the Haven until we return.'

Beth was there. As was Cook. But they needed some sort of oversight. 'Oh, dear. No doubt he will think me in dereliction of my duty.'

'He will not,' he said firmly. 'It is *my* task to make proper arrangements in light of our absence.'

'Tonbridge will not be pleased when he learns I left the Haven.' Shocked by the reason. Merry would be upset by her dissembling, her lack of trust.

Blade shook his head. 'You underestimate him. He would insist I not let you go alone.'

She got up and knelt before him, much as he had knelt before her earlier, and took his dear face in her hands. 'You missed your mother when she gave you up, didn't you?'

He drew her up and sat her on his lap, pressing her head to rest on his shoulder, nuzzling his lips against her temple, her cheek, her chin. A ploy so she would no longer see the pain in his eyes. She let him get away with it, because she understood the pain of one you trusted turning their back when you needed them the most. Now, because of him, she would not do the same to Tommy. She would argue her case until she had no breath left.

He breathed out a long sigh. 'Yes, I missed her. I had always thought I was important to her, you see. She called me her "little man". Her protector. It came as a shock when she'd handed me over so easily. My siblings were not exactly delighted by my arrival since I was now their elder. Nor was the countess thrilled with another child added unceremoniously to her brood. It was not a comfortable situation.'

At least Tommy would not have to suffer that indignity. There would be no sibling rivalry or hurt female feelings. 'Did *your* mother ever explain?'

'She said I'd become an inconvenience. A few days after my father took me, I ran away and went back to where we'd been living. She'd gone without leaving a forwarding address. Then I believed what she'd said.'

Her heart twisted painfully. He must have been so hurt. 'Did you settle in with your father after that?'

'I would like to say I did, but to be honest,

I left at the earliest opportunity and joined the army. It was better for all concerned.'

'And your mother? Did you ever try to find her?'

He kissed her lips.

And even as the passion of his kiss turned her mind to mush, she noticed that he hadn't answered.

Blade couldn't believe what had fallen from his mouth. He had never hinted at his desperate hurt at his mother's abandonment. Not to Charlie and certainly not to members of his father's family. The only way to stop himself from rambling on was kiss her until he could no longer think, let alone talk. And besides, he liked kissing her and, thank all the stars in the heavens, she seemed to like kissing him back.

Her hands were roaming his back and shoulders, and her breasts, unfettered beneath her dark-blue robe, were pressed hard against his chest. He tangled his tongue with the silk of hers. She tasted of tooth powder and smelled of lavender. And, yes, he understood she'd come to him for comfort and support in her decision even if he wasn't the sort of man she would want in her life on a permanent basis.

Nor should she. But comfort and support he could provide. Temporarily.

Pride that she would trust him to offer her something she needed, for she did not trust easily or often, sat strangely warm in his chest.

He broke the kiss and teased the shell of her ear with his tongue and the lobe with his teeth.

She shivered with pleasure. His shaft throbbed in response.

He cupped her jaw, revelling in the softness of her skin against his palm as he tipped her face up so she would meet his gaze. Her eyes were wide and clear and her lips were smiling. A positive answer to his unspoken question. She wanted this. Him. At least, she did now.

He lifted her in his arms and carried her to the bed, where he laid her down in her prim and starchy dark-blue cotton robe that covered her from throat to foot. He unknotted the belt with only a slight fumble of shaking fingers and the untidiness of having only one hand. He loosened it enough to unravel the knot with a tug. She didn't seem to notice his awkwardness; she simply lay looking up at him, the light from the branch of candles on the bedside table dancing in her eyes. He peeled back her robe to reveal a similarly prim and starchy white nightgown, this one embroidered with forget-me-nots. His shaft hardened to rock at the sight of her beaded nipples begging for attention beneath the fabric.

He licked his lips and cupped one of those lovely mounds of sweet soft flesh.

Her gasp of pleasure went straight to his groin. He climbed up on the bed and knelt beside her, resting his weight on his forearm while he kissed her throat, her chin and finally found her mouth, hot and wet and responsive. He stretched out beside her, kissing her lips and caressing her face with gentle strokes until he felt her melt, abandoning all semblance of reserve as her hands wandered his back and chest, likely without her knowledge.

He kissed his way down her throat to the rise of the breast until he found her nipple, hard and wanting. He breathed on it through the fabric. She arched up, seeking more, and he closed his hand around the sweet fullness of her breast and teased the peak with his thumb. She moaned.

He undid the bow at her neckline and opened it to reveal the bounty hidden beneath. 'Lovely,' he said and bent to taste.

Each time he made love to her, he managed to surprise and delight her. Never had she imagined there were such a variety of pleasures to be had with a man. The feel of his mouth on her breast, the insistent tug deep in her core that made her insides tighten and thrill, was astonishing. And lovely. And something she would remember for the rest of her life.

During all these years of playing the widow, she had been lonely for companionship. She hadn't known there was this other side to the partnership of a man and a woman. Oh, she knew men took pleasure in sexual congress, for otherwise why would they be at it here, there and everywhere? But she had never suspected that it was so wonderful. That it went far beyond the mere physicality of pleasure to a far deeper level of communication.

At least for her. With him.

She stroked her hands across the warm skin of his wide chest. Inhaled the scent of freshly washed man, the lemony essence of his soap and the aroma of the brandy he had been drinking beside the hearth. Those scents would always remind her of this night.

He raised his head, his gaze searching as he judged her reaction to his attentions, and when she smiled at him and parted her thighs in welcome, he moved over her, pressing one thigh between hers, while caressing one breast and suckling at the other.

The pleasure of it made her hips buck. And the pressure of his thigh against her mons only increased the fluttering ache in her core. The building inside her became almost unbearable.

His hand left her breast and slid downwards to her hip, where he began stroking her thigh and in the process bunching the skirts of her nightgown ever higher. It was wicked and it was enchanting.

He was not alone in his longing for a sight of bare skin. She wanted to see him. Touch him. All of him. One last time.

With trepidation causing her stomach to tighten, she reached between them and parted the robe. His erection brushed against the back of her hand. His groan of pleasure and the way he rolled his hips to one side to accommodate her efforts emboldened her.

She explored the rigid length with tentative fingers. It was hot and hard and silken at the tip.

He kissed her cheek and reached down to curl his palm around hers. 'Like this, love.'

Love. Such a sweet endearment even if it was not meant.

He set the rhythm of her hand on his member and a groan rumbled up from his chest.

She pulled her hand away. 'Am I too rough?'

'Never.' He took her hand again and returned it to his groin. 'Here, you need to be gentle.' He shifted her hand back to his member. 'This gentleman requires a firm hand.'

'Gentleman?'

His shoulders shook a little.

'Are you laughing at me?'

'Not at all. Most men have a name for it. Some are crude. Others are more affectionate. Mine is ironic. There is nothing gentlemanly about it, I'm afraid.'

She repeated the rhythm he'd shown her and he rolled his hips, pressing himself into her grasping fingers, and made a sound like a purr. 'You delight me beyond reason, but we need to slow down or I will be disgraced.' He shifted his hips out of reach, raised his head to kiss her lips. He stroked her stomach before dipping between her thighs and stroking her cleft to dizzying effect.

'Glorious heaven,' she murmured and ran her hands beneath his robe, wanting him closer. 'Too many clothes.'

He stood up and shrugged out of his dressing gown, pausing, looking down at her with his arms at his sides. The one forearm missing its hand and wrist was terribly scarred. She took it in her hand and lifted it to her lips. He made a soft choking sound in his throat. 'Don't.'

'It is part of you,' she said, reaching out with her other hand to trace the muscles of his upper arm, down his chest to toy with the hair around his nipples, which hardened into tight little buds, the way hers did in the cold and when he touched her there. She smiled at the feeling of power.

Then, unable to resist, her gaze dropped lower. His erection was magnificent, darker than the rest of him, jutting upward from a nest of crisp dark curls. She frowned.

'Am I not to your liking?' he asked, sounding amused rather than defensive.

Her gaze shot to his face. She blushed. 'I was wondering if all that—' she waved a vague hand towards his groin '—wasn't difficult to fit inside your clothes.'

He grinned. 'One gets used to it. And it is not always in such a state of arousal.'

Her face grew even hotter, but she could not stop herself from looking again and reaching out her fingers.

'My turn,' he said, his voice a growl that

made her melt inside. She lifted her hips to help him ease her nightdress to her waist, then crossed her arms and drew the garment off over her head.

When she glanced at his face he was staring at her, his gaze running down her length and back again until he was once more looking into her eyes with the sweetest, most boyish smile she had ever seen on his face.

'Perfection,' he whispered.

She opened her arms and he came to her on the bed, kneeling over her to kiss her, and when he was sure she was ready, he entered her and together they found darkness and bliss.

# Chapter Thirteen

Blade came awake to the unusual sensation of a soft, warm body entwined with his. Unusual for him. Delicious. Incredibly sweet. The sensuality of this woman astonished and delighted. And while he was not her first, he was the only man to have given her real pleasure. A thought that both pleased him and saddened him. Because likely he would not be the last.

She was both generous and loving. The sort of woman any man would want for a wife. He wished… He squeezed his eyes shut. Once a woman, any sort of woman, got to know him, really know him, they moved on, just as his mother had moved on. He preferred to be the first out of the door. There was nothing that made her different to any of the others. He gritted his teeth, knowing he was telling himself a lie. It didn't matter. He had to think of her and the best thing he could do was help ensure she and her boy could stay together.

How to accomplish such a thing was as yet a mystery.

While Charlie was heir to a dukedom, he could hardly interfere. His father would not be pleased.

His own father, the Earl of Hartwick, was certainly powerful enough and influential enough, should he choose to help. Blade gritted his teeth. He hated asking his father for anything. Yet for Caro, he realised he wouldn't hesitate to bury his pride. First thing in the morning, he would send off a letter to the earl, asking for his aid. His father was also a proud man and might not take kindly to a request from a son who had refused to have much of anything to do with him for years.

And thinking of pride, it would not sit well with Caro to be found in his bed when the maid came to make up the fires in the morning. Much as he would prefer to keep her with him all night, he climbed out of bed and shrugged into his dressing gown. It did not take him long to warm her sheets in the other bedroom.

With a heavy heart he carried her back to her own chamber with her snuggled against his shoulder. As he looked down into her peace-

ful face, his course of action was clear. For her
sake, he could not let this dallying continue.
He'd taken every precaution to prevent concep-
tion, but nothing was certain. While he would
offer marriage, should she become pregnant,
she would once again be robbed of her choices.
That he would not allow.

As he tucked her in bed, she shivered and
stirred, but then settled.

So…the dallying stopped now.

Regret left him feeling cold.

Even as nervous as she was at the thought of
meeting her son's grandparents, over the past
few hours Caro sensed that things between her
and Blade had changed. At every stop along
the way, he had been perfectly polite, but he
never rode in the carriage and he had refused
to stay inside the inn on their second night on
the road, preferring to lodge in the stables with
Ned and the horses. When he handed her into
the carriage whenever they stopped along the
road to eat, there was a coolness in his eyes.
A reserve in his manner. He was effectively
putting her at a distance.

She could only assume that upon reflection,
he had been shocked by her boldness these
past weeks. Or, which was more likely, hav-

ing had his fill of her, he was moving on, just as Merry had warned.

To tell the truth, she had shocked herself. If she was honest, she was glad he was able to draw back, since she certainly had no hope of doing so. To openly flaunt her affection for this man before Tommy's grandparents would ruin any hope of a truce. Fortunately, Blade, or rather Mr Read, was far less besotted than she. While her heart might ache for what could not be, it was for the best.

From now on, she would play the part of a respectable woman who had made one mistake in her life and could be trusted not to make another, while she prayed she could rein in her wanton desires.

The road they had travelled for the past few miles was badly rutted and she clung to the hand strap beside the door as she was bounced about like a dice in a cup. What if their undertaking failed? Could she return to the Haven? Merry and Charlie would know the truth about her past. Shame filled her at how she had lied to them. Merry hated lies and dishonesty and Caro would hardly serve as a good example for the young women who passed through the Haven's portals. No, whatever the outcome, she could not return to Skepton.

Decisions made, she could only await her fate at the hands of the Thorntons.

In the middle of the afternoon, the carriage drew up at a small inn with a thatched roof and timbered walls and Ned came and opened the door.

Of Blade…Mr Read, there was no sign.

'The captain's gone on ahead.'

She stared at the man blankly. 'Why?'

'He's going to reconnoitre the lie of the land, so to speak.'

As if it was some sort of military campaign. It certainly felt as if she was about to battle the enemy. Yet it was wrong to think of them that way. They were Tommy's family.

By the time she had washed some of the travel dirt from her face, tidied her hair and imbibed the pot of tea the landlady had happily provided, Blade had returned. He strode into the little inn's only public room.

Her breath caught in her throat at his grim expression. 'They won't see me.'

'It is not that,' he said.

'Then what is it?'

'Tommy ran away.'

Her heart stopped beating. Air seemed in

short supply. 'When?' she managed. 'How?' Images of her son lost and alone paraded across her vision. 'How could they possibly have let such a thing happen?'

'It seems Linette got distracted by a handsome stable lad when she took Tommy for a walk, and it was more than an hour before she reported him missing.'

'He can't have gone far.'

'Half the village is looking. The old earl and the countess are frantic. It seems young Tommy has quite stolen their hearts.'

Tears threatened to choke her. She sniffled. 'Why would he not?'

He handed her a handkerchief. 'I offered our help in the search.'

'They refused, of course,' she said, forcing herself not to collapse against his chest.

'They did not.' The expression on his face said he was perfectly serious. 'They are terrified harm has befallen him.'

She could not quite believe what she was hearing. 'They invite my help?'

'They are hoping you can shed some light on the sort of places he might choose to hide.'

She gathered her reticule, put on her bonnet and drew on her gloves. 'Then we must go at once.'

'I've paid the shot and asked Ned to have the carriage ready.' He glanced out of the window. 'It seems he has done so.' He held out his arm. 'Shall we go?'

It took but ten minutes to arrive at the gate to Thornton Manor and another five to reach the front door by way of a drive lined with lime trees that were showing the fuzz of pale spring green.

Several men milled about on the front lawn. All of them ceased talking and watched as she descended. One of them, an elderly man of imposing height, but with a stooped slender build, hurried across the grass and onto the gravel drive to greet her.

'Mrs Falkner?' It was an older, far more careworn version of the Lord Thornton she remembered.

She inclined her head in acknowledgement.

Mr Read leaped down from his horse and undertook the proper introductions.

Aware of a great many people watching them from a distance, she did her best to seem calm despite her heart racing. 'Where have you looked? How can I help?'

The old man looked relieved. 'Read said you were a sensible woman and not inclined to hysterics. Lady Thornton is inside, prostrate on her sofa.'

If hysterics would help find Tommy, she would be happy to indulge. She could certainly scarcely breathe for the fear invading her soul. 'When was he last seen?'

Thornton grimaced. 'Yesterday afternoon.'

Her heart lurched painfully. 'He was missing all night?' Without thinking, Caro shot a glance at Blade's face, her fear making her tremble. 'He would have been chilled to the bone and scared out of his wits.' She wanted to weep.

Blade stared at her, his face hard and uncompromising. 'Mrs Falkner, your son is missing. I suggest you put your mind to the task of thinking where he might have gone.'

His words were like a slap to her face.

In that moment, she hated him.

And was grateful for the anger.

God forgive him for his cruelty, but Blade could see that if she gave in to her fears, she would collapse. She was already teetering on the edge. Making her angry had snapped her out of her panic. At least for now. From the look on her face, though, she would never forgive him.

Likely it was just as well, for it seemed that Thornton in his guilt might well take in the mother to safeguard the child. There couldn't be a better outcome. As long as they found Tommy alive.

'Does Linette have any useful information?' Caro asked, her voice calm, but her face paper white.

Thornton shook his head. 'The woman is in a lather, thinking she is to be cast off without a reference.' His grey brows lowered and he frowned mightily at Caro. 'Seems she is not the sort of gel who one would expect to find in one's nursery, which likely explains her behaviour with the stable lad.'

'Not relevant,' Blade said.

'Perhaps I should speak to her,' Caro said. 'She might be a little more forthcoming.'

'A good suggestion,' Blade said.

A footman who had been hovering just out of earshot was sent to fetch Linette. While they waited, Caro twisted and untwisted the strings of her reticule, the only sign she was under an enormous amount of strain. That and the fear lurking in her eyes.

A distraught-looking Linette stepped up to Caro, clearly expecting a reprimand. 'I told him not to go anywhere, missus,' she said sullenly. 'He were happy enough looking at the horses over the fence.'

'The important thing is for us to find him,' Caro said kindly, clearly trying not to frighten the girl. Blade had to respect her effort. 'Was there anyone else nearby when you left him?'

'Not as I recall,' the girl said. 'I weren't gone but a minute or two.'

Caro put a hand on the girl's shoulder. 'Linny, it won't help us if you don't tell us everything you know, every little detail. No one is interested in placing blame. We simply want to find Tommy.'

'There weren't no one.' Her face crumpled and she gave a little hiccup of a sob. 'I lost track of the time. It were maybe a good half-hour I was with Mick.' She hung her head. 'I'm that sorry.'

Blade wanted to wring the foolish girl's neck. 'A boy can travel a good distance in a half-hour.' He scanned the surrounding parkland. 'How long before you let her ladyship know he was missing?'

'It were dusk,' she said, shamefaced. 'I was callin' and callin', but when it started to get dark I knew I had to tell.' Her shoulders curled inwards. 'I never meant for anything bad to happen. Truly.'

'Can you give us any idea of what sort of thing might attract Tommy as a good place to hide?' Blade asked Caro and then turned to Linette. 'Any places which caught his interest?'

Both ladies looked thoughtful.

'I'm surprised he left the horses,' Ned said, joining them while one of Thornton's lads took charge of the team. 'I had to chase him out of my stables more than once.' So had Blade. The lad had a habit of worming his way into the stalls. A dangerous thing when a creature outweighed you a thousand times.

'You did?' Caro said, looking completely nonplussed.

'Every boy likes horses,' Blade said, but worried that his voice sounded a little too hearty. 'What we need is an organised systematic search, so we aren't tripping over each other.' He turned to Thornton. 'Where have you looked so far?'

'The house. The outbuildings.'

'Set the indoor staff to looking again. And have two of the younger lads go through every nook and cranny in the stables and outbuildings. Places only they can squeeze into. The rest of us can spread out further afield. I will take the woods. Ned, you can go east. The stable master and grooms can go south towards the road.'

'I will go with you,' Caro said to Blade. 'He likes walking in the woods.'

'I will take the west,' Thornton said, eyeing the lake. 'Sims, you'll come with me.'

Blade tried not to think about dragging that benighted pond. It would be the last thing they would do. He certainly wasn't going to ask Caro if the lad could swim.

It took a few minutes to get the servants sorted into search parties and give them their instructions. Each group of men searching outside were given a pistol or a shotgun and told to fire once if they found the boy. One shot and everyone would return to the house.

Finally, he and Caro set off. It felt good to be doing something, though getting the search organised had been good, too. It had been almost like old times in the army, when he'd been a soldier with real duties and an enemy to fight. This time the enemies were time and the weather.

As they walked, they called out for the boy until they were breathless. Blade helped Caro over a stile set in a hedge between them and the woods.

'Why Tommy? If someone was to be punished, it should have been me.' Caro's voice was filled with anguish and the misery of loss and the agony of guilt.

He wanted to put his arms around her, offer his strength as comfort. Hold her and promise her all would be well. As a mere house steward visible to all and sundry, all he dare risk were words. 'He's a male of the species. As such he will wander off on adventures. We will find him. You will scold. And all will be well.' He offered up a prayer that he was right.

'I should not have been so selfish,' she muttered, quickening her pace as they marched across grass eaten short by sheep. The flock off in one corner of the field watched their progress with interest. 'It is all my fault.'

Clearly his homily had not reached her ears. 'It is not your fault.'

She glared at him. 'If I had given him up the first time they asked, he would have been safe here. Happy. There would have been no need for him to run off.'

His heart nigh broke for her. 'Your logic defies common sense. We have no reason to think he ran off. We will find him safe and sound and apologetic.'

She stopped and looked up at him, elbows akimbo. 'I would do anything to make it so.'

Tears ran down her face unheeded. 'They can have him, if we find him safe. I swear it. No conditions.' She picked up her skirts and ran.

His heart sank. These were the words of a desperate woman. He jogged to catch her up. 'Slow down, Caro. We need to look for signs that your son passed this way.'

She slowed her steps—somewhat. 'He has been gone all night. He could be hurt.'

But that wasn't what she was thinking. She was expecting to find him lifeless. And there was nothing he could do or say to change her mind until they discovered him otherwise. And if they did, the lad was going to have his breeches dusted for the worry he had caused his mama.

Even that thought didn't make him feel better.

# *Chapter Fourteen*

At the edge of the woods, Caro shaded her eyes and looked back down the hill to Thornton Manor. A beautiful old brick mansion in the shape of an H surrounded by green rolling park complete with sparkling lake. Here and there across the grounds were little groups of searchers. Her ears strained to hear the sound of a single shot. Instead birds twittered in the trees and sheep bleated barely loud enough to be heard above the sound of her own laboured breathing.

Beside her, Blade was large and warm and equally as helpless.

She plunged into the gloom of the woods and shivered. There were well-worn paths winding through the trees and the undergrowth of brambles. Would Tommy have walked such a distance from the house and been brave enough to enter such a dark and mysterious forest? She wished the answer was no. But what would have led him so far from the paddock and the horses she hadn't even known he loved?

How could she not have known?

Blade took her hand and threaded his fingers through hers. 'We will find him.'

Pain ripped through her chest. 'What if we do not find him in time?'

'Hush,' he said. 'We will find him.'

The feel of his palm against hers steadied her, gave her encouragement. 'Tommy,' she called again, her voice hoarse.

'Tommy,' he yelled.

Somewhere in the distance a dog barked.

Blade pulled her to a halt. 'Listen,' he said.

She heard nothing.

'Tommy,' he roared, his voice deafening to her ear.

A faint cry. Perhaps. And then the barking.

'It might have been a bird,' he said doubtfully.

'Which way?' she said, turning around. 'Which way is the dog?' She hadn't known about the horses, but Tommy had always wanted a dog.

'This way,' Blade said, pointing.

'Are you sure?'

He pointed at the ground. At the tracks of a dog in the loam. She peered closer. 'Are those boot prints?' Small ones.

He grinned. 'I believe so.'

She broke into a run. He caught her up, dodged around her, then went ahead. When she would have gone faster, he set a steady pace. 'Hurry,' she gasped.

He stopped short, grabbing at a sapling.

She ran into his back. 'What the deuce are you—?'

The path fell away right in front of them. A huge gouge in the soft earth. A landslide down the bank of a gorge with a small stream running in its bottom. On either side, the banks of the gorge overhung the valley.

'Tommy?' Blade yelled.

'Down here,' a thin little voice cried.

If not for Blade, Caro would have flung herself over the edge. 'We're coming,' she called out, pressing against his outstretched arm.

Blade glared at her. 'Hold still, madam,' he commanded brusquely. 'We already have one casualty. I do not wish to deal with another.'

'I'm not one of your soldiers,' she said, shoving at his arm and finding it immovable.

'Tommy,' he called out. 'I am going to fire

my pistol to let the others know you are found.'
He fired off one shot. Rooks rose from the
trees in a cacophony of objection, as did the
smaller birds.

Right then a large black dog appeared at the
bottom of the slope, barking madly. It shot off
to the right, following the stream.

'He must have followed the dog,' Caro said.
'Why did no one mention the dog? He was always begging me to buy him a puppy.'

A few moments later, the animal appeared
behind them, pink tongue lolling from its
mouth, tail wagging and looking very pleased
with itself.

'There's another way down,' Blade said.
'Take my arm and have a care where you put
your feet. This whole area looks unstable.'

While she would have run, he made her
walk and keep clear of the edge. The dog galloped down yet another earth-slide, this one
less steep.

'I suppose it's of no use my asking you to
wait here,' Blade growled at her.

'None.'

'Then hang on to my arm. You will be of no
use to Tommy if you are injured.'

Her heart full of affection and relief, she

went up on her toes and kissed his cheek. 'You are such a dear.'

He merely grunted and carefully worked his way down the loose earth bank, testing each step before trusting it with his full weight. And then they were at the bottom, walking alongside the burbling stream that had carved its way through these woods for what looked like centuries.

A few yards along, they came across Tommy lying against a tree.

'Mother,' he said, his dirty little face pale and streaked with tears. 'You came.'

'Of course I did.' She sat down beside him and put her arms about him. 'Thank God you are safe.'

'I hurt my ankle when I fell.'

Blade knelt at his feet and removed the boot from the indicated foot. 'It's badly strained, but not, I think, broken.'

'I couldn't get up the hill,' the little boy sobbed. 'I was so cold when it got dark, till Buster came back and cuddled me.'

'Buster?' she asked, suddenly terrified.

Tommy pointed to the dog. 'He's my friend. I didn't know dogs were so warm.'

'Buster has earned himself a roast dinner,' Blade said, removing his coat and bundling it around Tommy. 'You were fortunate, young man. You could have broken a leg or worse.'

His neck, for one thing. 'No need to scold, Mr Read,' Caro said. 'That is a task I will undertake with relish once I have Tommy safely back indoors and the doctor has seen him.'

'I w-wanted to c-come home,' Tommy said, clearly trying not to cry. 'But I got lost in the trees. You aren't going to leave me here, are you, like that man said?'

Her throat filled with a hot hard lump and she had difficulty speaking around it. 'Tommy—'

'We will talk about all that later,' Blade said harshly. 'First we need to get you back to the house and warmed up.' He picked Tommy up in his arms. 'Follow me, Mrs Falkner, and we will see if we can find a way up this bank that won't involve any more accidents.'

A house steward did not expect to be entertained in the parlour by the lord of the manor, even if he was an earl's illegitimate son and close friend to a ducal heir, but Caro had insisted he join her there once Tommy had received a visit from the doctor and been given a dose of laudanum for the pain.

Insisted out of gratitude for finding her son,

no doubt. And perhaps for moral support since there were now serious matters requiring attention. Like an abduction and the future of a child.

Lady Thornton had not come down from her rooms. Still prostrate, her husband had declared, though thoroughly relieved to hear that her miscreant grandson had been found alive and almost whole. As the only female present, Caro presided over the tea tray. If Thornton noticed that Caro did not ask Blade how he took his tea, he had the grace to give no indication of disapproval.

While of concern, the niceties of tea were the least of Blade's worries. He had a strong sense of impending disaster. And there was nothing he could or would say. It was not his place to interfere. Though to his surprise, he found he wished it were.

Wishes rarely came true.

Thornton harrumphed into the growing silence. 'I owe you an apology, Mrs Falkner. By any standards, my measures were draconian.'

The man went up a notch in Blade's estimation. Not for the apology, but for his continued use of her courtesy title.

Caro stirred her tea and put down the spoon. She folded her hands in her lap and gripped them tightly together as if she did not trust herself to raise the cup to her lips. Blade understood completely. Inside, he trembled for her.

'I understand an act of desperation, Lord Thornton,' she said coolly. 'Though your actions were inexcusable.'

Shame flashed in old eyes, before Thornton dropped his gaze to the contents of his cup.

'It would be unconscionable of me not to shoulder some of the blame, however,' she went on more gently. 'Had I been more accommodating...'

Blade ground his teeth. This woman had shouldered alone more than any woman should. 'Abduction is a serious crime,' he said.

Thornton stiffened, then shook his head, putting his cup and saucer on the table at his elbow. 'Butterworth overstepped his authority, but I make no excuses for the actions of the man I hired. He made the assumption I would be pleased with his efforts.' His lips pressed together for a moment, deep crevasses forming around his mouth. 'I cannot say I was not thrilled to see the boy at long last. As was my lady. He is not a bit like his father.'

Caro's eyes widened. 'Do you think I—?'

The old man put up a papery blue-veined hand. 'He is the image of his uncle, my oldest son, Redmaine. Lady Thornton almost fainted when she saw him.'

'I can assure you, I never met your oldest son.'

'I think what his lordship is trying to say,' Blade intervened, 'is that Tommy bears a strong resemblance to a beloved family member.'

'Exactly,' Thornton said. 'But more than that. Among my youngest son's effects that finally found their way back to us at the end of the war was your letter and the beginning of his missive to my wife and me asking us to take care of the matter as we saw fit.' He inhaled a deep breath. 'It had come to my notice that my youngest son was…wild at times.'

'Your son was spoiled rotten,' Blade bit out.

'Mr Read,' Caro warned.

Damnation, if she had not wanted his help, why the devil was he here?

Thornton tugged at his neckcloth. 'Harry was rackety. His older brother pointed this out on more than one occasion. It was the reason we bought him a pair of colours. He made an excellent soldier. He was mentioned in dispatches twice.' Pride tempered with sadness glowed in his eyes.

Harry Carothers's derring-do had been well

known, his recklessness boding ill for any fellow unfortunate enough to join his corps. But who was he to destroy a father's pride in a dead son? Fortunately, by the time Carothers had command of the unit, Blade had moved to another regiment. He sipped at his tea and wondered if it would be ill mannered of him to reach for a biscuit. He did it anyway.

Taking a deep breath, Thornton continued. 'On his deathbed, Redmaine exhorted us to find our grandson and bring him home.' He pressed his palms together between his knees. 'He had consumption, you know. He said we made a mull of it by trying to separate you from your child. He had looked into your circumstances, you see, Mrs Falkner. He said you were a decent gal before—' The old man wrung his hands. 'He placed the blame squarely with Harry. With Redmaine's passing I was left the last of my line. It has taken more than a year of searching to find you after you returned our last letter unopened.'

'Thomas cannot be your heir,' Caro said, lifting her chin. 'Your son and I never married.'

The old man's eyes looked watery and he passed a hand over them. 'He is all the family my wife and I have left. There is some unentailed property. Personal funds I can settle on the boy.'

'In exchange for leaving him with you, I presume.'

The heartbreak in her voice was hard to hear. Blade wanted to hit something. Surely she wasn't about to keep the promise she'd made when in such a panic of fear? He suppressed a groan of frustration. Not that the damage wasn't already done. His lordship's eyes had brightened considerably.

'Mrs Falkner, why not wait for his lordship to state his terms,' Blade said.

His lordship turned his gaze on Blade. 'Read,' he said musingly. 'The name is familiar.'

'I doubt it.' Blade had no wish to muddy the waters, though any number of gentlemen had *known* his mother.

The old man shook his head. 'It will come to me.' He turned back to Caro. 'As you see, we will offer your son every advantage.'

Apart from legitimacy and a loving mother. The latter being most important in Blade's mind. He kept his words behind his teeth. If she wanted his advice she'd ask for it, but right now he wished himself anywhere but here, knowing what this would cost her and her son. He reached for another biscuit. Anger made him hungry.

'I would not have my son spoiled,' Caro said slowly, frowning at her hands. She brought her gaze up to meet the old man's eyes full on. 'I insist on supervising his upbringing before he goes to school and I will be consulted on the choice of institution.'

Since he didn't have a hat, Blade almost threw the biscuit in the air at this display of courage.

'I am sure you will not object to his going to Eton, as our sons did,' the old man said proudly. 'And thence to Oxford.'

Caro's hands gripped so tightly about each other, the knuckles showed white. 'They sound suitable, but he is too young to go yet.'

The old man frowned. 'I cannot approve of him living at this establishment of yours. It is no place for a grandson of mine.'

The pain in her eyes was awful to see. Blade got up and went to the window, looking out on the drive, before he strangled one or other of them.

'I thought perhaps you both would stay here,' the old man finished. 'You and Thomas. With us.'

Blade spun around.

Caro made a sound between a sob and a cry of surprise.

Her eyes shone with unshed tears as she stared at the old gentleman who was offering her a hesitant smile.

'You are offering me a place in your home?' Her shock and disbelief rang in her voice, but also heartbreaking hope.

Blade held his breath.

'Mrs Falkner,' Thornton said, 'I regret nothing more in my life than turning you away the night you came to Grosvenor Square. Believe me when I say that if it were in my power to change *anything* I did in the past, it would be that. I would have insisted that my son make an honest woman of you, too, had I the opportunity. You were a decent gel and have been an excellent mother to our grandson. He is all that we have left of either of our boys and we are grateful to you for raising such a splendid, if adventurous, little chap. Our only request would be that he be permitted to change his name to Carothers. After all, recognition by a peer of the realm will do a great deal to smooth his path in life.' He gave her a gentle smile.

Blade knew what she was thinking, with her eyes full of tears and her expression full of doubt, and he wanted to curse. She was wondering if her son might not be better off without her. It was so like her to put her son before herself.

Unlike his mother, who had wanted her freedom.

Caro took a deep shaky breath. 'You mean this?'

The earl wagged a finger at her. 'You know, you aren't the first engaged couple in love to anticipate their wedding vows. Most will understand. After all, Harry was a hero.'

Bribery if ever he'd heard it. And perfectly feasible.

'You are very kind, my lord. May I think about it?'

The old man looked a tad surprised that she wasn't leaping at his offer, but he inclined his head. 'Of course. Take as much time as you would like, but let me say that it is our fondest hope that you will agree. For Thomas's sake.'

And on that parting salvo, the old man left the room.

Her gaze sought out Blade's.

He knew he should be happy for Caro. Ecstatic even. Instead his gut felt hollow. He was losing her to Thornton, who had status and wealth. Damn it to hell. This was the best possible outcome. That he was not delighted did not sit well with his image of himself, so he spoke more brusquely than he should. 'This proposal is all and more than we could have hoped. I beg you will excuse me. Ned needs to see me in the stables.'

He bowed and headed out of the door, aware of her puzzled gaze.

The door closed behind Blade. That was that, then. He clearly wanted nothing more to do with her and Tommy. She'd been as foolish over him as she had been over Tommy's father.

Except that Blade was twice the man Carothers had been. He was caring and generous and wonderfully kind to a small boy. He was also right about the earl's offer. It was far more than she had any right to expect. Far better than anything she had envisaged, certainly.

And yet she didn't feel…happy. She had an uncomfortable sense of something not being quite right.

Likely because if she accepted their offer, she would lose all her independence. Thornton was insisting she give up the Haven. Never had she envisaged her choice devolving down to her son or her dream of a better future for women like her.

The butler scratched and entered. 'Her ladyship will receive you now,' he intoned.

Butterflies took up residence in her stomach. Had his lordship consulted his lady before making his offer? Was she in agreement? Or had she been handed a fait accompli? The perspective of women was often very different to their menfolk. Caro had to know if Lady Thornton approved of all of this before she came to her decision.

She followed the butler upstairs to the ladies' withdrawing room, a light, airy room sprinkled with delicate gilt chairs and tables and fine porcelain knick-knacks. A boudoir from a previous age. Warm and heavily scented air made it difficult to breathe. The lady herself reclined on a chaise longue near the hearth. She regarded Caro from pale-grey eyes so like her dead soldier son's Caro was completely unnerved. Until now, she hadn't even recalled he'd had grey eyes.

The countess held out an imperious hand. 'Come closer. Let me look at you.'

Caro moved a few steps nearer and dipped a curtsy. 'My lady.'

'Miss Lennox,' the lady said.

Caro froze at the sound of her maiden name. 'Come,' Lady Thornton said. 'Sit.' She pointed to a chair set at right angles to the *chaise.* 'I do not bite.'

Inhaling a breath to steady her nerves, Caro sat.

The lady lifted a lorgnette and peered at her.

Caro had never felt so uncomfortable in her life.

'My word,' Lady Thornton said finally. 'I had no idea Harry had such good taste. You are positively lovely.'

Surprised and pleased, Caro blushed. 'Thank you, my lady.'

The lady swung her feet down and sat up straight. 'I think I am going to enjoy this coming Season.'

'I beg your pardon, my lady?'

'I always wanted a daughter. I envied my friends their come-outs and their forays to balls and Almack's. Sons are just not the same. You will be a big hit, my dear.'

Caro stared at the beaming elderly woman. Had she lost her reason? Forgotten that Caro was well past the age for a come-out and had born a child out of wedlock? Should she remind the countess of these facts? 'I do not think—'

'You did not think when you, a respectable

vicar's daughter, allowed my rakehell son to get you with child.'

Caro flinched.

'I beg your pardon, child. You will excuse an old woman for her plain speaking. In my day we did not mince words as they do today.'

'Then if we are to have plain speaking,' Caro replied, deciding to make sure there were no misunderstandings, 'you will surely see that I am not a candidate for the kinds of entertainments you describe. I am well past the age a girl can make her debut and I would never be accepted in polite society.'

'Perhaps not among the crème de la crème of society,' her ladyship agreed. 'But with a large enough dowry, there would be many more who would overlook the past, provided your manners are pleasing and your demeanour respectable.'

Caro's mouth dropped open. 'You cannot be serious.'

'Of course I am. A young woman as lovely as you cannot fritter away her youth. We need to find you a husband.'

A hollow feeling entered her stomach. Here was the serpent in the Garden of Eden. The woman planned to be rid of her, fob her off on some gentleman who would see only the fortune they no doubt intended to dangle before him.

She knew all about such arrangements from Merry, who had despised the idea and then fallen in love with the heir to a dukedom and he with her.

'And what of Tommy?'

'Thomas,' the older woman corrected. 'Why, I am sure you will allow him to visit with his grandparents from time to time.'

Astonished, she stared at the older woman whose wrinkled lips twitched suspiciously as if she was enjoying some sort of private joke.

'I do not understand why you are proposing this. I thought you wanted Tommy…Thomas.'

'We want him as part of our lives. But not at the expense of his happiness. Oh, I know Bertie would have you and him under his thumb here at Thornton, but he saw how well that worked with Redmaine. And Harry. He has come to regret his autocracy, though I would not put it past him to continue in that vein if he is not adequately checked, which is why we must find you a suitable spouse.'

'No respectable man would wish to marry me.' Take Blade Read for an example. He had been happy with a dalliance, but that was all he intended. All either of them had intended, to be truthful.

'Thornton is not without influence, gel. He has the ear of the Regent, and if we can convince Prinny to approve, then the rest of 'em will follow like lambs. We might even be able to convince the Crown to let Thomas inherit, in time.'

Thomas a peer? 'All this hinges on my marrying well?'

Lady Thornton pursed her lips. 'It is key. What? You do not wish for a husband? A home of your own? A man to serve as father and mentor to your son?'

There was only one man she could think of who could serve in that capacity and he had already indicated it was not what he wanted. Hadn't he?

The woman tilted her head on one side, like a thrush hearing a particularly tasty worm beneath the turf. 'My son treated you abominably and I believe he came to regret it. I would move heaven and earth to make up for his mistake, if you will allow.'

A husband, home and a father for Tommy seemed too good to be true. Something she had never dared aspire to. Now here it was seemingly hers for the taking. All she had to do was reach out. 'I don't know.' When had she been so indecisive?

'If not for yourself, then think of your son. He's no longer a baby. He needs a man's guidance and Thornton is far too old.'

'I wish to continue the work of the Haven. Women in trouble need help to find decent respectable employment, if they don't want to give up their children.' Their illegitimate children.

The old woman's eyes glistened with unshed tears. 'As you did for our grandson. We will help all we can. You will of course take a position on the Board of Governors, rather than an active role. We will find a good person to take your place.'

'A fair compromise.'

'Then you will promise to at least consider an offer of marriage. For the sake of your son.'

Heaven help her, the woman was manipulating her. Perhaps there was a man out there she could love and respect. But would he be willing to ask for her hand? 'I promise. But if there is no offer to which I can agree…'

'Then you will have a comfortable settlement upon which to live.' Lady Thornton rose to her feet. 'It is agreed, then. As soon as Thomas's foot is strong enough, we will hie to London.'

\* \* \*

When Blade arrived in the stables, he found his henchman looking as grumpy as he himself felt. 'A problem with the horses?'

Ned shook his head and left the horse he was grooming to hand Blade a letter. 'From your father.'

The missive had followed him from York to Skepton and now here.

Blade cursed. 'He's heard the news, I assume.' He broke the seal. As he had guessed, the earl wanted an accounting of his recent *contretemps*, as he labelled it.

He and his father had never been close. Blade's fault entirely. 'I am summoned to London.' The only question in his mind was whether he stuck to the official version of why he had resigned or gave him what his father would consider the shameful truth. Blade knew his father's political machinations—the earl was likely already in possession of the facts as presented by those in charge. It seemed he was to face the music of his errant behaviour sooner rather than later.

'What of the missus?' Ned asked, going back to his brushing.

'Mrs Falkner is well settled. She has no need of our continued presence.' His presence could only cause her embarrassment. It would not do for Thornton to sense there was more between them than a common employer.

Ned looked a little sheepish. 'What?' Blade asked, interpreting that look.

'I would like to return Tonbridge's carriage and team to Skepton. One of us should be at the Haven with all the rising-up talk going on.'

'Need to assure yourself Beth hasn't run off with the grocer's boy, do you?'

Ned grinned. 'She wouldn't do that.'

He sighed. 'I agree. You should be on hand, ready to pass the information along to Tonbridge should the threats become more than talk. I will return as soon as I am able.'

Ned looked pleased. 'I will set out in the morning.'

'As shall I. I can be in London before day's end whereas you will take it in easy stages with Tonbridge's cattle.'

'I will,' Ned agreed.

'I will inform Thornton of our imminent departure.' Hopefully, the old gentleman would pass the information along to Caro before they sat down to one last dinner.

While he wasn't particularly glad of the reason he needed to depart, he was nevertheless glad to have a reasonable reason to depart

Thornton Manor that would not leave Caro wondering if it were somehow her fault. The woman seemed prepared to shoulder a great many burdens.

That he must go was an unassailable truth. He had done all he could in his limited power for Caro and her son. Next she would be giving him thanks and his congé. Cowardly though it was, he would sooner forgo that particular scene.

## Chapter Fifteen

Two weeks after Caro arrived in London, and after numerous visits to dressmakers, milliners and other such worthies, she was deemed fit to make morning calls. Her first was to Merry and her husband, Lord Tonbridge, at the Duke of Stantford's London town house. It was not really an official morning call, since she had walked over with her maid, who was now being entertained in the kitchen.

At their request, she had told her friends everything—everything that was not too personal to mention—that had occurred over the previous several weeks.

At the conclusion of her tale, Merry raised a brow towards her husband. 'If it wasn't you telling me this tale, Caro, I would assume it was a story from a novel.'

'Precisely,' Caro said. 'I was so sure the

Thorntons despised me and I would never see Tommy again, when instead they have been wonderfully kind and treat me as they would a real daughter-in-law. Honestly, though, the idea of me going to balls and attending routs—' she shook her head '—it doesn't make any sense. Surely the members of the *ton* will turn their backs when my story is known. For it will be. I have a son and I was never married.'

'Your mother was the daughter of an earl and your father the third son of a baron,' Merry said. 'Two things you didn't tell *me*, by the way. As I understand it, the story is that you were engaged to be married and your betrothed's untimely death prevented tying the knot. Given that the Thorntons recognise both you and Thomas, and with the support of others of influence—' she smiled at her husband, who was sitting beside her on the sofa '—Lady Thornton is right. It should be very possible for you to contract a suitable marriage, should you so wish.'

'I wish my father was alive to hear the news.' It had been a shock to learn her family had been wiped out by an outbreak of smallpox in the village more than two years before and all because her father had insisted her mother and sister do their Christian duty by those who were ill. Had she not left, she would likely have suffered the same fate.

'Bah. Your father blamed the wrong person,' Merry said. 'If Carothers was not already in his grave, I think I might want to kill him myself.'

'Dearest wife,' Tonbridge said with a look of deep affection in his eyes, 'given your condition, you will leave such violent actions to your dutiful spouse.'

Merry snorted. 'I'm expecting a child. I'm not an invalid.'

She was indeed expecting a child and soon, Caro judged. 'How are you feeling?'

'Like a barge in need of two tugs,' Merry grumbled, placing a hand to the small of her back.

'I believe it is time for your nap.' Tonbridge took her hand in his and kissed her knuckles.

'It is your enjoyment of napping in the afternoon that landed me in this situation,' Merry snapped, but her smile belied her sharp words.

Caro couldn't prevent her laugh. She'd missed Merry and her down-to-earth ways.

'Madam, you are shockingly outspoken,' her husband admonished with a twinkle in his eye.

'Only among friends,' his wife said.

The thought of friends brought someone

else to Caro's mind, though he was far more than a friend and very dear to her heart, which seemed to have spent a great deal of time missing him. 'What do you hear from Mr Read?' Her face warmed. 'Did he return to Skepton?'

Tonbridge shook his head. 'No. His family have requested he remain in town. He has a sister who is coming out this Season and he has been dragooned into escort duty, much to his horror.'

Did that mean she would see him at one of these balls or routs she was anticipating with such dread? Her heart gave a little thump. Would he pretend they were meeting for the first time? Or would he be forced, for the sake of his debutante sister, to turn up his nose at a woman who was no better than she should be and who had forced herself into the midst of the *ton*? She was, after all, quite scandalous. A fallen woman. Her father had called her a strumpet and others would, too, though not to her face when she was accompanied by the Thorntons, accepted by the Tonbridges and indeed by the Duke of Stantford, who, while still recovering from his illness, had signified his approval by hosting the ball in her honour.

The Duchess of Stantford had also promised to send tickets for Almack's when she had called on Lady Thornton earlier in the week.

'You do know Mr Read is a—' Merry pressed her lips together at a warning look from her husband. 'Was born out of wedlock and only because he is recognised by his father is he accepted everywhere.'

'Up to a point,' Tonbridge added. 'He would not be found suitable as a prospective husband by the most discerning of papas with hopeful daughters, though he would be fine as a dance partner.'

'It seems so unfair,' Caro said, 'when he served his country so bravely.'

'I agree,' Merry said. 'What do you hear from the Haven?'

A kind change of topic. 'Beth has come into her own. She and Ned are managing very well. Cook's rheumatism has subsided and she is back at her post and three girls arrived last week. One of them with a child. Everything seems to be running like clockwork.' While she was pleased for the younger woman, it made her feel…unnecessary. And not only at the Haven. Tommy loved his new tutor and was happy with his Linny, as he called her, no matter how often Lady Thornton instructed him to use her last name. And then there was

Blade, who had walked out of her life without a backward glance.

There was no one who really needed her any more.

It was lowering and disappointing.

Though, she thought with a surge of joy, Tommy still would not sleep unless his precious mama read him a story and tucked him in.

'I am sure Beth will continue to need your guidance,' Merry said, as if sensing some of those feelings of loss. 'Now we have one established so successfully, I am thinking we should find a similar institution here in town. I would love your help.'

'Not until after the child is born, I hope,' Tonbridge said. 'You will run yourself ragged, my dear. And besides, Caro will need to establish herself before she can begin such a venture.'

Such a venture would be doomed to fail if she was not accepted by the members of the beau monde.

She glanced at the clock. She had been here far longer than the fifteen minutes allotted to such calls, though Merry was not actually receiving calls as a general rule, so there was no one to notice. 'I should leave you to your rest,' she said, rising to her feet.

Tonbridge followed suit and escorted her to the door.

It opened before they reached it.

Blade stood before her. Warmth rushed into his expression, but was gone so swiftly she might have been mistaken.

For long seconds they stood, staring at each other.

For two long weeks she had been in London and not once had he called. No doubt her knight, having completed his quest, had moved on to the next maiden in distress. But she wasn't a maiden, was she?

'Mr Read,' she said, her voice sounding chilly, colder than she had wanted, though cold was the only way she could survive seeing him so unexpectedly.

'Mrs Falkner.' He bowed with that lovely elegance that always struck a chord low in her midriff.

She dipped a curtsy to Merry and Charlie. 'I bid you farewell until tomorrow night.'

Merry looked as if she wanted to say something, but Charlie took her hand and looked down at her before he spoke. 'It will be our greatest pleasure, Mrs Falkner. I will ring down to let your maid know you are leaving.'

'Thank you.'

'Blade, will you walk Mrs Falkner to the front door? My wife needs my help up the stairs.'

Blade stood to one side, presenting his arm. 'I would be honoured.'

A lady had the right to refuse a gentleman's escort and she could see in his eyes he half-expected that she would. But he was Tonbridge's friend and it would make their lives awkward if she was to behave with anything but cordiality to this man. Angry she might be. Hurt at his indifference. But it wasn't the first time she had been cut loose from those she cared about. She'd survive.

Despite the ache in her heart.

She took his arm and they promenaded out of the door and down the stairs to the ground floor.

'Caro,' he murmured softly. 'You are well?'

She tried not to put too much import on his enquiry, though politeness had never been his forte. 'Exceedingly so,' she said with as much enthusiasm as she could muster.

'You look fagged. Have they been trotting you too hard? You must not allow yourself to be run off your feet. You will want to be in your best looks for the ball.'

'Will you be there? At the ball?' Oh, why

did her pride have to desert her now? 'It is to be quite a grand affair, I understand.' She hoped she sounded polite, rather than desperate. As if she did not care if he came or not.

'I will be there.' He hesitated. 'Your adopted in-laws do not care for me, I think, or I would ask you to save me a waltz.' His voice was low and seductive and her insides fluttered wildly. As he no doubt intended.

Memories of their first dance chased across her mind. Her heart hammered against her ribs. Thoughts of good behaviour almost deserted her. Almost.

'I do not waltz, Mr Read.'

His eyes widened a fraction and then he nodded tersely.

Surely he understood that she would not be waltzing with anyone. There was no further time for talk of a personal nature, for they had reached the front door, where a footman stood ready with her maid.

Blade took her hand in his and bowed low, then kissed her knuckles in a way that felt like possession, but could only be old-fashioned courtesy. Or so she must tell herself, because if he was toying with her, as he apparently toyed with so many other females at the edge of society, she really could not bear it.

'Until tomorrow,' he said.

Her heart lurched. She forced a smile. 'To-morrow.'

And then she was out on the street and her maid was scurrying along, trying to keep up.

It was the day of the ball. Blade glared at his reflection in the pier glass. Charlie had kindly lent him his valet to help him dress, but he missed Ned's practised skills and ap-plying the false hand to his wrist had been an exercise in gritted teeth, ill-concealed embar-rassment and utter futility. Until Charlie had come along to help.

If not for Charlie and his bride, Blade would have left London for points far away. They had convinced him that Caro needed as many friendly faces as possible, though in his opin-ion, he was likely to be more of a hindrance than a help.

And she was not going to waltz.

Something he and Charlie had plotted to take advantage of. Yet more misery to add to this day.

He twitched at the bottom of his coat, took a breath and wended his way to the drawing room, where Charlie and Merry had gathered their exclusive guests attending the dinner ahead of the ball, important people in the world of the beau monde. They were to present a united front. To prove that, in their view, Caro was another unfortunate victim of Bonaparte's ravages across Europe. Had her fiancé lived, Caro would have married her sweetheart with the full support of the Thorntons.

He ignored the sour taste in his mouth at the thought.

Blade had brought his own big guns, courtesy of his father's eldest legitimate son. The earl, his father, and his countess were a force to be reckoned with among the denizens of the *ton*.

Knowing Caro had not yet arrived, he strode into the drawing room, pretending, as he always did, that he belonged. As society dictated, he greeted his hostess and host, then moved on to his father. Blade bowed. 'My lady. My lord. Thank you for coming tonight. Your support is greatly appreciated.'

'Blade,' his father said gruffly.

A surprise, to be sure. His father rarely used any form of address but his last name. A reminder that they were only peripherally related, Blade had always assumed.

'I was delighted to be asked,' the countess said, her gaze fixed intently on his face, disappointment shadowing her eyes as it always did when she looked on him. Who would blame her? What wife wanted her husband's by-blow dropped into her pretty nest?

'I hope Tonbridge can carry it off.' Victor, Blade's next brother in age, joined them. He was very much like the earl, with his dark hair and eyes, whereas Blade took after his mother. 'Having Stantford here would have set the seal,' Victor continued. 'Too bad his Grace is not yet well enough for public functions. Good to see you here, Brother.'

He shook Blade's hand, his grin infectious. The fact that he raked around town to his family's dismay was neither here nor there, in Blade's opinion. He had years before he needed to think about his duties as heir. 'I thought you had decided to hare off north again.'

Blade liked this new adult version of his half-brother, whom he'd played with when they were children, though they'd had their share of childhood rivalries. They had seen little of each other since Blade took the King's shilling. He was surprised to realise how much he had missed him.

'I'll be leaving soon,' Blade said.

'And how do you find the wilds of Yorkshire?'

'Seething with discontent.'

His brother's face became grave. 'Hardly surprising. Prinny is an idiot. As are the rest of them. Do they want to start a revolution?'

Blade cocked his head. 'I am surprised to hear you voice such an opinion in public.'

'Think I am an idiot, too, do you?' He glanced over at his father. 'Even the earl is baulking at the Six Acts.'

Blade was pleased and proud to hear it. 'Too bad he didn't put a stop to them.'

The butler opened the door. 'Lord and Lady Thornton and Mrs Caroline Falkner.'

At his side, Victor drew in a sharp breath. 'My word, what a diamond she is. And a widow, too. She will take the town by storm.'

Caro looked magnificent. Beautiful. The gown, a lovely shade of lavender, showed her milky skin off to perfection, and her hair had been pinned into an elaborately charming style. Blade couldn't have drawn a breath if he'd tried. He jabbed an elbow in his brother's ribs. 'A little more respect, if you please.'

His brother rubbed at the offending part of his anatomy and gave him a cheerful grin. 'Like that, is it?'

Annoyed, Blade glared at him. 'It is not *like* anything.'

In case others fell into a similar misapprehension, he edged out of the centre of things and let Charlie and Merry do the necessary courtesies to those who mattered.

Like his father and his brother.

From where he stood he could see the courage with which she endured the introductions. For the sake of her child.

He wanted to hit something.

Or run away. As he had run from his father all those years ago, but it had done him no good then and would not do so now. Besides, he'd never run from a fight and Caro was fighting for her son and the right to the life that had been ripped away by a fellow who hadn't recognised a treasure worth a king's ransom.

Finally, she was standing in front of him flanked by her guardian angels, Charlie and Merry. 'And of course you and Blade are old friends.'

Far more than friends. The thought flickered in her eyes before she dismissed it.

'Indeed,' she said, inclining her head at the perfect angle for the illegitimate offspring of an earl. She was magnificent. She would carry the whole thing off without any help from him.

'How are things going at the Haven?' he

asked in a low voice as the ducal heir helped his wife to a seat near the hearth.

'Swimmingly,' Caro said, twiddling her fan. 'We have three new occupants and one of them has a child.'

'I assume you will not be returning there.'

'No. Merry has asked me to help her establish a similar institution here in London.'

He had thought the whole idea for her remaining in London was to find herself a husband. 'You will enjoy the Season, then.'

She looked doubtful. 'Merry would have it so. I am not sure I am up to the rigours of town life, but Lady Thornton wants to make sure Tommy, I mean Thomas, has every advantage.'

He couldn't contain his smile. 'He will always be Tommy to you, even when he reaches maturity.'

Her eyes sparkled. 'He will. In private.' She glanced around the room. 'It is so very kind of everyone to turn out in support of the Thorntons. I hope I do not let them down.'

'How can you? You have given them their hearts' desire. Returned a part of their son. Remember, many of those here came for your sake.'

Her gaze darted to his face and away, a

slight stain of colour on her cheeks. Damn, did she think he was only talking about himself?

She gathered her composure with her lovely cool smile. 'Merry agrees with Lady Thornton that I should seek a husband as soon as possible. Thomas needs a father. I can see that now.'

A pang pierced his heart. 'How is his ankle?'

'Oh, he is hopping around on crutches and feeling very much the wounded hero.' She closed her eyes briefly and winced. 'I beg your pardon. I had no intention of belittling—'

'Caro,' he murmured urgently. 'Between us there should never be awkwardness. Cannot be. The *ton* watch with eagle eyes.'

The butler was again making a grand entrance. 'Lord and Lady Robert Mountford.'

The most fascinating petite woman entered on the arm of a gentleman who looked exactly like Charlie, if it wasn't for the sun-bronzed skin of his face.

'Robert,' Charlie said, surging forward. 'I had no idea you had returned from Italy.' He shook his brother's hand and was pulled into a manly hug complete with the obligatory thump to the back.

'We arrived yesterday,' Lord Robert said, grinning broadly and being thumped in return. 'I had no idea you were entertaining until

Mother sent us a note. Oh, and by the way, I brought reinforcements.'

'His Highness, the Prince of Wales,' the butler trumpeted. 'And his Grace, the Duke of Wellington.'

Brilliant. Charlie had done it. Clearly, Blade had been right. He really wasn't needed. He would have left right then, if it wasn't for Caro hanging on to his arm like a lifeline.

'The first ball of the Season,' Lady Thornton said, watching a set in full swing. 'And everyone will remember it as the best, too.'

'Do you think so?' Caro was beginning to feel overheated by the press of people and there was no respite to be had, for she was on display. Indeed, people were still lined up down the stairs from the front door to the first-floor ballroom, waiting to get a look at her. If dinner had been terrifying, the ball was horrendous.

'With both the prince and the duke in attendance? It is a coup,' exclaimed her mother-in-law. For that was how Mrs Thornton had introduced her at every turn. *My daughter-in-law.* When Caro had objected the truthfulness of this, she had waved her off, saying it only wanted the little detail of a ceremony.

The prince had been charming and very

condescending to Caro at dinner and at the ball had held her in conversation for several minutes after the first dance had been completed. Then he had left.

But the point was made.

There couldn't possibly be a scrap of scandal in Caro's past or the prince would have refused to acknowledge her.

The fact that the Duke of Stantford had offered the prince the stupendous gift of a work of art he had bought in France immediately after the war had sealed his co-operation. How would she ever repay her debt to all these people?

She understood why Tonbridge and Merry were so keen on her acceptance by the *ton*. She was their good friend. A person they wanted to have as part of their social life. This was their way of ensuring that very thing.

And she could not be more grateful.

But…ever since the start of all this fuss to make her entirely respectable, Blade, her friend and her lover, had become more and more distant. Was it that he did not approve of what his friends were doing? Did he perhaps feel she was getting above herself?

*Strumpet. Shameful jade.* Her father's condemnation rung in her ears.

She shivered.

'I believe the next dance is a waltz,' a deep voice murmured close to her ear. Blade had come up behind her to stand at her shoulder.

Lady Thornton stiffened. 'Mr Read, Mrs Falkner has no intention of waltzing this evening.'

Could his timing have been any worse? Could he not have waited until she was standing with someone else like Merry or Tonbridge, which would have allowed her to refuse in a less public manner? She took a deep breath. The challenge in his gaze, the edge of pride, said he expected her refusal. Blast him, he was asking her now so she could show the world she was not the sort of woman to fall for a man renowned for his seduction of lonely widows and bored wives.

'It is an age since I waltzed, my dear mama-in-law,' Caro said sweetly. 'Having watched the last one, I believe I remember the steps perfectly well.' She dipped a curtsy to Blade and held out her hand. 'I would love to waltz, Mr Read.'

He led her onto the dance floor.

Ripples of shock stirred the air around them.

'You should have declined,' he said in a voice too low to be heard by their nearest neighbours as he whirled her around. 'Now I will be forced to dance with every wallflower in the place, to stop tongues wagging.'

She stiffened. 'If you did not wish to dance with me, you should not have asked.'

'I am surprised Tonbridge did not warn you.' He smiled at her with seductive charm for the sake of those watching. 'Tongues are wagging. They know we are both friends of Tonbridge and that I recently returned from York. They know you hail from somewhere nearby. Someone let the cat out of that bag. Probably one of the Thorntons. They are very well meaning, but not exactly sharp. You told me you were not going to waltz.'

'There you go again. Saving the damsel in distress at the risk of your own life,' she said, a little buzz of anger humming along her veins, making her say what she thought and not what she should. She almost added the word *idiot*, but it was hard to be furious with a smile on her lips.

He twirled her under his arm and gracefully brought her alongside him for the traverse. 'You waltz divinely,' he said.

'I'll wager you say that to all of your ladies.'

'There are no ladies,' he said. 'Not any more.'

Something inside her seemed to shatter, but

in a good way, as if a fear had broken away and diminished.

'You really were not supposed to dance with me.' He spoke truculently, as if he was annoyed that she had robbed him of the chance to…to what? Fight her dragon?

'I could not be that cruel to a man—' She broke off.

'A man?' he prompted.

Now was not the time for such honesty. Or the place, when it was full of strangers and she did not know how Blade might respond. 'A man who is my good friend, whom I admire and respect.'

Was it disappointment she saw in his eyes? Or merely acceptance.

He sighed. 'And so you consign your good friend to the wallflowers.'

'I am sorry,' she said as the waltz came to an end. And she was. Dreadfully. But she did not think he truly believed it. And she wished she knew how she could make him understand.

## Chapter Sixteen

Blade took a sip of the brandy Tonbridge handed him. It was three days since the ball and Tonbridge had asked Blade to drop in after dinner.

'To our success.' Charlie raised his glass in a toast. He sounded smug. As he should. The lady was successfully launched. The brief appearance of Prinny and the extended stay by Wellington meant that Mrs Falkner's reputation as a respectable widow was assured. No one would ever query the death of Mr Falkner. Not when Thornton had arranged for such a healthy settlement in that dear departed individual's name to be available when she married again. She already had several suitable men sniffing around, at least one of them with an ancient title.

Blade toasted with his glass in response.

The fact that *he* didn't feel the slightest bit smug was neither here nor there. His duty was done. He took a healthy swallow of some of the best brandy it had ever been his privilege to imbibe. 'I'll be getting back to my stewarding in Yorkshire on the morrow.'

Tonbridge gave him an odd look. 'It won't be necessary. Merry and I will be returning there next week, now that Stantford is on the mend.'

In other words, his services were no longer needed. 'I'll let Ned know.' The man would be disappointed to leave his fair Beth behind. 'Unless you have a position for him? He's a good man with a horse and you haven't yet replaced your coachman.' A bit of a comedown for a man of Ned's talents, but at least he would be able to stay near his sweetheart. Blade certainly didn't have any work for him. Or much in the way of funds to pay him.

'He could take your old position, I suppose,' Tonbridge mused. 'In a more limited capacity, though. Merry will expect him to marry the lady in charge. Less gossip that way.'

'Beth will be in charge at the house?'

Tonbridge inclined his head.

The duke-to-be didn't miss a trick and the idea he proposed cheered Blade. Somewhat. At least it relieved him of his obligation to Ned and he knew it would please the man no end. 'An excellent solution.'

'I am glad you think so. So what will you do now?'

His only thought had been to leave London, given that the Season was in full swing. The bastard son of an earl was always at a loose end in polite society, unless he had an interest in cutting a swathe through the new crop of bored matrons and widows in need of comfort. The thought made him feel tired. He certainly did not want to be around to congratulate Caro on her conquests or for any other reason for which a woman received congratulations, like engagements and forthcoming weddings. 'Perhaps I shall go to France for a while. See Paris as she is meant to be seen. Sample more good brandy.' He raised his glass a fraction. 'There are other armies in Europe in need of soldiers.'

Tonbridge's lips tightened. 'What about the offer to serve as land steward on your father's estate in Kent?'

'Heard about that, did you?'

'From your brother Victor.' The legitimate brother and heir moved in the same circles as Tonbridge. Belonged to the same clubs. Gossip had never been Blade's friend.

The brief interview with his father on the subject of his resigned commission had made him feel like an *ungrateful* bastard. To say the subsequent offer of employment had come as a shock was putting it mildly.

He shook his head. 'It holds no appeal.' Or rather, it was too close to the temptation of Caro Falkner. Perhaps France was also too close. India might be better.

'I don't see myself as a farmer,' he said. 'Nor do I wish to become his dependent.' He still owed his father the cost of his commission.

Tonbridge raised a brow. 'I rather thought you would be relieving him of a worry and thus putting him in your debt.'

Blade cracked a laugh that sounded false to his ears. 'Relieving him of the worry of how to support me, you mean.' Or the guilt that he'd ever been born.

'Something of the sort.' Tonbridge refilled their glasses. He sipped reflectively for a moment. 'I apologise for this next, Blade, but I am required to ask, because my countess will take me to task if I do not. What of Mrs Falkner?'

He froze. It was the last thing he had expected to be questioned on. The recollection of her at the ball whirling around in several lordlings' arms had his hand tightening around his glass. 'I am not sure what you mean. The gossip was scotched.' Barely, after that waltz. 'The lady successfully launched, as you so recently pointed out, and the matter is satisfactorily resolved.'

'You are satisfied?'

'Of course,' he lied. Knowing his early departure from that long-ago assembly because of his adolescent hurt feelings had allowed Carothers a free rein with Caro burned a hole in his chest. As did the knowledge of how more recently he had taken advantage of her loneliness.

Except he could not stop thinking about his time with her, over and over. They were memories that would keep haunting him for the rest of his life.

'I presume the fact that she is right now upstairs taking tea with my wife is of no interest to you?'

He shot to his feet. 'This is why you asked me to come by this evening? Some sort of ambush you have concocted between you? And I thought you a friend.'

Charlie's expression darkened and he looked down his lordly nose. 'I'll forgive you that, Blade, but only because you are acting like a dolt. For heaven's sake, the woman is breaking her heart wanting to know what she did to drive you away.'

'What *she* did?'

'You have to talk to her, Blade. Face to face. Explain yourself.' He muttered something under his breath that sounded suspiciously like 'stubborn idiot'.

His heart began to race. 'I can't give her what she is entitled to. Her or her son.' What had been taken from her by another thoughtless male. The respectability she craved.

'Entitled? Or what she wants? Because what she seems to want—which personally I cannot understand—is you.'

Something inside him shifted. No one that he could ever remember truly wanted him. His mother certainly hadn't. His very existence had been an unpleasant shock to his father. He'd learned to accept that as his due. But Caro—whom all those years ago he'd let down so badly because he'd known what Carothers was like— 'Taking tea, you say?'

'A three-handkerchief tea by the time I left,' Tonbridge said, looking disgruntled.

She was crying? Over him? The idea pained him. Badly. 'Perhaps we do need to clear the air.' He'd honestly thought she would be glad to see him gone. She as well as the Thorntons. It seemed she needed convincing.

'Wait here while I scout the terrain.' Tonbridge sauntered from the room.

Tonbridge, ever the careful soldier. It was what had made him such a good commanding officer. He had a brain and he cared about his men.

Damn it all, Caro was here? Blade paced from one end of the room to the other, rehearsing what he should say. The list of advantages now open to her and Tommy. His lack of prospects. Although there was the estate in Kent, where he wasn't well known. He'd been there once or twice as a boy. It was part of the settlements for the countess's children. He'd loved the place because it was nowhere near as grand as the earl's other holdings. How could he ask Caro to bury herself in the country when she had such dazzling prospects before her?

No. He would not allow her to sacrifice herself in that way. Thornton had made it quite clear Blade's antecedents and youthful peccadilloes would reflect badly on Caro as well as the name of Carothers. A name Tommy would adopt as his own if the Thorntons had their way.

At a sound, he glanced up, expecting to

see Charlie come to escort him up, but it was Caro entering in a swish of silks. She looked lovely. She'd always looked lovely to him, but now, fashionably dressed, her bronze-coloured gown cut seductively low, her hair in the latest style, she was magnificent and utterly calm. Perhaps it was Tonbridge who had needed the handkerchiefs.

'Mrs Falkner,' he said, trying to keep his tone teasingly light. 'First you waltz with me and now you meet me unchaperoned—have you no sense at all of self-preservation?'

'Mr Read.' She glided deeper into the room. 'I heard you were thinking of going away. To France. Is it true?'

'I did not realise my business was of such concern to the world, but, yes.'

She stared at the carpet as if gathering her thoughts, then lifted her gaze to his face. Her skin was luminous in the light of the candles, paler than usual. 'There is something I wanted to tell you. Something I think you should know.'

He closed his eyes briefly at the stab of pain, before forcing a smile. 'You have an offer of marriage. I wish you well and you have no need for concern with regard to my discretion.'

She drew in a breath, as if he had shocked

her. 'No. That is, yes, I have had an offer, but that is not what I wanted to say.' She hesitated, and despite the pain behind his breastbone at her news, he couldn't help drinking in her beauty, memorising each delicate curve, the line of her neck, the turn of her elbow.

Her voice trembled as she spoke. 'Blade, I want you to know that I love you.'

Everything inside of him stilled. His heart felt suddenly too large for his chest. Too big to allow breath into his lungs. He loved her, too. But... 'You are a lovely generous woman. You deserve far more than I could ever provide.'

'You already gave me so much.'

'You are not saying you are...?' He glanced down at her stomach. 'You did not conceive?'

She swallowed, her eyes sad. 'I have not.'

He didn't know whether to be glad or sorry. For he would have married her had it been the case. 'I am not what you need. Not what Tommy needs. I told you I have no interest in marriage.' She flinched and he wanted to strike out. Most likely at himself. 'Caro, you will find someone else upon whom to shower your affections. I do not believe in what the poets call...love.' He forced the word out.

'Why not?'

Blast the woman. When had she become so

deuced persistent? Since always. He smiled wryly to himself. It was one of the things he liked about her. What on earth could he say in answer to such a question? 'I find the whole concept strange. I am not sure I could ever confine myself to only one woman.' Though of course he had and would likely continue to do so for some time to come.

Her eyes glittered. With anger? Tears? Her self-containment didn't allow him to be sure. 'Blade, I love you. I promise I would never abandon you.'

The words tore a hole in his heart. What on earth could have made her pick on the one thing he feared in the deepest reaches of his soul? The one thing he barely admitted to himself. How could she even make such a promise? Circumstances changed. People changed.

'Caro,' he whispered. His arms longed to embrace her. His fingers itched to ease the tightness of his collar almost as much as they itched to furrow through the careful ordering of her locks so he could see them in disarray about her shoulders one last time. He held himself under rigid control. He forced what he hoped was a smile. 'I really am sorry.'

After a long considering look, she inclined

her head. 'You will come and say goodbye to Tommy.'

He wanted to howl. And he wanted to strangle Tonbridge. But a soldier knew when he had been given an ultimatum. 'I will.'

She turned and left. He gave her a moment to go up the stairs and departed before his so-called friend could arrive with more stories of handkerchiefs.

'I don't like London,' Tommy said, banging his one good heel against the leg of the breakfast-room chair.

'Please do not kick the chair, Thomas. This is our home,' Caro said quietly. He was trying to be good, but his changed circumstances, the restrictions, were difficult for him to accept. 'Please eat the rest of your eggs. Would you like a slice of toast?'

'Only if it has strawberry jam,' he said crossly.

'We only have marmalade at the moment. Orange jam. You know you love oranges.'

'I want strawberry jam.'

Tommy was never grouchy. 'Is your leg paining you, darling?'

'No.'

Grandpa Thornton lowered his paper and

revealed equally lowered bushy grey brows. 'Perhaps it would be better if he took breakfast in the nursery.'

He was already taking luncheon, afternoon tea and dinner in the nursery. It was a long time since the Thorntons had lived with small children, and to hear them tell of it, their children had lived most of their lives in the care of others. From this happy state of affairs they'd developed the notion that boys aged eight were perfect little gentlemen when in the company of adults.

Tommy cast her a look. Daring her to agree. He'd already threatened to run away again.

'The sooner you finish eating everything on your plate, the sooner we will be on our way to the park.' Every morning after breakfast they visited the ducks in Green Park. Children needed routine.

Lady Thornton glanced up from one of her many pieces of correspondence with a frown. 'Is it right to reward—?' She stopped, clearly realising her words were not being well received. 'I beg pardon, Caroline. I am sure you know what is best.'

She was right. Granting him a treat *was* bribery in a way, but Tommy was spending far too much time in the nursery when boys of his age needed to be outside. She would be glad when they returned to Thornton Manor with its extensive grounds where a young lad could breathe.

Tommy finished his breakfast in short order and it wasn't too long until they were off in the open carriage. Linny had complained of female pains and had begged off the outing. Caro had no doubt her pangs were genuine. The poor girl had looked so dreadful, Caro had sent her back to bed with a tisane and a hot water bottle. So they were accompanied by one of the Thorntons' rather stuck-up footmen.

On arrival at the park, it took a moment or two for Caro to organise the footman and the blanket and Tommy's ball. When she turned around to take Tommy's hand, he was already entering the park, hopping along on his crutches, no doubt heading straight for the pond.

She picked up her skirts and ran after him, leaving the footman to fend for himself.

'Tommy, wait,' she called out.

'Stop, Thomas.' A male voice of authority. Not her footman.

Tommy halted immediately, then changed direction, heading for two men on horseback. 'Mr Read,' he yelled, stopping to wave a crutch. How had he got so nimble on those things? They should be slowing him down.

Caro dropped to a walk. This was a meeting she had been dreading, but she had not expected it to happen here. She had thought he would send round a note asking for permission to call on her and Tommy, giving her time to compose herself. She pulled together the shreds of her dignity, going first hot, then cold at the memory of the way she had thrown herself at him a few nights before.

Blade jumped down before Tommy was anywhere close to his horse, tucked him under one arm and spun him around in mid-air. Tommy squealed with delight.

The other man also jumped down, taking both horses' reins, and while he was just as tall as Blade, his features were more refined and his eyes were dark and his hair sable. Blade's half-brother, Victor, she remembered. Blade swung Tommy to sit on his shoulders.

She smiled at both men. What else could she do? 'Thank you. Once more you have rescued my runaway son.'

'Look at me, Mama. I'm riding a horse.'

Blade made suitable clip-clopping noises.

'Well met, Mrs Falkner,' his brother said. He

flashed her a charming smile. 'Duvane, at your service. We met at the Tonbridges' ball. May I say what a pleasure it is to meet you again.'

The man had charm to spare.

Blade glared at him.

Caro dipped a curtsy. 'Of course I remember. Tommy and I were on our way to visit the ducks. I must thank you for your intervention. I and my entourage only turned our backs for a second.' She looked up at Tommy high above her head, his crutches tucked beneath Blade's arm. 'You really should not run off like that, Thomas. London is so very much bigger than Skepton. I would not want you to get lost.' Again.

'Apologise to your mama, lad. It is what a gentleman must do when he is in the wrong,' Blade said.

Some gentlemen apologised when they were in the wrong. Others left.

'I'm sorry, Mama,' Tommy said and he sounded genuinely remorseful.

She nodded her acceptance.

He clutched at Blade's hair. 'Why don't you ever come and see us any more, Mr Read?' His feet drummed a rhythm on Blade's chest. 'Don't you want to be my papa?'

Caro nearly fainted in mortification. 'Tommy,

Mr Read is a friend. He has been busy…' She gestured vaguely to signify all sorts of important things.

Blade's expression shuttered. She could only be glad that Tommy could not see it from his perch. 'I am here now,' he finally said.

'Yes,' Tommy replied, apparently satisfied.

The three of them strolled side by side towards the pond, Blade carrying Tommy and holding her arm with Lord Duvane on her other side leading both horses.

'I am trying to dissuade my brother from leaving us again so soon,' Lord Duvane said, clearly looking for a topic of conversation to fill the awful awkwardness. 'His sisters have seen little of him these past many years.'

His brother, too, if the regret in his voice was anything to go on. 'Mr Read is not an easy man to persuade,' she said, hoping she sounded more teasing than petulant.

Blade cast her a look she could not interpret, but said nothing, for they had arrived at the lake and Tommy was struggling to dismount.

The footman rushed forward with the bread they had brought and handed it over. Trying to balance on crutches and throw the bread proved to be a frustrating exercise. The ducks who had rushed to greet them, quacking and splashing, were less than pleased to find that their treats ended up in the mud on the bank.

Caro went to lift him.

'Allow me,' Lord Duvane said. He looked at his brother. 'Leave me to deal with this little chap and take the lady for a stroll, brother dear.' He smiled at Caro. 'Perhaps you will have better luck than I.'

Blade shot him a glare. His brother winked at Caro and to hide his smile he picked up Tommy, balanced him on his hip and headed down the bank. 'Come on, lad. I'll hold you and you throw. You'll discover the advantages of growing as tall as me.'

Blade held out his arm. 'Would you care to walk?'

She accepted with a smile, tucking her arm beneath his elbow.

The footman hesitated, not sure which of his party he was supposed to guard, but a glower from Blade had him deciding to stay put.

'Why did Tommy say that?' Blade demanded, sounding so grumpy and put upon, she had the urge to laugh when saying goodbye was no laughing matter. She patted his gloved hand where it rested on top of hers as if he feared she might run.

'We clearly were not as discreet as we

thought. Children hear things and see things and draw their own slanted conclusions about a world that, to their eyes, revolves around them.'

He grunted as if considering her words and glanced over his shoulder with a puzzled frown. 'I am glad I ran into you today,' he said when they were out of earshot.

'We come here every day.' She frowned. 'You planned this meeting?'

He looked a little shamefaced. 'Tonbridge mentioned that you came here each morning.'

She glanced back to where his brother was handing lumps of bread up to Thomas. Had he planned that, too? In order to speak to her alone. Her heart thumped harder in her chest. 'Your brother seems sorry to see you go.'

He shrugged. 'He is sorry I have refused to take the employment my father is offering. It means more work for him.'

There was an edge to his words she could not quite understand. She frowned. 'You dislike your brother?'

'Half-brother. We have different mothers. You know this.'

'He does not make the distinction. And you did not answer my question.'

Blade stopped and stared into the pond's murky water. 'I like him well enough, but…'

'But?' she prompted, watching a little moor-hen dabbling its red beak among the reeds along the bank.

'I invaded their home and he didn't like it. Father told him that I was a duty and a responsibility there was no getting around.' He swished at the rushes with his riding crop, sending the moorhen off with a startled squawk and a splash. 'I didn't need their charity then and I don't need it now.'

'Something you overheard?' she guessed.

'I was outside the library window. Victor and I had fought over who would ride the pony first.' He grimaced. 'It was his pony, but I was bigger and stronger.'

'So a fight between two annoying little boys. One trying to find his way in a new home, the other trying to find a new place for himself with the arrival of an older brother. And a papa trying to keep the peace.'

He looked at her askance and started walking again.

Caro glanced back to where Duvane was showing Tommy how to skip stones across the pond. 'It is not easy raising children. One never knows if one is making the right decisions.'

'You were right to keep Tommy with you.'

A small smile curved her lips, but there was an ache in her chest. 'I have you to thank for that piece of advice. Tommy and I will remain together until he is old enough to go to school. I have explained to him about his father. He will understand better when he is older.'

'You are happy.' He sounded pleased, but there was something else in his eyes, something watchful.

'I am content.' It was all she could expect, really. She certainly wasn't going to marry when her heart belonged to a man who didn't want her. But nor was she going to go into a decline. She had her son. She had security. What more could she need?

Suddenly she could not stand all this polite conversation. It was hurting too much to pretend that all between them was well. 'It was very kind of you to come to say goodbye to Tommy, Blade. I really think we should be getting back.'

'I—' He took a deep breath and stopped walking, looking into her eyes. 'Actually, I wanted to speak to you about something else. About what you said the other night.'

Her chest felt tight. Was he going to take her to task for her foolish declaration? Warn her for her own good, as the Thorntons had done? If so...

'Caro, I do care for you. A great deal.'

Caring wasn't enough. 'You are going to request my friendship. I understand. I will be your friend. Please, let us go back.' She tried to walk on, but he held her back.

'That is *not* what I intended to say.' He glanced across to where the footman hovered, clearly trying to keep both parties in sight, and led her towards a willow tree overhanging the bank.

When they were obscured from view, he took her left hand in his right and stroked her palm with his thumb, sending fiery little tingles down her back. Eyes wide, she stared at him. 'Blade, you are scaring me. What is wrong?'

His expression tightened, but he did not release her hand. 'I've spent my life expecting those I—I love to turn their backs on me. I learned not to care. To always leave first. It hurt less.'

Her insides melted, he looked so wounded. 'Oh, Blade,' she whispered, her heart in her throat.

'The other night, when you said you would never abandon me...' He shook his head and swallowed. 'I believed you. You have proved your loyalty to those you love, over and over again.' He swallowed. 'Old habits die hard, Caro. I couldn't make myself speak. I do love you. I always will.'

She swallowed a lump in her throat. 'But?'

'I will understand if I've spoken too late. I understand if you have already accepted another offer. I had to tell you, that was all. I love you.'

'Then why are you leaving?'

'I'm not sure I know any longer.'

He sounded so hopelessly lost tears welled in her eyes. 'Then don't go. I love you. Tommy loves you. Stay.'

'Darling. My dearest love.' His voice was husky and broke a little on a laugh. 'You won't ever leave me?'

'Not if wild horses tried to drag me off.'

He brought her hand to his lips with a tender smile on his face. 'Dearest Caro. You give me such courage. Will you marry me?'

Her heart tumbled over. She flung her arms around his neck and kissed him.

When they finally broke apart, he was looking at her quizzically. 'Caro, will you?'

She had answered, hadn't she? Not in words, no, but in her actions. Laughter, love and all kinds of emotions bubbled up in her. 'Yes, you idiotic man, of course, yes.'

He breathed a long sigh of relief and kissed her again, deeply, seductively. Finally, they took a breath and she rested her head on his shoulder.

'We should go and tell Tommy I will be his papa after all. I hope the Thorntons aren't going to cut up rough.'

'Tommy will deal with them. They were so relieved when I said he and I would move to the dower house.'

He grinned. 'They find him hard to handle.'

'As a barrel full of monkeys.'

He laughed out loud. 'Come, let him be the first to hear our news.'

'Him and your brother, who is deserving of sainthood after all this time.'

'Victor is all right. He's used to young children. The countess and the earl have quite a few.'

Arm in arm, they returned to the path, strolling in perfect harmony.

'Oh, hell,' Blade said. 'I beg your pardon, Caro, but it seems we are about to run into Hartwick and the countess.' He glanced back to where his brother was now playing ball with Tommy. Cricket with crutches, if Caro wasn't mistaken. 'The devil. No wonder he was hell-bent on coming with me. And I thought it was to help with Tommy.'

Now Blade knew why he had always preferred being an only child. Less people to interfere with his business. Friends were bad enough.

A few yards away from them, his father lifted his silver-topped walking stick in greeting as if Blade might not have seen him. Or perhaps—Blade felt a stab of guilt—the old fellow thought Blade would simply pass him by. For the first time in an age he looked at his father. Really looked at him. When had he become so old, so bowed down? And when had the countess's golden hair acquired so much silver? Regret at lost years caused his gut to clench.

As they came abreast of each other, Blade bowed. 'My lord,' he said. 'My lady. You know Mrs Falkner, of course. You met at Tonbridge's the other evening.'

Caro curtsied.

His father bowed. The countess held out her hand and Caro shook it.

'How lovely to meet you again, Mrs Falkner.' The countess tucked Caro's hand beneath her arm and turned and walked with her. Gritting his teeth, Blade followed at his father's side.

'Was there something you wanted, sir?' he asked after a moment or two of silence. 'I cannot believe your presence here is a coincidence.' Any more than his had been.

His father harrumphed like a schoolmaster about to deliver a lecture on manners. 'I won't have you haring off to join some foreign army. Nor will your mama.'

'Stepmama.' The word came automatically. Then his brain caught up with the meaning. He stiffened. 'I don't see—'

The old gentleman stabbed his cane at an unfortunate dandelion. 'I know, it is none of my business. Or so *you* think, but hear me out, my son. I heard back from a friend at Horse Guards. Tried to turn 'em back, did you?'

Chill ran in Blade's veins. 'Unsuccessfully, I am afraid,' he said, trying not to sound defiant. He'd beaten a couple of the militia with the flat of his sword, trying to stop them charging into the crowd at St Peter's Field. He could have been court-martialled and shot for that alone.

'Damned fools should have listened.'

Blade's jaw dropped. 'My commanding officer did not see it that way.'

'As I said, damned fools. The lot of 'em.

And so I told Arthur. He's agreed to tear up your resignation, if that's what you want.'

His stepmother turned around and shot a glare at her husband. 'Jemmy, that is not why we came here today. Get on with it, do.'

His father waved his stick at a pair of benches. 'Sit down with me, my son. I have something important to tell you.'

Caro looked at him with eyebrows raised and he shook his head. He wanted to hear what his father had to say before broaching their news. He and his father took one bench, Caro and the countess the other.

His father pulled something from the inside pocket of his coat. He thrust it at Blade. 'A letter. From your mother.'

Blade blinked and looked over at the countess.

'*Your* mother, Blade,' his father said.

Blade sagged back against the seat. 'What? You've known where she is all these years and never seen fit to tell me?'

His father put a hand on his arm. 'Not is, my boy.' His voice thickened. 'She died a year or so after you came to us. Consumption. She knew she had it. That was why she sent for me. I promise you she was well looked after throughout. The countess and I made sure of it.'

'You and the countess?' He could not keep the incredulity from his voice. Or the grief from burning in his throat.

'Me and your stepmama, if you must be formal.' The earl showed the mettle of a man used to ordering his life the way he wanted it. 'I'd have done more, had she allowed.'

'She sent for you to fetch me because she was ill?' Anger coursed through his veins. 'I would have cared for her.'

'She didn't want you seeing her suffer,' his father said grimly. 'Her mother died of it. She knew what was going to happen.' He pressed his lips together. 'It wasn't only that. There was a man who used to visit her. A friend, she thought. She caught him dandling you on his knee and—' He cursed softly. 'I assume I do not need to draw a picture? Naturally, she threw him out, but she was terrified. He was a powerful man. She had no choice but to send you to me.'

He gazed at the toes of his shoes. 'I was furious she'd kept me from you all those years. And I was right. It was too late. You never took to us, did you?' He sounded disappointed. He had always sounded disappointed. Blade had always thought it was because he was lacking.

Pain blocked his throat. 'You should have told me.'

'I couldn't. She made me swear.' His voice was thick. He swiped at his eyes. 'Believe me, boy. Don't you think I would have married her, if I had known she had conceived? It would have been a scandal, but I wouldn't have cared.'

Blade pulled out his handkerchief and handed it to his father. 'You couldn't have married her. She was a courtesan.'

'That was what she said. Puppy love, she called it, and she was right. But I was devilish fond of her all the same. I would have done my duty.'

Blade glanced over at the countess. 'And lost out on the love of your life.'

'When did you become so understanding?' his father said gruffly.

He patted his father's arm and smiled. 'When I fell in love.'

The earl gestured at the letter Blade had placed on the bench between them. 'She wanted you to have that when I thought you were ready. Your stepmama has been after me to pass it on for years, but—' He gripped his walking cane more firmly. 'I worried you might leave us, if you knew she was alive, and then I thought perhaps it was best if it was all forgotten. You were doing so well in the army. After Waterloo, I thought it might be too much to bear.'

Blade had been in poor shape, grieving the loss of his fellows and his hand. 'You thought it might be the last straw.'

'Something like that. Your mother—' he winced '—your stepmother says it's time for a new start. A new understanding.'

He used the head of his cane to push himself to his feet. 'Read it. I don't know what it says and I don't want to, but believe that she cared for you, my boy. She cared more than life itself.'

Blade stared at the letter. At the handwriting, so prettily formed. *Bladen Jeremiah Read.*

When he looked up, his father and the countess had already walked a fair distance and Caro was standing in front of him. Waiting.

'Do you want me to leave you?' she asked softly.

'God, no.'

'Will you read it?'

'The countess told you?'

'She did.' She sat down and rested her cheek on his shoulder. The comfort of it unmanned him.

He swallowed the lump in his throat and crushed the letter in his fist. 'I'm not sure I want to do this.'

'You need to,' she said softly.

His hand was trembling too much for him to break the seal and hold on to the paper. 'Open it. Please.'

She took it and unfolded it.

Blast. The wind was making his eyes water. This was ridiculous. All over a stupid letter from a dead woman, when he hadn't even heard what she'd written. Just knowing, though, that she had not forgotten... 'Will you read it? Please.'

She opened her reticule and handed him a handkerchief. 'It is yours. I want it back.' She began reading.

'My dearest darling little gentleman, best of all sons,

You cannot imagine with what trepidation I write this note. I leave it to your father, dear man, to judge when the right time would be for you to receive this, or rather to his lady. She has been kindness itself, promising to bring you up as her own. And so understanding, given your father's rantings when he discovered I have kept you from him all these years.

That I do not regret. Selfish woman that I am, I have had you to myself and you are growing up to be a fine young man. Nor do I regret the error on my part that resulted in your birth. I do regret that I was not able to protect you as well as I should have and pray that you have no bad memories of me or the life I constrained upon you.

I hope you will forgive me, my darling boy, for not seeing you again. To see you and not be able to hold you without...'

Caro put the paper on her lap. 'Oh, Blade, are you sure you want me to continue?'

'Go on,' he managed.

'...without having you see the ravages of this horrid disease. It takes one from the world yet leaves one to linger.

Your father loves you. His countess loves you. Be happy. Forgive me.

Your loving mother...'

She folded it up and enclosed him in her arms while he wept. He wept for his mother and for the boy who had never understood.

Feeling ashamed, he averted his face. 'I beg your pardon,' he muttered.

Her arm snugged around his waist. 'There is nothing to forgive. I love you.'

He swallowed. 'There are a great many admissions of people loving me today,' he said, trying for lightness and failing. He just felt so humble. And grateful.

'Loving you back, you mean,' she said softly. 'You are a very loving man, aren't you? It hurt you badly when you thought she didn't want you any more.'

'Worse than losing my hand,' he said, finally relieved to be able to admit it freely. He put his arm around her waist and they stood together while he composed himself. Finally, they began walking towards Tommy and his brother, who were now rolling in play on the ground.

'I love you so much, Caro,' he said, finally able to form words again. 'Will you marry me soon? I am not sure I can wait even three weeks for the banns to be called.'

'A special licence would solve that problem, I believe.'

He grinned at her. 'I give you my heart and my soul, but you will find them badly bashed around.' He bent and kissed her cheek. 'Will you take them into your care?' he whispered in her ear. 'For there will never be another for me.'

She stopped and rose up on her toes and kissed his mouth.

When they finally broke apart, people were staring at their shocking behaviour.

'Disgraceful conduct, Mrs Falkner,' he said.

'I know. How soon can we do it again?'

They repeated their disgraceful behaviour all the way home, to the shock of the footmen and passers-by and to the disgruntlement of Tommy and the amusement of Victor.

Blade took the offer of employment from his father on the understanding that the lovely estate in Kent would become another Haven for children like him and mothers like Caro.

\* \* \* \* \*

*If you enjoyed this story, don't miss these other great reads from Ann Lethbridge in her* RAKES IN DISGRACE *miniseries.*

*THE GAMEKEEPER'S LADY*

*MORE THAN A MISTRESS*

*DELICIOUSLY DEBAUCHED BY THE RAKE* (UNDONE!)

# MILLS & BOON®

## &HISTORICAL

**AWAKEN THE ROMANCE OF THE PAST**

# MILLS & BOON®

Mills & Boon have been at the heart of romance since 1908… and while the fashions may have changed, one thing remains the same: from pulse-pounding passion to the gentlest caress, we're always known how to bring romance alive.

Now, we're delighted to present you with these irresistible illustrations, inspired by the vintage glamour of our covers. So indulge your wildest dreams and unleash your imagination as we present the most iconic Mills & Boon moments of the last century.

Visit **www.millsandboon.co.uk/ArtofRomance** to order yours!

a deep breath as his hand went to the buttons of his falls.

There would be no going back after this night. No pretence of being virtuous or honourable. But at least she would know something of what a wife would know. She sat up. 'Let me help?' She knew that since Merry and Charlie had been married, they rarely used a maid or a valet, instead helping each other to undress at night. Surely the same could be done by a...lover? Even the thought of that word sent a shiver down her spine.

His hand dropped away from the button he'd been working at and she busied herself with the fastenings. After all, with a son, she knew how this went. On a swallow, her throat rasping and dry, she pulled the fabric down over his hips. He was magnificent, his shaft standing erect from dark curling hair against his flat stomach. As he stepped out of his pantaloons, she leaned back on her elbows, the better to observe what was a miracle of nature.

Slowly becoming aware of his gaze, she glanced up at his face. He was smiling, seductively, winsomely, waiting for her to look her fill. No shame at all, the devil. Ach, more fiery blushes. She inched backwards on the bed to give him room to climb up.

He stretched alongside her and cupped her jaw in his large warm hand. Then his mouth plundered hers until she was dizzy with wanting. His hand wandered her body as if he would learn every inch of her skin beneath her nightgown, and she strolled her fingers down his broad back, down his spine, to his muscular derrière.

Such a lovely lithe body.

His thigh pressed between hers and she arched into him, wanting more than the sweet pressure he offered. He broke their kiss, looking down into her face with a smile. 'My turn.'

She gazed at him blankly, in too much of a sensual haze to comprehend his words, but feeling him drawing her nightgown upward towards her hips, she understood. She lifted her hips to aid his efforts, then sat up and, as he had done with his shirt, drew her nightgown over her head and tossed it aside. She forced herself not to close her eyes, but sank back amid the pillows.

This was what she had wanted and it would happen only this once and she was not going to hide from it. If she trusted him to do this, then she had to trust him to make the experience pleasurable.